MOUNTAIN WILD

Stacey Kayne

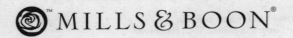

DID YOU PURCHASE THIS BOOK WITHOUT A COVER?
If you did, you should be aware it is stolen property as it was reported
unsold and destroyed by a retailer. Neither the author nor the publisher
has received any payment for this book.

All the characters in this book have no existence outside the imagination
of the author, and have no relation whatsoever to anyone bearing the
same name or names. They are not even distantly inspired by any
individual known or unknown to the author, and all the incidents are
pure invention.

All Rights Reserved including the right of reproduction in whole or
in part in any form. This edition is published by arrangement with
Harlequin Enterprises II BV/S.à.r.l. The text of this publication or
any part thereof may not be reproduced or transmitted in any form
or by any means, electronic or mechanical, including photocopying,
recording, storage in an information retrieval system, or otherwise,
without the written permission of the publisher.

This book is sold subject to the condition that it shall not, by way of
trade or otherwise, be lent, resold, hired out or otherwise circulated
without the prior consent of the publisher in any form of binding or
cover other than that in which it is published and without a similar
condition including this condition being imposed on the subsequent
purchaser.

® and TM are trademarks owned and used by the trademark owner
and/or its licensee. Trademarks marked with ® are registered with the
United Kingdom Patent Office and/or the Office for Harmonisation in
the Internal Market and in other countries.

First published in Great Britain 2010
Paperback edition 2010
Harlequin Mills & Boon Limited,
Eton House, 18-24 Paradise Road, Richmond, Surrey TW9 1SR

© Stacey Kayne 2009

ISBN: 978 0 263 87566 9

Harlequin Mills & Boon policy is to use papers that are natural,
renewable and recyclable products and made from wood grown in
sustainable forests. The logging and manufacturing process conform
to the legal environmental regulations of the country of origin.

Printed and bound in Spain
by Litografia Rosés, S.A., Barcelona

Stacey Kayne has always been a daydreamer. If the comments on her elementary school report cards are any indication, it's a craft she mastered early on. Having a passion for history and a flair for storytelling, she strives to weave fact and fiction into a wild ride that can capture the heart. Stacey lives on a ranch near the Sierra Nevada with her high school sweetheart turned husband of eighteen years and their two sons. Visit her website at www.staceykayne.com.

Recent novels by the same author:

MUSTANG WILD
MAVERICK WILD

Dedicated to my critique partners,

Sheila Raye,
who's always there for emergency brainstorming,

Marlene Urso,
for her speed-of-light proofreading,

and Carla Capshaw,
whose insight is always an inspiration!

Special Thanks to:
My husband—Happy 20th Anniversary!
Tanner and Ethan for always being there
to help their mom out.
My mom and mom-in-law
for their never-ending support.
My pals at Writers at Play.
Lucy, my fabulous editor,
for her faith and understanding.
My readers—I hope you enjoy this final addition
to my WILD series!

Prologue

Southwest Wyoming Territory—1875

"There's nowhere to run, Margaret Grace. I'm going to find you."

He was too close. Desperate to escape her brother's rage, Maggie's fingers dug into the dirt as she struggled through the thick brush. Thorns scraped across her cheeks, snagging her braids, ripping at her dress.

"Thirteen is a bit too old for hide-and-seek," Nathan called out, his taunting voice sounding merely a foot away.

Maggie froze. She tried to control her jagged breaths and the tears burning for release. Her face and belly throbbed from his heavy fists crashing down on her. Their daddy hadn't been dead a full hour, and her brother had lost his mind. He'd exploded from the house in a rage, their father's will in his hand.

He'd gone after her like a man deranged.

A twig snapped behind her. Maggie held her breath as his shadow moved over the dense scrub, blocking out bits of sunlight breaking through the twisted branches as he walked past. The crunch of his footsteps faded deeper into the woods. Her heart thundered as she waited. She had to make it back to the ranch before him.

She scrambled from the bush, biting back a scream as thorns ripped at her skin. Shaking, she hurried back down the hillside. Through a maze of tall timber she could see her home below and those who'd gathered in the yard— stable hands, housekeepers, the nanny who'd raised her.

Why didn't they come for her? She had screamed for help. All of them had looked on with horrified expressions, shrinking away as Nathan struck her again and again, forcing her to run for the woods to get away from him.

"There you are."

Maggie swung around. Fear gripped her chest, stealing her breath as her older brother towered over her. A wedge of black hair covered one eye. The other sparked with anger. Their father's will was still crushed in his grasp, her blood marring the pages.

Until today, no one had ever struck her. At twenty-two, Nathan was now her legal guardian.

"Look at you, Margaret Grace." He shook his head as though he weren't the one responsible for her tattered state. "What would your daddy think of his precious little girl crawling through the dirt in her fancy pink clothes?"

A smile curved his lips, and tears blurred Maggie's vision. He'd never liked her, but she never guessed her brother harbored such hatred. "What have I ever done to you?" she cried.

"You were born. My life was perfect before you came along. You killed my mother and have been nothing but a drain on my inheritance. And now I'm supposed to waste what's left of *my* money on some finishing school and a dowry so you can be pawned off on some aristocratic fool?"

"I don't have to go. I won't go!"

"It's in the will!" he shouted, waving the crumpled pages. "His lawyer has a copy. I'm his only son, the rightful heir! All this talks about is preparations made for *you, Margaret Grace!*" He swung his fist.

Pain exploded through her cheek. A scream ripped from her lungs as she hit the ground. She curled up, defending herself as best she could.

When the next blow didn't come, she opened her eyes and saw a pair of Indian boots just inches from her nose. Her gaze traveled up a giant wearing a thick fur coat. A full beard covered most of his face, but didn't hide three long scars twisting through his cheek.

Maggie gasped and scrambled back until she bumped into something. Fingers twisting into her hair, popping strands at the root, reminding her she faced a greater threat—her own brother.

"Who are you?" Nathan demanded.

The beastly man stared at her a moment before he glanced at her brother. "Trapper."

"You're trespassing on my property."

"I come to trade."

The trapper looked directly at her. Maggie shivered, his vacant brown eyes increasing her fear. She was scraped, bruised and bloody, one of her braids had unraveled, yet he stared as though her brother held a dog by a leash.

"You want her?" Nathan asked, laughter in his voice.

The trapper's shoulder shifted and a bound clump of fur landed on the ground beside her. "Give you six beaver pelts. Fair trade."

Maggie gasped in horror. She couldn't be sold! *"Nathan."* She tried to stand, shaking her head despite the pain in her scalp. Her brother wrenched his hold. Pain pierced her scalp, forcing her back onto her knees with a sharp cry.

"You live around here?" he asked.

"No," the trapper answered, his gaze fixed on her. "I follow the rivers."

"You can't sell me!" she shouted. "I'm your *sister!*"

He released her hair. Pain exploded across her back as he kicked her into the dirt. "Take her."

Long, grimy fingers reached for her. Maggie screamed as she was hoisted up and tossed over the giant's shoulder. "No! *Nathan!*"

She kicked and screamed as the trapper carried her deeper into the woods. Her thrashing didn't slow his strides. He broke from the trees and ran across a wide clearing. Reaching the other side, he stopped and swung her forward, pinning her against the rough bark of a tree.

Fear choked her. Her breaths came in short gasps.

"Hush your mouth, lest you want to die," he said in a harsh whisper.

She stared at the jagged scars rippling across his cheek and into his thick beard.

"I seen lots of death, little miss. That man has killin' in his eyes."

He lowered her to the ground and steadied her. "You want to live?"

Tears burned hot against her cheeks as she nodded.

"Then you bes' move fast and keep quiet. He may not be finished with us yet."

Her mind reeled as he tucked her against his side, his gaze scanning the ground he'd just covered.

He was afraid. Afraid her brother would come after them.

"Goddamn cowards on that ranch," he murmured. "Even wolves defend their young. Goes to show why I don't trust my back to no one."

Maggie gazed up at his tawny, withered face and the matted brown hair poking out from beneath his battered hat. He smelled bad and was old, but not so old that his hair had grayed like her daddy's.

"I done my good deeds in this life," he muttered, taking a step back. Fisted hands twice the size of her brother's slammed onto his hips. His angry dark eyes narrowed.

Maggie stumbled back, beyond his reach.

"I got a mule a half mile from here. We're headed north. You can go my way or find your own way. It ain't my worry."

Find her own way? "I—I'm only thirteen."

"Only two ages in this world that matter. Either you old enough to survive or you ain't." He held his hand out to her.

Maggie stared at his large, filthy palm then glanced at her own scraped hands. Twigs and leaves clung to dirty pink satin and the frazzled black hair draped over her shoulders. She was suddenly aware of the ache in her swollen lips, the burning in her eyes.

Her daddy was dead. Her brother had tried to kill her.

"You old enough, Margaret Grace?"

Only Nathan called her by her first and middle name.

"My name is Maggie," she said, taking the trapper's hand.

"I'm Ira."

Low murmurs carried across the meadow, drawing his gaze. Ira's fingers tightened over hers, tugging her after him.

"*Run,* Maggie."

Chapter One

Central Wyoming Territory—Fall, 1889

She moved with the caution of a doe caught grazing in an open meadow. Her dirt-stained fingers quickly secured a rope behind her saddle, binding her supplies as she discreetly watched the men filing out of the newly constructed town hall.

Following a roomful of grumbling cattlemen out onto the boardwalk, Garret Daines spotted the woman they called Mad Mag the moment he stepped into the crisp evening air. Her mangy bearskin coat and battered brown hat was hard to miss in the fading light of an otherwise deserted street. Murmurs of recognition and surprise rumbled through the crowd of men.

Garret had seen the mountain recluse in a town only one other time in the eight years he'd lived in these Wyoming hills, some years back in a settlement further north. The bushel of tangled black hair beneath her hat suggested she could still benefit from a lesson or two in hygiene. Known for having a temperament on the far side of crazy, Mad

Mag tended to avoid folks altogether. She obviously hadn't expected all the cattlemen within fifty miles to spill out onto the streets of Bitterroot Springs at five o'clock in the evening. He glanced around at the men watching her with an equal measure of curiosity and caution.

"What's the plan?" Duce asked, clapping a hand on Garret's shoulder as he stepped beside him.

Garret glanced over at his business partner, the man's wide grin striking him as a pure wonder. The past two hours of heated debates and near brawls, two of which had included Garret, left an ache in his shoulders, the frustration winding inside him still burning for release. In the fourteen years he'd been riding with Duce the wiry cowpuncher had never known a sour mood.

He doesn't handle the account books, he silently retorted. Duce had signed on as his partner in name only, refusing to take a cut or responsibility for a business he hadn't funded. At the age of forty-two, Duce still lived for Saturday nights and blowing his paycheck on weekend benders. In the past six years of running his cattle ranch, Garret had come to envy Duce's carefree attitude and figured the past few winters had closed the wide gap in their ages.

Garret felt old. Nothing like a failed marriage and Old Man Winter cramming his boot up your behind to age a man.

He glanced out at a pink-streaked sky. "Sun's about down. Might as well spend the night."

Duce gave a nod. He raked his fingers through his bushy red hair glowing bright beneath a streetlamp then tugged on his hat. "Think I'll head over to the Gilded Lady. Winter snow will be piling up soon and my girls are bound to miss me. Care to come along?"

"Not in the mood." He shook his head, a weary sigh breaking from his chest. "I feel like I've just been ambushed by seven cattle barons."

Duce chuckled.

Garret didn't share his humor. To secure his place in the stockyards come spring he'd signed over a small fortune to the wealthy bandits of the newly appointed Cattlemen's Association. They'd seemed rather disappointed in his ability to meet their demands. He wasn't about to be pushed off his land. He'd faired better than many of his colleagues, men who'd lost all their stock in the freeze a couple of winters back, a blizzard that had damn near wiped out the cattle trade across the state. Now the railroad and invading cattle barons circled like vultures, ready to pick off the smaller ranches struggling to make ends meet.

"I'll settle for a pint of whiskey and passing out in a hotel room."

"You can do that over at the Gilded Lady," Duce persisted. "What you need is a night in the saddle with some wild women. Ain't no reason for you not to." He moved closer as they stepped into the street. "Amanda's not coming back, you know?"

Garret rolled his shoulders against the surge of anger and resentment tightening his muscles. "I sure as hell hope not." Staring at that outrageous cattlemen contract reminded him of the divorce papers he'd finally signed last spring—cutting his marital ties to a woman he'd not seen in nearly three years. A wife walking out on a marriage left a man with no small amount of humiliation. He didn't see the need to announce his divorce.

Life sure hadn't gone the way he'd planned. Having acquired his ranch at the age of sixteen and marrying at nineteen, he truly thought he'd be settled in with his own family by now, not contemplating a night at a brothel. Damned if he could figure out what he'd done wrong. One thing he did know: he was through chasing women. If he was to have another wife, she'd have to run him to ground first.

"You can slug me for saying so," said Duce, "but you're lucky to be rid of that one. All that pretty was wasted on a woman who don't do nothin' but sniffle and pout 'cause you're too busy to sit and stare at her all damn day."

The truth didn't keep Garret's chest from burning at the thought of Amanda Billings standing on his sister's front porch bound and bustled in the fanciest gear he'd ever seen. The daughter of a Southern banker, she was a true belle, her soft-spoken voice never reaching much above a whisper, her long, lithe body and graceful movements *mesmerizing*. The fact that she'd looked twice at his weather-beaten hide had lit his fire, and he'd sure as hell lit hers.

Passion hadn't been enough to hold her. After eight months of marriage Amanda had her fill of him and Wyoming winters—a winter like nothing he'd ever seen. He wasn't new to tragedy or hardship. Raised on cattle trails by his older sister, he'd survived raids, floods, droughts and damn near being washed out of a Colorado Canyon—none of it had prepared him for watching his livelihood go to hell in a frozen handcart.

Murmurs buzzed from the men around him as Mad Mag guided her horse along the main strip. The top of her hat was barely visible beyond the large bay she led by the reins. A fine horse, its golden coat gleaming in the low light. His gaze stopped on the Morgan brand singed into the animal's haunch—the brand of his sister's ranch. He glanced again at the horse's golden coat, black socks, the burst of white on the horse's dark frock—*Star.*

"Is that Star?" he said to Duce as they stopped beside their own mounts.

"Yep," he answered, not bothering to shift his gaze toward the woman and her horse. "Chance sold his mare to the trapper, Ira Danvers just before you bought your ranch and we moved onto the Lazy J."

That was six years back and he and Chance Morgan hadn't been on good speaking terms, Chance having stolen his girl right out from under his nose. Still, he found it hard to believe Chance would sell his prized mare to someone like Ira Danvers. Garret had never actually met the mountain man, but had heard he was far less sociable than his woman.

"How can filth like that own a Morgan horse?"

Garret glanced back at the newest member of the Cattlemen's Association standing on the landing of the town hall, his expression filled with disgust. Strafford, the newly elected mayor of Bitterroot Springs, gripped the sides of his shiny blue jacket and stepped onto the walk, his group of ranch hands moving with him like a clutch of chickens scurrying after a peacock.

"Folks call her Mad Mag," said one of his men. "Ain't ever seen her in town before."

"Mad Mag?" Strafford's gaze narrowed. He stepped off the boardwalk into the dusty road. "You there? Come back here."

The woman increased her strides and urged the mare to move faster.

"Uh... Boss?" his man called after him. "I wouldn't—"

"Hey!" Strafford shouted. "I'm talking to you!"

"He's barkin' up the wrong tree with that one," Duce murmured.

Mad Mag turned into the alley beside the mercantile. Strafford hurried after her.

"Someone might ought to fetch the sheriff," suggested one of the men.

"Who wants to bet Mayor Strafford just got a new mare?"

The large group erupted with laughter.

Anger snapped at Garret's nerves. He'd disliked the overdressed rancher the moment he'd met the man. Nathan Strafford had moved into these hills with the greasy finesse of a snake-oil salesman, forcing out the smaller ranchers while pouring his money into this town. He'd funded a new school and the first courthouse in Bitterroot Springs, which had gotten him elected as the new town mayor.

Garret started across the road, damned if he'd stand by while that arrogant jackass took advantage of some poor deranged woman.

"Garret?"

Leaving Duce to chase after him, he rounded the building. Mag was near the far end of the alley, Strafford closing in on her.

"We got new laws in this town," Strafford announced, his long arm reaching for her. He grabbed a fistful of fur.

Mag spun to face him, the rifle in her hands forcing him to take a backward step. "Back off," she growled.

Strafford's six-plus frame towered over the small woman. "What business do you have in *my* town?" he demanded. "Aside from reeking up the streets and stealing our horses?"

The woman's cold, throaty laughter echoed through the hallow shadows of the narrow alley. "Oh, that's rich. *You* calling *me* a thief."

Strafford leaned closer to her. *"Mag—?"*

The butt of her rifle connected with Strafford's gut, ending his words in a hard cough. He doubled over. She swung again, her rifle cracking against his skull, sending him staggering back. Another swift blow to the brow, and Strafford hit the ground like a fallen timber.

Damn. Her reputation wasn't just rumors. She stood over Strafford, the barrel of her rifle pressed to his chest. She trembled. Jagged puffs of breath lifted the tangled black hair covering most of her face. Her finger flexed over the trigger.

If she shot Strafford, provoked or not, she'd hang before sundown.

"He's not worth it," Garret whispered, slowly moving in beside her while keeping an eye on that rifle.

Rage shaking her, Maggie couldn't think of a single reason why she shouldn't put a hole through Nathan's black heart. He had no right to touch her—no right to be in this part of Wyoming!

His town? Her gaze raked over his fancy suit. Bile burned in her throat. Did this town know the vile measures he used to acquire his wealth? It was past time for Nathan to be stomped back down to the devil.

She startled at a light pressure on her shoulder. Her gaze snapped to the long fingers touching her fur coat. She glanced up at wide shoulders creating a clear line on the pink horizon.

"Careful," he said. "Sheriff's coming."

Pale blond hair glowed white against the sunset, instantly identifying the man beside her.

Garret Daines. Recognition broke across her senses like a crack of lightning, shattering her tattered nerves.

She'd spotted Daines and his cow dog often enough in the hills around her mountain, but never so close. He appeared rather like the Vikings she'd learned about during her studies as a young girl, his pale hair wavering in the cool breeze, the span of his chest blocking out the world. A colorful sky outlined his profile, defining the sharp lines and intriguing contours of his face.

"Ma'am, you'd better git." The hand on her shoulder urged her aside, jarring her from a mental stupor. Not that he noticed. His hard gaze never strayed from the murmur of voices growing louder by the second. He glanced to his right and his friend moved in beside him, completely blocking her from view of the approaching mob.

"What's going on?" a man shouted.

"What happened to Mayor Strafford?" called another.

"Not much that I could see," said Daines. "Ol' Strafford didn't mind his footing. Tripped over his own boots and bumped his head."

Maggie stared up at Daines's broad shoulders, staggered by his outright lie, his offer of protection. Seizing the opportunity, she grabbed Star by the reins and stepped around the corner of the building. She wouldn't be back to this town.

Garret glanced over his shoulder as the crowd descended on Strafford, and was relieved to find the woman had fled. He looked at Duce and nodded in the direction she'd gone. They prudently made a swift exit. Garret scanned the surrounding hills and tall grasses spotted by patches of trees and scrub. Mad Mag was nowhere in sight.

"You got some kind of death wish I should know about?" asked Duce.

"Why would you think—?"

"You're lucky that woman didn't fill you full of buckshot. Or didn't you see the way she laid out Strafford?"

"She had a rifle, not a shotgun. And he likely frightened her, grabbing her the way he did."

"Frightened *her?* That's it," Duce said, shoving him across the road. "We're headed to the whorehouse before you end up dead or courting a mountain shrew."

Garret laughed, and didn't argue. Watching that woman knock Strafford down a few notches had lightened his mood.

Finally a bit of justice in this world.

Chapter Two

A soft swirl of snowflakes cold against her face, Maggie tugged her hood low and tightened her hold on the rope of her sled as she increased her stride through the soft powder. Her body ached to hunker down in her warm bed.

Two more miles.

The crunch of her snowshoes pressing through the soft ground echoed across the silent countryside. Dark clouds loomed to the north, telling her this was only a small reprieve in the blizzard. The late-winter storm had come on strong and without much warning the prior evening. Maggie barely had time to skin and dress the big buck she'd shot before having to bury her kill in the snow and seek shelter. Huddling in a dank alcove near the river had been no way to pass a frigid February night.

Despite the inconvenience, her hunt had been worthwhile. The frozen deer meat on her sled would last her the rest of winter, and then some.

A streamer of sunlight pierced the thick gray sky and glistened against an embankment of fresh snow up ahead. The silver sparkle captured her attention. As she drew closer she noted the metallic gleam was a *spur*. A spur attached to the vague outline of a boot buried beneath the snow.

Maggie slowed her stride. Her breath hit the cold air in a puff of white as her gaze moved across the long, lumpy mound.

Some fool cowpoke had gotten himself caught in the storm. He'd likely ventured up here looking for strays. High country weather was nothing like the lowlands. Lying on his side, the bulk of him was covered by a foot of snow.

The storm hadn't been *that* bad—nothing like the freeze two winters back. The deadly cold had caught beast and man in its clutches for miles around, reaching deep into the plains. The stench of death had lasted long into the spring. Any cowboy worth his salt would have learned from such disaster, and sought shelter or at least dug himself in to wait out the blizzard.

She shook her head and pressed on. As Ira used to say, she'd leave it to God to have sympathy for the men too stupid to save themselves. The world could get by without another cowpoke. Hundreds littered the lowlands around her mountain, whooping and hollering at their herds of cattle. At the rate things were going, she'd soon be crowded out of her mountain home just as the Indians had been forced from theirs.

A whimper broke across the winter silence. The snow-covered mound shifted.

Maggie hitched her shoulder, slinging her rifle forward, into her hands. Caution prickled at her skin as she watched the long shape rise up near the center.

A dog stood and gave a vigorous shake. She recognized the mutt's shaggy black fur and four white paws. *Boots.*

The sound of Garret Daines calling after his dog was as familiar to her as a meadowlark's song.

Oh, no. Maggie's breath stalled as she cautiously approached the figure partially buried beneath a blanket of white. Something inside her softened at the sight of pale hair and familiar features.

Why did it have to be Daines?

She crouched beside him. He had the pallor of a dead man. Blood matted his pale hair. A dark bruise protruded on his forehead—suspiciously shaped like the blunt end of a rifle.

Someone had knocked him out.

She glanced around the clearing. Undisturbed snow coated the ground, blanketing wide-spaced shrubs and trees. Any tracks had long since been snowed over.

How long has he been here?

She brushed away some of the packed powder and noted the slight movement of his chest. Relief swamped her. Biting the fingertip of her glove, she pulled the lined leather from her hand. She slid her fingers along his stubble-coated jaw. The man didn't so much as flinch. His skin was cold, but still soft. She didn't see any blackening signs of frostbite. His dog had likely kept him from freezing, but his shallow breathing didn't make even a slight mist in the frigid air.

He wouldn't live long if he didn't get out of the cold.

She reached for his coat and his dog barked, the sharp sound echoing through the winter silence. His master's eyelids fluttered, but didn't open.

She glanced at the dog prancing nervously beside her. The dog had distinctly different colored eyes. One deep green, the other pale blue.

Peculiar.

"Come'ere, Boots," she said, holding out her bare hand.

The dog's damp nose bumped against her palm.

"You stay friendly," she said, scratching behind its ear, "and we'll see about waking up your master."

She fisted the front of Daines's thick jacket and tugged him up, out of the snow. "Daines!" she shouted, giving him a shake. "Wake up, Daines!"

Pale lashes lifted. Glazed green eyes stared up at her. "Ma'am?"

For being half-frozen, his vision was keener than most. Not too many folks looked at her long enough to determine her gender. "You've got to get up," she said.

"Cattle…Duce…" His lids drooped.

"You don't get out of this cold, you're gonna lose more than cattle," she said, certain she was talking to herself.

His head tipped back and Maggie fell forward, his dead weight dragging her down with him. She landed flat on top of him. Her bare hand plunged into the bite of ice-cold snow.

"Damn it, Daines," she shouted, pushing off him. *"Wake up!"*

He blinked, but didn't move another muscle.

He'd already been exposed to the cold for too long, addling what she knew to be an otherwise sharp mind. Ira had fallen into an icy river once and had emerged from the frigid water dumber than a rock and helpless as a babe.

Maggie sat back on her heels and knocked the snow from the cuff of her white fur coat. The cold breeze snaked inside her sleeve, sending a chill across her warm skin. She quickly pulled on her glove. Her gut burned as the true extent of his situation sunk in. He wasn't going to make it.

He was too far from his ranch, at least six miles. The last thing she wanted was to take this Viking cowboy inside her home. There wasn't a soul alive who knew the location of her cabin. She lived up in the dense wild country for a reason—she didn't want to be bothered. The one time she'd had unexpected company she spent a whole spring and summer relocating.

The fact that her visitors had been relatives of Garret Daines didn't ease her reluctance to help him. By her account, his relation to Chance and Cora Morgan made him more of a threat. Morgan and his wife knew too many of her secrets already and she knew too well how a helpful hand could turn to a threat in the blink of an eye.

Don't trust your back to no one. Ira's mantra was embedded in her mind.

Thanks to her run-in with Nathan a few months ago, wanted posters now hung in surrounding settlements featuring a poorly drawn sketch of a mountain shrew, announcing a five-hundred-dollar reward for the capture of Mad Mag.

Why should she put herself in further danger by helping a man she barely knew?

"M-m-ma'am?" His unfocused green eyes blinked up at her. "Are y-y-a…all right?"

Was *she* all right? She wasn't the one lying half-frozen in the snow.

The blatant concern in his expression prodded at her usually silent conscience. Garret Daines seemed to have more charm than sense. Despite his intimidating size, he had a kindness to him that had struck her right off the first time she'd spied him in the low country. With his unusual pale hair and a deep laughter that could carry for miles, he was always easy to spot. Her Viking protector hadn't been smiling a few months back—a vision that had been plaguing her dreams ever since. His gaze had been hard and focused as he had stood between her and the riled citizens of Bitterroot Springs.

He'd defended her. *Her.* Mad Mag, the local lunatic.

I can't just leave him here to freeze. Unlike those who'd betrayed her, Garret Daines wasn't a man who'd stand by while harm befell another. He'd do as Ira had done, taking on a burden he didn't want to save the life of a stranger. She'd also been small enough for a grown man to toss over his shoulder and cart off into the woods. She couldn't carry Garret Daines five feet, much less up this mountain through the snow. She had to get him up.

"Help me, Garret," she said in her best damsel voice. "It's so cold. I need to get home. Can you help me?"

He nodded, muscles bunching beneath his thick coat. He tried to push up, and groaned, his stiff body rebelling against the movement. She gripped his arms and helped to tug him up. Snow clung to his thick coat and buffalo-hide chaps—clothes that should have kept him warm. His hat lay crumpled in the top of the outline of his fallen form. She noted the creases pressed into his left cheek. His dog and his hat had protected those handsome features from hours of exposure. But the icy weather had taken a toll on his mind. He stared blankly at the ground before him.

He swayed, his eyelids drooping.

She reached for him, her arms sliding into his open coat. His shirt crinkled like a sheet of ice.

Alarm squeezed her chest. His clothes had gotten wet.

The rain from yesterday, before the heavy snowstorm had set in. No wonder his coat and woolly chaps weren't holding heat—they were likely keeping him as chilled as an icebox.

"Come on, Garret," she urged, trying to guide him toward her sled. "Stay with me."

His expression contorted with pain. His boots barely

moved in the deep powder. With a rumbling groan, he fell from her grasp and landed face-first into the snow.

Boots yapped at him and nudged his tangled hair with his nose.

"It's no use, dog. We'll have to get him on the sled."

Working quickly, she pushed her supplies and the frozen meat wrapped in deerskin aside and rolled Garret onto the wooden slats. After shoving her supplies beneath his legs to keep his boots from dragging on the ground, she bound a strip of rope across his middle, pinning his arms against his sides. Finished, she fetched his hat, shook off the snow and tugged the dark felt over his white hair.

She glanced at his dog standing up to its chest in snow. She'd seen the cow dog jump onto the back of Garret's horse more than once while roaming through the lower hills, settling in a spot behind the saddle as though curling up on a porch rug—one of the oddest sights she'd ever witnessed.

"Come on, Boots," she said, patting his master's coat.

That was all it took. The hound curled up on Garret's chest and laid its head on his white paws, his two-toned eyes watching her as she grabbed the sled rope and slipped it over her shoulder. Using all of her weight, her leg muscles burned as she began to haul her heavy load toward home. She'd be drenched in sweat before she reached her cabin, creating a nice layer of ice between her skin and her clothes. Risking her life for a stranger only to catch her death with pneumonia.

She glanced back.

Bound and unmoving, Garret looked like a big prize buck strapped to her sled. The ache in her gut intensified.

"You better not die."

* * *

By the time she spotted the gap in the stone leading to a secluded meadow, every muscle in her body burned despite the increasing chill in her skin. A freezing wind whipped at her back as snow swirled around her in a flurry of white. She clenched her jaw to keep her teeth from chattering. She hadn't slowed to check on her cargo, but kept her focus on the mountainside rising beyond the trees.

She always missed her horse over winter, never so much as the past two hours. But she had no way to house and feed Star once the long freeze set in, forcing Maggie to leave her with the man who'd given her the mare. Chance Morgan's generosity didn't keep her from resenting having to depend on his services. Life had been so much simpler when she could keep to the rivers, bartering with only the Sioux and other trappers. Ira had warned her. It was past time to move on.

Barely visible through a thick forest, she spotted her cabin front built into the stone alcove. *Home.* Relief dragged a groan from deep within her chest.

She dragged the sled through the tight maze of trees then stopped before the snowed-in door topped by a stone overhang. After releasing the bindings on her snowshoes she cleared away the snowdrift then lifted the lock. Her cabin door squeaked open. The small dark space inside was no warmer than the brisk cold blowing through the trees. She hurried to the stove against the stone wall and reached for the matches.

Within moments flames licked over dry wood, illuminating the darkness. She'd expected to come home cold and had left her cabin prepared. She lit the lamp sitting atop her storage shelves beside her stove then moved her full teakettle to the warmest spot on the range top.

Movement beside her made her jump. Boots gave a vigorous shake, spattering a fine spray of melting snow across her cabin floor. She followed a trail of dirty paw-prints across the polished wood. Irritation burned through her.

You brought them here, she silently berated. *You'll have to deal with the messes.* She turned and took a small throw from the foot of her bed. She tossed the thin blanket into the corner beyond the stove.

"Lay down," she said, pointing to the rumpled fabric.

The dog went right to the corner and curled up.

Easy enough. She glanced through the open door at the lump of leather and man bound to her sled. Snowflakes swirled down from a storm-darkened sky.

Dread pooled in her belly and seemed to settle like a lead weight in her deerskin boots. She forced herself to move toward him. Despite her anxiety, she hoped she hadn't endured that exhausting climb for two-hundred-plus pounds of dead cowboy. She stepped back out into the whipping wind and a shiver moved through her, the biting cold a prelude to the storm rolling in with the dark sky. She released the rope and brushed the fresh snow from Garret's face. His eyelids fluttered, but didn't quite open.

"Couldn't just come home with deer meat," she lamented, pulling her supplies and the bound venison from beneath his legs. His boots dropped over her threshold. She tossed her gear inside then carried the meat bound in fresh deer hide to the cold box buried beneath a foot of snow just outside her cabin. She dug up the lid and dropped in the whole hide-bound parcel. Salting and stewing would have to wait.

She pushed the sled up to the narrow door frame and climbed over Garret's legs to get into the cabin. Gripping one of his boots just above the spurs, she pulled off the stiff leather. After placing his boots beneath her table she gripped him by the ankles and noticed a hole in the heel of each thick wool stocking. Either the man wasn't married or his wife wasn't worth the food to keep her fed.

"No gentle way to get this done," she said, firming her hold.

Using all her strength, she hauled him inside. His head bounced against the hardwood floor, the sickening thud making her cringe. No time to worry about his bruised skull, she hurried past him to shut out the chilling wind and bar the door. Tossing her gloves onto the table against the front wall, she quickly shrugged off her fur coat and hung it from a hook beside the door. Cold stagnant air seeped through her clothes, but her heavy coat would get in the way of tending her guest.

Low moans sounded behind her as Garret began to rouse. He filled the space between her bed and the stove, leaving little room to walk around him. His eyes clenched tight, his face contorting with pain. She imagined the meager warmth of the stove was starting to penetrate his cold skin. She'd been on the verge of frostbite more than once. Flesh coming back to life felt like needles searing through bone.

She knelt next to him and pulled the leather gloves from his hands.

Greenish-blue eyes glazed with pain blinked up at her.

"Hurting is good," she said, lifting one of his hands into the lantern light. "Means you're not froze through." She caressed each of his fingers, testing for frozen patches of skin. She didn't feel anything but long, strong fingers and hard-earned calluses.

"You'll get to keep your hide." She pushed back the sides of his sheepskin coat and started working the buttons on his shirt. Ice melted beneath her fingers, saturating his two wool shirts by the time she had them unbuttoned. She pulled the thick layers back, his skin cold and damp beneath her palms as she tried to work the fabric over his shoulders.

"We won't get these off with you lying down." She eased back and tugged at his arm. "Garret, I need you to sit up."

His expression contorted with pain. His big body didn't budge.

"You think this hurts?" she said, moving over him, patting his pale stubble-coated cheeks, forcing him to focus on her. "Wait till the shivers set in. We need to get you out of these wet clothes before your muscles start to spasm." She tugged on his arms. "Come on, cowboy, give me some help!"

He curled forward, groaning as she gripped his shoulders, pulling him the rest of the way up.

In a burst of movement, he shrugged off her hold. Wild, angry eyes stared deep into hers. He slurred words she couldn't make out. Judging by his fierce scowl and harsh gaze, he was swearing at her.

Fighting her own fatigue, Maggie sat back on her heels and tried to assess his state of mind. She was in no shape for a bear fight. His narrowed eyes began to drift shut. His head tilted toward the cast-iron stove.

Maggie lunged onto him. Her knees banged against the floor as she straddled his lap. "Garret!" She gripped his shoulders and struggled to hold him upright.

His dog barked, likely startled by her quick movement. Her arms ached in her attempt to hold Garret steady. His chest pressed against hers like a block of ice.

Boots kept barking at her back, the sharp sound echoing across the high stone ceiling. She looked over her shoulder and glared at the mutt. "I skin bigger beasts than you. *Lay down.*"

Boots pranced for a moment then went back to the blanket, lying down with a whimper. The weight in her arms eased, muscles firming beneath her hold. Maggie looked back at Garret and found him staring at her. His face so close, she could see each tiny fleck of blue and gold in his green eyes. Her skin prickled, the rush of sensation awakening what felt like a field of butterflies in her belly, and suddenly she was startled by their closeness.

What the hell was she thinking to bring him here?

She eased back. Even with his complexion as pale as his shaggy white hair, he was a handsome specimen of a man, the finest she'd ever seen.

"We'll get you warmed up," she said. "Then you can get the hell off my mountain. All right?"

His eyes narrowed, as though he struggled to comprehend her words. She had to get him bundled in some warm, dry blankets.

She peeled his jacket and shirts from his arms. His thick muscles began to bunch and quiver. He remained silent as she removed his gunbelt and worked the buckle on his chaps. She tugged open his trousers and glanced up at his vacant stare. She smoothed his hair away from his face. His tremors increased as her hands cupped his stubbly cheeks, forcing him to meet her gaze.

"Garret, you have to stand up."

He gave a slight nod and she eased back. His quivering muscles flexed in an attempt to do as she asked. The pain in his expression made her chest ache. Halfway up she wrapped her arms around his cold chest, giving him added support as he straightened his legs. His wet chaps and trousers fell to the floor in a heap. She slid her arms down to his bare waist, guiding him forward, helping him step out of the tangled clothing.

Trembling beside her, Garret stared down at his naked form then glanced at her, a look of sheer confusion on his face.

"This is no great thrill for me," she said, and nearly laughed at the outright lie. Garret Daines in the buff, his muscles flexed and quivering, was a sight to behold. *Long, lean, chiseled to perfection.*

A startling stir of new sensation shimmered inside her. Maggie forced her gaze up to the startling view of his bare chest.

Good gracious. Heat flushed across her skin, and suddenly her damp clothes weren't quite so chilling. She reached past him to pull back the quilts and buffalo hide covering her bed. Unnerved by her body's reaction, she knocked him onto the feather-stuffed mattress and began pulling blankets over all that shivering brawn.

His gruff voice sounded in a slur of words. He growled with frustration and grabbed her hand.

Maggie froze, startled by his strong grip. His eyes burned with questions.

"It's the cold," she said, pulling her fingers from his grasp and tucking his hand back beneath the covers. "Addles the mind for a time. You've just got to warm up."

As though she'd given the answer he needed, a sigh broke from his chest. His eyes drifted shut—which was how she preferred them, she decided. Unease swept through her at the thought of a fully conscious Garret Daines standing in her small cabin.

Oh Lord. She hadn't thought that far ahead…and tried

not to think of it now. Wasn't anything she could do—he was here, shivering in her bed. The wood frame creaked with his violent tremors.

She stepped back. All she could do now was keep the fire stoked. His body needed to hold heat. She pulled her coat back on and grabbed her gloves from the table. She'd have to make sure the stovepipe atop the hillside hadn't snowed over before she fetched an armload of wood.

By the time she returned to the cabin, her teakettle was steaming and she was trembling nearly as much as the man curled up in her bed. She shut the door against a fierce wind, the storm having fully arrived. She fed the fire another log then took a cup from the shelves beside her stove and opened her tea canister.

Exhausted, she dropped onto the only chair beside her narrow table with her tea and two shortbread cookies. Her shivers reminded her that her clothes were still damp. Taking a sip of tea to wash down the cookies, she told herself she needed to string a line to dry Garret's clothes and start some stew. Her supply of meat needed to be thawed, cut and salted. She took another deep drink, the warm liquid soothing her chill. Completely worn-out, her mind and body balked at the idea of going back out into that storm to bring in the venison.

She watched Garret shiver in her bed and his dog sleeping soundly beside the stove as she drank the last of her tea. Suddenly she could barely keep her eyes open. Her tea no longer warming her hands and her belly, the chill crept back into her skin. Her own clothes needed to dry out, and she needed warming. All her blankets were wrapped around Garret. Lying on his side, he left just enough room for her to squeeze in beside him. A couple hours to warm up and regain her strength and she'd be ready to dry his gear and start a stew.

She lit the small lamp at the center of her table then dropped to her knees before her trunk at the end of her bed. Stacks of brightly embroidered shirts and dishcloths filled three quarters of the space—a winter's worth of work. She didn't have use for such colorful garb. Since Ira's death, she bartered the fancy stitched dishcloths and clothing instead of animal pelts. She pulled out her flannel night-shirt and dropped the lid. Changing into the dry garment she hung her damp clothes over the chair and placed it before the stove. She'd be needing her clothes long before Garret would have use for his.

The fire stoked, her clothes drying, she stood beside the bed in her thick wool socks and nightshirt. She held her belt and sheathed blade, but was hesitant to crowd in beside Garret. Didn't matter that she'd watched him in the lower hills more often than she should have in the past few years or that he seemed a fine man. She'd once been foolish enough to trust those who'd been ready to watch her die at her brother's hands.

Ain't enough of you to fight off man or beast. Ira's gritty voice sounded in her mind. *Don't bed down without a weapon at hand.*

If she didn't get some sleep she'd be dead on her feet by the time Garret awoke. *Not smart.* His slow, jagged breaths assured her he was in a deep sleep just this side of death.

She went to the foot of the bed, stepped onto her trunk and eased into the sliver of space. She draped her belt over the bedpost and angled her knife so it would be within easy reach. She burrowed beneath the heavy blankets, lifting Garret's arm to make room. The chill of his skin stole her breath as she settled beside him. Even so, her tired muscles rejoiced at the feel of the mattress beneath her.

Garret moaned. His big body shifted, his arms closing around her.

Maggie braced her hands against his cold chest. "Garret?" she whispered, forcing her voice past her constricted throat.

Several minutes passed. His eyes remained closed. The pressure of his hold didn't change despite the tremors of his body. His heart thumped slow and steady beneath her palm.

The man's practically an icicle, she reasoned. Instinctively he was trying to get warm.

She relaxed against his hold and tried to scoot into a more comfortable position. With every shift, her bare legs brushed against the coarse hair of his masculine body. She'd never lain with a naked man. The few times she'd snuggled up with Ira for warmth they'd been fully clothed and she'd been too cold to be bothered by Ira's stench. Cleanliness wasn't Ira's way. He frequently grumbled about her sweet-scented soaps attracting bear. But he respected her way, making sure she had lye to make soap and seeking out a hot spring when she needed a long soak. She could use one now. So could Garret.

She yawned again, drawing in the musky scent of Garret's skin. The hair on his chest tickled her cheek. Garret Daines didn't smell bad, she noted. Her hand slid over his side to the smooth skin of his back as she settled against him. Despite his cold presence, a pleasing warmth spread through her as she gave in to sheer exhaustion.

Chapter Three

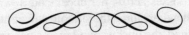

She spoke to him through the darkness. Her soothing touch pulled him from the cold depths of a nightmare. Heat suffused across his body as images of delicate ivory features and piercing blue eyes flickered through his mind.

Garret knocked a weight from his shoulders then shifted against the warmth pressing against him. His hand slid over a distinctly feminine form. A bare leg, a smooth hip curving into a narrow waist. He snuggled closer. Silky hair brushed his face. Her fresh, floral scent swirled across his senses as a soft, satiny breast filled his palm.

His body stirred, increasing the heat radiating beneath his skin. Her sensual moan dragged him toward consciousness. He wanted to open his eyes, to see her before she slipped back into the darkness. He blinked, letting in a flicker of light, then forced his heavy lids to open.

She was there, in the soft glow, sleeping against his chest just the way he'd always imagined a woman should sleep with her man. Relaxed against him, her head on his shoulder, her silky black hair fanned over his arm. His other hand was tucked inside her shirt. The bunched gray wool revealed a trim belly and the deep curve of her hip. It had been far too long since he'd had a woman in his bed.

I must be dead...or dreaming.

Looking at her pretty face, he didn't much care which. She was a vision to be marveled, *cherished.* He leaned in, touching his lips to hers in the lightest caress. His thumb bushed over the firm peak of her breast and her breathing deepened. He dusted light kisses across her cheek and down her slender neck as his hand explored the smooth silk of her abdomen.

She moaned, the husky sound increasing the heavy beat of his pulse. He pressed a kiss to the hollow of her throat as the satin fullness of her breast filled his palm once more.

Her breath broke, her back arched.

Starving to taste what she offered, he nudged at the fabric with his mouth. A button gave way, revealing the soft, supple swell of her breast and beaded pink crown.

Garret gave up on trying to breathe. His lips closed over her and he simply tasted. She stretched and shifted beneath him, twisting against his caressing mouth like a gentle flame. His body warmed to a fevered pitch as he drew his dream lover from sleep in the sweetest way he'd ever imagined.

"Oh! What are...!" Her fingers drove into his hair and tugged.

Groaning with regret, he released her. Despite her hold on his hair, he brushed his lips over the glistening peak once more before easing up. Wide blue eyes stared at him.

Blue as sapphires, just as he knew they would be.

"Garret?"

A tingle of surprise rippled through him. Of course she'd know his name.

"You are...*so beautiful.*" He brushed his mouth over her parted lips. She tensed against him and gripped his shoulders.

"Gar—"

His name became a muffled cry as he deepened the kiss. He wasn't ready to give up this dream. His fingertips lightly skimmed her breast, her waist, her thigh.

A pleasing groan was lost inside his mouth. Her tight hold on his shoulders became an arousing embrace as she shuddered against him. Her fingers slid over his back as she returned his fiery kiss. Triumph roared through him. The rush of passion and the pounding of his pulse forced him to release her mouth. He dragged for breath as he trailed kisses across her throat.

"You're *perfect.*" He wanted her; he wanted to know her name.

An intense pain throbbed through his mind, blurring his vision. He gathered his dream lover close, his body aching for her. *"Stay,"* he said, but her delicate features began to fade. Darkness closed in around him, pulling her out of reach.

Trapped beneath Garret's unmoving weight, Maggie's eyes burned with unshed tears as she fought for breath. Her mind spun in a tangle of overwhelming sensation and utter confusion. One moment she'd been dreaming of floating in a hot spring, the soothing heat of the water rippling over her sensitive skin—in the next moment Garret Daines had his lips on her, creating a kind of heat she'd never felt before.

She was sure she'd opened her mouth to tell him to stop, but had only managed a strangled moan as he had flooded her body with sensations she'd never experienced in her life.

"Don't go," he whispered against her ear, the vibrations rekindling the wild tingles in all the places he'd touched. His arm tightened over her ribs.

Suddenly she was frightfully aware of her exposed

damp skin, the warmth of his thigh wedged between hers, the very male portion of him pressed firmly against her hip.

Damnation!

She shoved his arm away and scrambled for the end of the bed. She stumbled over the trunk and fell to the cold floor. She sprang up, tugging her wool nightshirt closed as she bumped against her table, wobbling the lit oil lamp. Light shifted over shadows and the naked man sprawled in her bed.

She inched toward the stove, grabbed her now dry clothes then backed toward the door. How long had she slept?

Too long, she reminded herself, still trembling from Garret's touch. She wasn't about to look away from the man before her to search for signs of daylight seeping around the door. She shoved her feet into her warm buckskin pants and jerked them up. The shift of fabric against her damp flesh made her shudder. What had he done to her? She tugged on her buckskin tunic over the wool shirt. Her shaky fingers cinched the ties.

Ira had warned her about the violent intentions of randy men. He claimed she was his woman to those they encountered to keep her safe from such advances, but she hadn't always traveled with Ira. She'd been chased more than once by men with such intentions to hold her down and hurt her—they'd never caught her.

Keeping her gaze on Garret, she slid her foot into a tall moccasin. She should have left him in the snow! *Shot him,* and then left him in the snow!

After lacing both boots she stuffed the bottom of her shirt into her pants. His coloring had returned. The light hair on his legs stood out against the darker skin beneath. Her gaze trailed across his bare backside.

The heated swirls he'd conjured rose up, stealing her breath.

She strapped her arms around her trembling middle and realized her belt and knife were missing.

Her gaze landed on her belt hanging from the bedpost. Why hadn't she reached for her blade?

Boots stood up in the corner and stretched. The black shaggy dog trotted toward her and bumped her leg. Keeping her gaze on Garret, she reached down to pat the dog's head.

"What's the matter with him?" she whispered. How could he still be sleeping when her pulse hammered erratically from the things he'd done to her?

He hadn't actually hurt her. He'd *kissed* her, in ways she'd never imagined a man would kiss a woman. Her teeth clamped down on her trembling lower lip. The memory of his mouth on her breast, his tongue moving against hers added to the violent stir of her pulse. His touch had been tender, his kisses…overwhelming. She recalled the time Morgan and his bride had invaded her old cabin some years back. She hadn't meant to watch them; she'd been mesmerized by their gentle embraces and tender kisses as Morgan had convinced Cora to marry him.

No wonder they seemed to enjoy themselves. Kissing Garret so intimately… She drew a deep, ragged breath and had to wonder if a man would have courted her with such tenderness, had she been allowed to grow into the proper lady her father always believed she'd become.

Bitter sentiment squelched the thought.

She wasn't some gentile lady full of ignorant fanciful notions. She didn't entertain suitors. At twenty-seven she was well into spinsterhood and had put such notions behind her. Garret Daines had no call to touch her in such a manner!

He continued to lie there, his back rising slightly with his deep, even breaths. Could a man put his mouth on her one moment and be unconscious the next?

She moved toward the bed. His dog stayed beside her.

"Garret?"

He didn't stir. Her stomach dipped at the sight of his sleeping face and flushed lips. *Far too handsome.* She stepped closer. Heat radiated off his body. She touched his shoulder. His skin fairly scalded her hand. He moaned at her touch.

He's raging with fever.

"Garret?"

When he didn't respond, she reached over him, grabbed her belt and quickly strapped it around her waist. She picked up one of the blankets he'd knocked to the floor and draped it over the firm slope of his bare backside. Fever or not, her sensibilities could only handle so much.

"Thaw him out to cool him off," she muttered on her way to the door. Outside she was stunned to discover night-time encroaching on a stormy gray sky. She'd slept nearly the whole day.

A short while later she was packing snow into the embroidered hand towels she'd intended to sell. Garret moaned in his sleep as she placed them over his super-heated body but didn't fully rouse. The snow melted quickly against his shoulders and the back of his neck. As she swabbed his flushed skin with the cool cloth a troubling thought increased the unease welling inside her.

He'd been out of his mind with fever, and she'd nearly succumbed to his hallucinations. He'd called her beautiful and she'd lost her mind right along with him.

Thank goodness he'd passed out. She could just imagine

his reaction when he awoke to discover it was Mad Mag he'd been kissing in that bed.

Her hands paused on his back, the thought of facing his scorn twisting her stomach into a painful knot. She hadn't just allowed him to kiss her, she'd reveled in the bursts of pleasing sensation, the shocking intimacy of his deep kiss.

Shame washed through her. *Good God.* What would he think of her?

Same as everyone else, she supposed. Tears stung her eyes, a reaction that stunned her.

This time she'd finally earned the moniker *Mad Mag*.

Chapter Four

Garret woke to the aroma of stewed meat and the telltale bubbling of something simmering on the stove. He blinked several times, and still he stared up at a high stone ceiling. His gaze swept over rock walls, a black stove to his right...none of it the slightest bit familiar.

His stomach growled, the tantalizing scent drawing his gaze back to the bubbling kettle. Licking his dry lips he glanced at the wood front of what appeared to be someone's home. A lamp to his right and another beyond the foot of the bed created soft circles of light, brightening the dank surroundings.

Where the hell am I?

He pushed up onto his elbows and had to stifle a groan. His body ached as though he hadn't moved in ages. Pain pulsed through his skull, radiating from the left side. He reached up and touched a tender spot above his forehead and discovered a small lump and what felt like a gash beneath his hair. The movement wafted him with a clean, sweet scent. He paused and sniffed his arm.

"Wildflowers?"

Sapphire eyes and black hair against delicate ivory skin surfaced in his mind.

The woman. She'd stayed nearby, stroking his skin, encouraging him to drink.

Rest, Garret. You have a fever.

The soft, husky voice tantalized his memory with the alluring scent of her skin, her silky softness beneath his lips.

"A dream," he muttered. *The only safe place to love a woman.*

He pushed the wool blanket aside and froze, surprise prickling through him. He wasn't wearing a stitch of clothing. His gaze skated around the room, searching every shadowed corner. He was alone. In the corner beside the stove was a rumpled blanket and tooth-scrapped bone. Wherever his caretaker had gone, she'd taken his dog. Why was he here? If he was sick, why wasn't he in his own bed? And yet…he didn't recall getting sick. For all he knew some woman had knocked him from his saddle and dragged him to her bed.

Her delicate feminine features surfaced in his mind.

A man could suffer a worse fate.

Another glance around the rough rock walls snuffed that thought. He doubted the delicate creature of his dreams would live in such desolate surroundings. Had he dreamed up her pretty face to match the soothing voice and gentle hands that had been caring for him?

He shifted his feet to the floor with silent caution. His bare toes touched down on a cold, smooth surface.

Polished wood? He glanced again at the tidy space, noting the canisters, boxes and stacked dishes lined up all nicelike on the wide-set shelves, the stack of blankets folded at the foot of the bed. He'd known a couple of miners who'd carved out similar dwellings—but he'd never known any miner to be quite so tidy. Every breath drew in a clean floral scent and the mouthwatering aroma of stew.

How the hell had he gotten here? He closed his eyes, trying to remember. Last he could recall he'd been riding range... he'd ridden home at noon and—*Duce.* He'd been looking for Duce. His business partner hadn't made it in for the noontime meal. The way the countryside had been strewn with violence and mishaps lately, too many ranchers turning up dead and a storm rolling in...

Chills prickled his skin as he recalled the cold, whipping rain washing out horse tracks he'd followed into the hills—old panic clenched his chest.

He hadn't found Duce.

Garret shot to his feet, pulling the blanket around his waist as he stood. The quick movement made him light-headed and wafted him with the scent of spring flowers, reminding him that whoever lived here had done more than simply tend his fever. He'd been *bathed.*

He moved toward the door, each step a slow stretch of tense muscles. The way his head and body ached, he could have been struck by lightning. Maybe Duce had found *him* and brought him to this place.

Spotting his boots tucked beneath the small table beside the rickety door, he pulled them out and stepped into the tall leather shafts. His clothes were nowhere in sight. Surely he'd been fully dressed when he'd arrived. He scanned three large barrels stacked on top of the other in the far corner and a large chest at the foot of the bed. He was tempted to search their contents for his britches. A pinch in his bladder urged him to search out a privy first. After he relieved himself, he'd find whoever had taken his clothes and his dog and demand some answers.

He pulled open the door and had to shield his face from a flurry of snowflakes. Cold wind buffeted against his bare chest, sending an instant chill shivering across his skin. He stared gap-jawed at the snow piled some three feet high on either side of the door, a path having been recently shoveled.

"What the hell?"

Through the haze of swirling flakes tall timbers reached toward a gray sky. White-topped mountain peaks rose up from all sides.

He was in the high country. He wouldn't have ridden into these snow-packed mountains.

A familiar bark echoed over the rush of wind and Garret stepped into the brisk cold. "Boots!"

Snow burst from the embankment up ahead as his dog bounded onto the shoveled path. Garret grinned, relieved to see his shaggy friend.

"Hey, boy," he said, reaching down to pat his furry head while keeping his gaze on movement near the end of the path. He narrowed his eyes, trying to peer through the falling snow as the stranger drew near. The small form slowly emerged through the flurry of flakes, a white hooded coat blending with the winter landscape. He couldn't make out more than a faint outline and a shotgun clutched in the left hand.

Caution tensed his muscles as the stranger drew close.

Mad Mag was the first thought to his mind, until she looked up. The deep blue eyes and delicate, feminine features lurking beneath that hood stole his breath.

She's real. The passionate woman from his dream.

"You should be inside."

Her voice was low, *husky,* and flooded his mind with the

sounds of breathy moans, the image of her rose-tipped breast straining toward his mouth.

"Move."

Her harsh tone and stern gaze jarred him from the tantalizing vision. He stepped back, allowing her to rush him through the doorway. She quickly shut out the wind and wisps of snow.

"Go lay down." She pointed toward the far wall, her stern tone commanding as she stared him right in the eyes.

Maybe this bitty thing *had* clubbed him over the head and dragged him to her bed. Shock rippled through him…along with an undeniable stir of attraction.

Boots brushed his leg on his way to the corner, and Garret realized she was talking to his dog, not him. He scrubbed a hand over his stubble-coated jaw. He obviously wasn't working with a full deck. His brain struggled to take hold of the notion that his dream lover stood before him. He stared at her, his mind lost somewhere between reality and a *really good* dream.

She propped her gun beside the door and glanced briefly at the floor. Her supple pink lips pressed to a firm line as her gaze moved over puddles of melting snow. He'd left the door wide-open.

"Sorry about that."

Sharp blue eyes narrowed, her expression bordering on lethal. Not quite the passionate woman from his memory— *his dreams,* he silently amended. He eased back toward the warmth of the stove, his instincts warning him not to crowd the little filly. Her soft, delicate features were a clear contradiction to the hard blue eyes watching him with calculating caution.

She stayed beside the door, her posture stiff, defensive. The hand hovering near her waist made him wonder if she wore a gun beneath her coat. She pushed her hood back, revealing silky black braids tucked behind her ears. In his mind her hair was loose, fanned out across his arm, his chest—

"How do you feel?" she asked, her smooth voice washing over him like a sensual caress.

Uncomfortably aroused. He shifted his hold on the blanket and had to remind himself he didn't know this woman. Other than the alluring images in his mind, he'd never seen her before.

"Alive, I suppose," he answered. At the moment he wasn't certain of anything else. His dreams blended with reality, distracting him from the questions he should be asking. Like why he'd awakened in the high country, where were his clothes and…had he actually bedded this woman? Best to start with something simple.

"Where am I?"

"About eight miles north of your ranch."

Eight miles? Most of them straight up by the looks of the mountainous terrain he'd glimpsed outside.

She shrugged off her heavy fur. Garret wasn't sure what he expected to see beneath the long coat, but the vibrant red flowers stitched across the shoulders of her white shirt took him by surprise. The garment hung to mid-thigh, cinched at her narrow waist by a beaded belt. She wasn't wearing a gun. A leather sheath secured a long bowie knife at her hip.

Tiny but fierce, he thought, noting how her gaze didn't stray from him as she hung her coat beside the door. Buckskin britches encased her slender legs, the bottoms tucked into her tall Indian-style boots. He only knew of one mountain woman to frequent these ranges, had been close enough to the old woman called Mad Mag to catch her stench, to see the filth on her hands as she had held a rifle to a man's chest. The wide white cuffs of this woman's shirt were etched with red thread and hid her hands, revealing just enough of her fingers to see her clean, short fingernails. She smelled as fresh as a spring rain.

"You were caught in the storm," she said, drawing his gaze back to her young, pretty face.

He remembered a rainstorm, and the cold...waking to a beautiful woman sleeping in his arms. His gaze slid to the bed, a sense of dread tightening his gut.

"Do I have you to thank?" he asked. "Or was it your husband who brought me here?" A husband would be good. He needed some reassurance that the visions in his mind were just that—*visions.*

"You can thank your dog. If not for him, you likely would have froze before I found you."

"*You* found me?"

Her posture stiffened. "That's right."

"Begging your pardon, ma'am, but...I don't recall your name or riding up to this..." His gaze slid over the stone walls. "*Cabin.*"

"I'm not surprised. You were froze out of your mind when I found you. That was the day before yesterday. Once your chill wore off a fever set in."

He had the vague memory of a cool, damp cloth stroking his skin, her smooth, husky voice encouraging him to drink. Incapacitated for nearly three days, it wasn't a wonder he was starving and his bladder about to burst.

His shock wearing off, he was hit by the renewed urge to step outside.

"You've been sick," she said. "You should lie down."

"What I need are my clothes." *And an outhouse.* At this point, his clothes would be a waste of time—he had to go *now.* He took a step forward.

The woman's hand went for her blade. The glint in her eyes told him she wouldn't hesitate to fillet him.

"Easy, honey," he said, raising his hand, the other gripping the blanket at his hip. "I'm just headin' for the door. No reason to get jumpy."

"You can't leave," she said, her hand still on the hilt of her long knife.

"I need to step outside for a spell."

Her stance widened as though she thought she could stop him. "It's still storming."

"Lady, *I've got to take a leak,*" he all but shouted, the pressure becoming downright painful.

"Oh." Her eyes widened, understanding easing her tense expression. God bless her, a pink flush flared into her cheeks. "There's a chamber pot under the bed." She rushed past him.

Garret watched her kneel beside the bed and figured she must be out of her pretty little mind. It was bad enough he stood before this woman in nothing but his boots and a blanket. He'd damn well risk the frostbite.

"You can—" A burst of cold air hit Maggie's face as she sat back. Her guest slammed the door shut behind him.

"Of all the fool notions!"

His dog scampered after him and barked at the closed door.

"He's going to freeze," she spat. And this time she was not going to tend to his warming! Boots bumped against her leg as she stood, his tail wagging wildly. He was obviously happy at seeing his master up and around. Maggie reached down to pet him and noticed her hands were shaking.

He's awake.

She didn't know why Garret's size had come as such a shock—but it had. Tending him while unconscious hadn't prepared her for looking up at those flexing muscles, his eyes clear and alert. The way he'd stared at her...

He remembers.

If her cheeks blazed any hotter they'd catch fire. She pressed her hands to her flushed skin. *Hellfire.* She was actually *blushing.* The fact that he'd flustered her so increased her worry. He'd taken one step toward her, his eyes dark and turbulent, and she'd damn near drawn her knife against him.

A natural reflex, she reasoned. *For someone who lives in the wild.* She'd spent most her life hunting, skinning and shooting at anything that came at her baring teeth, whether it be beast or man. And there'd been plenty of both.

She'd suffered her share of scratches, bite marks and bullet wounds. Even so, she ventured that most folks, *sane folks,* didn't greet a request for an outhouse with a knife wound.

Biting out a swear word she grabbed one of the blankets at the end of her bed and dropped it onto the wet floor. It had been too many years since she'd been so close to anyone. She'd never had cause to be cordial with any man since Ira. She wasn't sure she remembered how. After so much effort to keep Garret alive, she'd sure hate to harm his handsome hide.

I ought to bar the door while I have the chance.

Instead she draped the damp cloth over her chair and hurried to the stack of barrels she'd turned into tall cupboards. Opening the hinged side of the center barrel she took out Garret's clean shirts and trousers. She pulled his coat from the bottom barrel.

He'll rest up and be gone by tomorrow.

Her stomach flopping something awful, she tossed the stack of clothes onto the trunk and pressed a hand to her belly. The sight of black braids lying over bright red blossoms made her groan as the heat in her face intensified. She felt foolish wearing the ornate nightdress she'd hemmed, her hair woven into the only style she'd ever done on her own. No respectable townswoman wore braids at the age of twenty-seven, but Maggie didn't own any hairpins and wouldn't know what to do with them even if she had. She'd done the best she could to appear feminine, normal.

She hadn't convinced him. His expression had creased with confusion as his gaze soaked up her attire.

"I don't give two shakes what he thinks of me," she muttered as she hung his coat beside hers and went to the stove. *So long as he doesn't think I'm Mad Mag.* With Nathan hunting her and wanted posters boasting a reward for her capture, she couldn't risk anyone knowing where she lived.

She glanced warily at the door. Boots stood vigil, whining as the wood creaked against a gust of wind. Hopefully he hadn't gotten too close a look at her that day in town.

She dragged in a shaky breath and lifted the lid off her stewpot. Thick brown gravy bubbled around tender meat and potatoes. Her appetite soured at the memory of Nathan grabbing her in that alleyway. Her surprise had paled to his. He'd been shocked to see his little sister alive and well— a shock that had given way to *undeniable fear.* She'd relished the fear and had spent the weeks before the first heavy snow checking out his new place. Had she caught him alone she would have finished what he started in Bitterroot. But Nathan was a coward. He didn't take a step out his door without being surrounded by his hired guns.

Before winter had set in she'd taken care to give Nathan the welcome he deserved. There wasn't a holding pen on his ranch that could stay latched. Rattlers had become a common inhabitant of his outhouse. She'd spent quite a few nights bedded down in the tall grasses around his place, gazing at the night stars as she listened to her brother's yelps and shouts echoing across the plains. Her brother hadn't changed a lick in fourteen years—he was still a thief and a liar. And folks still turned a blind eye to his treachery. His band of cattle thieves spent more time skimming off neighbors stock than tending their own. She'd followed along on a few of their late-night roundups, watching intently as they gathered and moved nice tight herds, tucking the longhorns into canyons and valleys on Circle S land. It sure didn't take much to spook a herd of cattle. She grinned, recalling just how high-pitched a man's scream could hit.

She'd move on, just as soon as she settled her business with Nathan.

A burst of cold air announced Garret's return.

"Damnation! That is a cold wind." He slammed the door shut as a gust lifted the edge of his blanket, giving her a glimpse of his rounded backside.

Nothing I haven't already seen, she lamented, which didn't do a damn thing to settle the sudden stir of her pulse.

Boots pawed at him, demanding his attention, and nearly stripped him of the blanket he struggled to keep around his waist. "Easy, boy." He knelt down, briskly rubbing his hands over the dog's thick coat. "Glad to see you, too, but we don't want to offend the lady."

Lady? A pleasing stir moved through Maggie at the un-expected title. She watched the bunch and flex of muscles beneath his bronze, knowing full well there wasn't anything offensive about Garret's body.

"Worried about me, were ya?"

The dog hadn't been the only one to fret over him. After all her toil and trouble, he'd traipsed off into the storm!

"Sick as you've been, you shouldn't have risked the chill," she said. "I would have given you some privacy."

He straightened and shoved a hand through his tousled hair, giving her a clear view of his green eyes. The curiosity she saw in those gentle depths stirred a tingling surge of sensation she'd first felt when she'd awakened in his arms.

"No sense in you getting a chill, as well," he said, taking a slow step toward her.

"I'm not the one who's been abed the past two days," she said, her tone sounding hateful to her own ears.

Be civil, she silently berated. She'd been schooled in good manners and proper etiquette, though she couldn't clearly recall a single lesson. Her life before Ira was nothing but a distant dream.

"Your clothes are on the chest behind you," she managed to say in a mild tone. "I hung your coat by the door. Your chaps are stored outside."

He glanced at the stack of clothes and then looked back at her. "I'm much obliged."

She would be, too, once he buttoned that chest into a shirt. Not that it would matter much. She'd memorized all the contours of his muscular form as she'd tended his fever, soothing him when he thrashed around, murmuring names in his sleep. Some she recognized, most she didn't.

"Come here, Boots," she said, patting her thigh. She rubbed the mutt behind his ear then pointed to his blanket. "Go chew on your bone."

He stood beside her, watching his pet curl up in the corner. His lips curved into a grin as he met her gaze. The unexpected smile caused an equally unexpected surge of sensation low in her belly.

"I hope Boots hasn't been any trouble for you."

"Get dressed."

His grin widened. "Yes, ma'am."

She waited until he moved around the bed before she turned back to the stove. She watched the play of shadow cast on the floor as she took two bowls from her shelf and began serving stew.

"I sure appreciate you taking care of him," he said, followed by the sound of his boots thumping to the floor as he pulled them off. "He's been with me a long time."

The care he showed for his pet was something that had always intrigued her. She couldn't recall a time she'd spied Garret in the hills without his dog along.

"He hasn't been any trouble."

She could feel his gaze upon her, could tell he was watching her by the stillness of his shadow.

"Glad one of us hasn't." Fabric snapped as he shook his trousers out.

She set the steaming bowls aside as his shadow swayed, his hand reaching toward his head. She turned as he slumped forward and reached for the foot of the bed.

"Garret." She was beside him in a flash.

"I'm all right," he said, easing down to sit on the trunk.

Maggie curled her fingers into her palms, fighting her urge to soothe him. His complexion had paled. Wearing only his trousers, his shirt clutched in his hand, he rested his elbows on his thighs and blinked as though clearing his vision.

"You shouldn't have gone out into the cold," she scolded.

He glanced up, his gaze dark, burning with frustration. Maggie took a step back, beyond his reach.

"Why in hell am I so weak?"

"You nearly froze to death. You've been abed for two days."

His green eyes scanned her from head to toe and back again. "This may sound rude, but…should I know you?"

"I don't see why you should," she said, relief easing her stalled breath. "You were hardly conscious when I found you."

"You seem to know me…and my dog."

"I'm sure most folks around these parts are familiar with you and your cattle ranch, Mr. Daines."

He shrugged on his shirt, his gaze never wavering from hers. "I thought I knew most folks around these parts. And I sure—" He paused, turning his face toward the collar. He sniffed loudly, his eyes widening as he met her gaze. "You *washed* my clothes?"

"They were already wet." She wasn't about to put dirty clothes in her cupboards. "I figured adding some soap couldn't hurt."

A slow grin eased his tense expression. He stood and stuffed his shirttails into his waistband. "I smell like a field of flowers."

"It's the only soap I have," she said, realizing now that a man may not care to smell like wildflowers.

"I suppose it's better than carrying the stench of sweat and horsehide."

While tending his fever, it made sense to add some soap to that water, as well. Hopefully she'd rinsed him enough since then that he hadn't noticed.

He sat on the side of the bed and Maggie felt some relief. He wasn't quite so intimidating when he wasn't towering over her. Perhaps she could tie him to a chair until he was strong enough to leave.

"I'll be damned," he muttered, staring at his mended sock.

Maggie silently cursed the heat in her cheeks. "They were in a sorry shape."

"You're more than a thorough nursemaid. I'm indebted to you, Mrs.…?"

"Didn't take much to mend them."

He stared at her a moment, his narrowing gaze telling her he hadn't missed her failure to give her name. "I was also wearing a gun," he said.

"You'll get your holster back when you leave."

"I didn't see any other structures outside. Where are you keeping my horse?"

"There was no horse."

"No horse?" He surged up. Maggie forced herself to hold her ground, not that she could have backed any closer to the stove.

"I found you and your dog buried in the snow about two miles from here."

"Buried?"

"Covered by a foot of fresh powder. I nearly walked right past you. If your dog hadn't stood up, I would have. You'd been hit in the head and had been on the ground for a long while."

He touched the spot on his head that had been caked with blood when she'd found him.

"Perhaps you should sit down, Mr. Daines. You were suffering from the cold when I brought you here. You had a high fever all of yesterday and most of today. You'd slept so long I was starting to worry the cold or the fever had damaged your brain."

"It must have. I don't remember riding into these mountains. And I can assure you I am not prone to falling from my saddle."

"I didn't assume that you were. Looked to me like someone struck you with a rifle. By the time I found you any other tracks had been long-since snowed over."

He'd been attacked? Garret tried to jar his memory. Shouldn't he remember something like being knocked from his saddle? Had he been ambushed? The last he could recall was watching Duce's tracks fade in the heavy rain.

"I was looking for my partner," he said. "I followed Duce's tracks into the hills. What little snow had been on the ground was washed out by the rain."

"That's why you nearly froze to death. It didn't rain long before snow set in, just before sundown. I found you about an hour past dawn. Have you been feuding with anyone?"

"Only half the state," he said, shoving his hands into his hair. "The cattle trade has been more akin to pirating as of late."

"Desperation and greed tend to have that effect on men."

The chill in her husky voice drew his gaze. Why was it her face that filled his mind instead of his attackers?

She nodded toward the front wall. "Go sit at the table."

She sure didn't have any trouble passing out orders. His first memory after the storm was *her,* those blue eyes ablaze with passion, her sweet body arched beneath him as she'd awakened to his touch, his kisses…

"Mr. Daines?"

He blinked, and realized she stood before him with a bowl in her hands, his stern nursemaid, not the lover from his dream. The hearty aroma penetrated his dazed mind, initiating a growl in his empty belly.

"The table," she repeated.

She obviously didn't trust him to not end up on his face, staying at his side until he sat in the chair. She plunked the bowl of stew down in front of him and his mouth watered at the sight of steaming chunks of meat in dark gravy. Despite his hunger, he waited for his hostess to join him. Realizing he sat on the only chair, he grabbed the trunk from the foot of the bed and slid it forward.

She stayed by the stove, her bowl in hand, her sweet face pinched in a frown. He gathered she hadn't planned on joining him at the table. Her steps seemed to drag as she approached him. She nudged the trunk to the far side of the table then hesitantly took her seat.

"I swear I don't bite," he said, forcing a smile.

"I don't usually have company."

"I don't usually get lost in snowstorms. I am sorry for putting you out."

"I'm just glad I didn't have to bury you in the frozen ground." With that, she took a bite.

He didn't wait for further invitation. He heaped a big bite into his mouth and nearly groaned as venison melted against his tongue, the flavorful gravy nothing short of heaven. He emptied the small bowl in a few hearty bites and would have thumbed out the remaining gravy had the bowl not been snatched away from him.

"I'll get you some more."

"I don't want to leave you hungry," he said, while hoping that big pot was filled to the brim.

"I have plenty," she said, refilling his bowl. "Luckily I brought more than a frozen cowboy home from my hunt."

"Thank you," he said, unable to pull his gaze away from her graceful movements as she sat across from him. Had some sorry excuse of a man left her up here to fend for herself under such harsh conditions? Catching his gaze, she paused before taking another bite. Her tense expression suggested she'd rather be dining alone.

"You were out hunting in that storm?" he asked.

"That deer meat didn't jump into my stewpot on its own."

Garret grinned. The flat line of her lips didn't so much as twitch.

"I don't imagine it did. Guess you caught more than you bargained for."

"I did indeed."

"You must have been at the end of your food stores to be hunting in this storm?"

Her jaw tightened.

"I'm stocked up just fine," his nameless savior insisted.

He wasn't new to stubborn women. Wasn't a woman born more stubborn than his older sister—or so he'd thought.

"A tracking snow can be real useful. It was—before the storm hit. You were the one so far from home."

If he'd ended up here, what had happened to Duce?

"My business partner didn't ride in at noon. Duce wouldn't have stayed out in that weather unless he was having trouble or had found trouble."

"I'd been hunting in those lower ranges the whole day. I didn't come across anyone or hear any other gunshots."

He hoped Duce had made it back to the ranch. "How long have you lived up here?"

"A while."

Boots pounced up beside her, his front paws landing in her lap. "I already fed you," she said, her lips hinting at a smile.

"Sorry about that."

"I'm used to it by now." She scratched at his ears, turning his cow dog to a limp pile of fur.

"You've spoiled him. Boots usually has better manners."

"You've been far more trouble than he has."

God save him, her smiling eyes sent a whisper of sensation across his skin as images flooded his mind. Unnerved by the rush of desire, he swept his gaze over the small space.

Simple, clean, the nicest cave he'd ever seen. Small and dank, yet livable—*for a miner.* So where the hell was he?

"More?" she asked, reaching for his bowl.

The first two servings had taken the edge off his hunger, but he could easily put away another. "Only if you're sure you can spare it."

She pushed his dog aside and went to the stove. His gaze followed her dainty form, trailing down the part of her braids to her slender, *kissable* neck.

He pinched his eyes shut. If he'd actually made advances on her in her sleep, she'd be tossing him out on his ear, not serving him stew. And yet…he could practically feel her arms around his neck as she had kissed him into unconsciousness. He looked up as she stepped beside him, her eyes full of caution as she slid the bowl and mugs onto the table—she sure as hell didn't like being near him.

"You've saved my life," he said. "And I still don't know your name."

"I couldn't rightly leave you in the snow." She turned away and he caught her by the wrist.

"That's the second time you've avoided telling me your name. Who are you and where is your husband?"

"If you value that hand," she said, the chill in her tone raising the hair on the back of his neck, *"move it."*

Garret had lived with temperamental females long enough to know when his hide was in danger. This wasn't a woman who took kindly to being backed into a corner— or grabbed by the wrist. She didn't move to pull away but the cold clarity in her eyes told him her other hand was already gripping the hilt of her blade. A sudden move on his part would have painful results.

Biting back a swear word, he opened his fingers.

"My apologies."

She took a step back, glowering at him as she rubbed her wrist. He knew he hadn't used enough pressure to bruise her soft skin.

"Well?" he persisted. "Why isn't your husband here? You are married, aren't you?"

"I don't see how my life history would be beneficial to you, Mr. Daines."

"Considering I've been lying naked in your bed for the past few days," he said bluntly, "asking your marital status seems a fair question."

She crossed her arms, her pointed little chin raising a few notches. "Are you suggesting I should have left you in the snow for the sake of propriety?"

Her crisp speech carried a hint of formality that reminded him of Amanda's. This woman's sharp gaze and graceful mannerisms belayed her odd attire. She'd been properly schooled. Must have been a sweet-talking sonu-vagun who'd convinced her to come all the way out here.

"No, ma'am," he said. "I'm grateful for your help. But your husband may not appreciate—"

"I don't have a husband, so you can relax."

Relax? With the thoughts that were filtering through his mind. Not likely. Why the hell didn't she have a husband? "You live way up here alone?"

"You should be focusing on getting your strength back. You'll be leaving as soon as the weather allows."

Her hostility and evasiveness gnawed at him. He was obviously making her nervous. Hell, he was making himself nervous!

"I know for certain I wasn't near any homestead when the storm hit," he said, hoping a less invasive question would get him some answers. "At least none that I'm aware of. I've lived in this area for nearly nine years."

"Do you really think you're on a homestead?"

She wasn't buying any of it.

"No, ma'am. More of a miner's claim, I suppose."

Her single arched eyebrow wasn't a denial or a confirmation. The sheer challenge in her gaze caused a discomforting stir in his britches. He was starting to think he had a thing for sassy women. *Sassy, stern and pretty beyond measure.*

Her cheeks flushed to a soft pink before she hooded those blue eyes with thick lashes.

And passionate, his mind added. She'd been hesitant at first but had quickly turned to sweet fire in his arms.

Garret dropped his spoon, the provocative images in his mind driving him to the brink of insanity.

"Did I bed you?"

Her gaze snapped up, pinning him with those vibrant blue eyes.

Well hell, that hadn't been the smooth delivery he'd hoped for.

Chapter Five

"*No*, you didn't!"

Garret heaved a sigh of relief and shoved his hands through his hair. *Oh, thank God.*

Her angry glare cut his relief short.

"I didn't mean to insult you. I'm a little…out of sorts."

"I dragged your sorry hide two miles through the snow," she raged, her crossed arms locked tight over her chest. *"I was tired!"*

Garret's breath stalled, the tremble in her voice confirming his fear—he hadn't been dreaming.

"Had I known you'd awaken with such intensions, I can assure you I'd have left you in the—"

"I'm sorry," he said, lunging to his feet. "Honest to God, I wouldn't have—"

"Sit! Down!"

He obeyed the command only because he recognized her fear. Beneath the anger in her gaze, he saw panic.

"I took advantage," he said quickly. "I wasn't in my right mind."

"Neither was I."

The stain of embarrassment on her cheeks stabbed at his conscience. He hadn't given her a chance to refuse him, having coaxed her body into passion while she slept. "It was all my fault," he said. "You were sound asleep. Your body was on my side before you even woke up and I—".

"Enough!" she shouted, her fingers clamping over the hilt of her blade. Garret carefully regarded the hostility in her posture poised to strike.

"I swear I'd never force myself on you." *Holy hell.* He wasn't rightly sure what he'd done before he'd passed out. He knew what he'd wanted to do.

"Oh God," he groaned, horrified at the thought of shaming the woman who'd saved his life. "Did I hurt you?"

The concern in his soft tone caught Maggie off guard.

Did he *hurt her?* She'd never felt anything so exquisite in all her life. "Ma'am? If I—"

"You kissed me," she said. "And then you blacked out with fever."

"That's all?"

That's *all?* "That was enough!"

"I was afraid...the thought of forcing you—"

"You didn't," she clipped. Remembering just how willingly she'd responded to his kisses increased the fire beneath her cheeks. The sheer relief in his expression doubled her embarrassment. His eyes no longer clouded by fever, the thought of such intimacy with someone like her likely repulsed him. Alarmed by the moisture burning her eyes, Maggie turned toward the stove.

"I was disrespectful."

Startled by the voice directly behind her, Maggie spun around. He stood a foot away, his fingers tucked into his pant pockets, his expression nothing short of miserable.

"I am truly sorry."

The ache in her chest intensified. "Okay," she said, hardly able to breathe the word.

"It ain't a wonder you've looked on the verge of skinning me. I'd be gunning for any man who'd treated my sister in such a way. Honest to God, I thought you were a dream. I couldn't imagine why else I'd be in bed beside such a…"

Maggie steeled herself for the insult. *Hag? Shrew?* She'd heard them all, whispers of townsfolk when she'd venture into a settlement.

"*Beautiful woman.* I figured I must be dead or dreaming."

Surprise rippled through her. Was he mocking her?

He took a step back, caution darkening his gaze—the effect she was used to having on folks—and Maggie realized she was glaring at him.

"Did you really drag me two miles through the snow?"

She wanted to rage at him to keep backing up, to sit down and shut up until he cleared out…but she couldn't. His solemn gaze choked her anger and put an ache in her belly. He felt bad—she didn't know why that should soften her rage, figuring he ought to feel real bad and then some for all he'd put her through. It had been sheer hell, having her hands all over him while fighting the memory of his sweet words and even sweeter mouth.

"I had a sled," she told him, his silent guilt wearing on her nerves. "Not that it made the climb an easy one."

"Thank you."

His gaze held hers as an unfamiliar surge twisted through her, feelings she couldn't identify.

"Guess I can't blame you for not wanting to share your name after the way I shamed you. Don't blame you a bit for reactin' so hostile. I'll admit, for a moment there, I thought you might be the woman they call Mad Mag. I swear, I—"

"Grace." She blurted out her middle name, the first that came to mind.

"I beg your pardon?"

Realizing she'd shouted the name at him, she dragged in a calming breath. "My name is Grace."

His stormy eyes warmed as his lips curved into a grin. *Sweet mercy.*

"You look like a Grace."

"What's that supposed to mean?"

"That it's a pretty name."

She blinked against a sudden burning in her eyes. She had to get out of here. She couldn't breathe with him standing so close. "You still have food on the table."

He gave a nod and turned away from her. "I have a niece named Grace. She and her sister are six years old and cute as buttons."

The moment his butt touched down on the chair she made a dash for her coat and shrugged into the heavy fur as she reached for the door.

"Where are you—?"

"Wood box," she said, stepping into a burst of cold wind. "Boots!"

Garret watched his dog dash outside. She slammed the door before he could offer another word, much less any assistance.

His elbows hit the table as a hard breath broke from his lungs. He rubbed a hand over his face and the four days' worth of growth on his chin. He must look like a polar bear. He'd clearly displayed all the manners of one.

Maybe Duce was right and he needed to find himself a

steady girl at the Gilded Lady. He'd given it a shot, but after having his own woman in his own bed, weekend romps just didn't appeal to him. A hell of an inconvenience for a man with no wife. The thought of seeking out any of the single young ladies in town left him cold and irritable. He flat didn't trust those inviting smiles and batting lashes.

Instead of carousing or courtship, he'd assaulted a decent woman who'd saved his life.

What a fine mess.

He ate the last of his stew wondering all the while what had happened to Grace for her to end up alone in this cave. Done up as it was, the stone enclosure was still a cave in the heart of wild country. And she shouldn't be out there in that wind!

He stood, his sore muscles complaining as he collected the empty dishes on the table. It would take another day before he'd be of any use. A full stomach didn't do anything but sap the last of his strength. Not that she'd welcome his help.

Damn it.

Spotting her shotgun still propped inside the door, he knew he was lucky she hadn't reached for her gun and loaded him full of buckshot after the liberties he'd taken. Would have served him right.

He stepped up to a washstand wedged between her pantry and the empty wood box. Finding a jar of dishrags, he took one and wiped out the bowls then set them in the basin. He lifted the kettle from the stove and scalded the tin with the hot water. Grace returned as he was stacking the dishes in her pantry. Didn't take but a glance at her wide blue eyes to gauge her wariness.

Boots trotted in before her, his wet paws tracking prints across the floor she'd already mopped up once today.

She kicked the door closed behind them and stood there, her arms loaded down with wood.

"I'll wipe up the floor," he said, turning to find another rag. *"No."*

The single words stopped him.

"You should lie down."

He figured that was her way of telling him to get the hell away from her. Tiny thing that she was, he didn't doubt his size made her nervous. He backed toward the bed. His dog seemed to know the routine, having lain back down in his corner without prompting.

She didn't take a step forward until Garret eased onto the mattress. She dropped the firewood into the box beside her stove, her gaze moving over the sink basin and the dishes he'd rinsed and put away. She fetched the drying sheet from the back of her chair and dropped it on the damp floor. Her foot dragged the cloth across the puddles as she watched him.

"If I can help with anything—"

"You can help by resting."

"Two days abed should have been enough," he said, hating that he felt so damn useless.

"You were sick."

Red rimmed her eyes. He imagined she hadn't slept much in the past three days.

"Doesn't look like you've had much sleep at all."

"I'll sleep just fine once you're gone."

"I can kick back in that chair if—"

"You'll stay in the bed. I'm not taking the chance of your fever coming back."

Her cut-and-dried delivery of orders sure could go against a man's grain. Aggravated by his weakened state and aching with exhaustion, he was in no shape to argue with her.

"Rest up," she said, picking up her shotgun on her way to the chair. She settled back like a guard on watch duty. "You've got a long walk home."

Garret kept his eyes on Grace as he stepped into his second boot and reached for his coat. He hated that he'd slept in her warm bed while she'd huddled over a table all night. Her cheek rested on her folded arms, one of her hands gripped a white cloth. Her expression was peaceful in the dim light of the lamp, yet he knew the quilt draped over her shoulders couldn't be keeping her warm. A hard wind blew outside, the cave growing colder by the second.

He'd attempted to stoke the fire, but hadn't been able to do more than clear out ashes. Grace had already burned the last of the wood she'd brought in. With no natural light in the place he couldn't tell the time, but judging by the cold stove and empty firebox, it was near dawn or shortly thereafter.

Boots bumped his hand as he reached for the gloves tucked in his coat pocket. Anxious to go outside, his dog pranced impatiently.

"Easy, partner," he whispered.

Grace jerked up as though he'd shouted. Her eyes wide, disoriented, she shot to her feet, the chair scraping across the floor as her gaze wildly searched the room.

"It's just me," he said, watching recognition ease her fright. "You're a jumpy little thing, aren't you?"

"I don't usually wake up to voices." Still clutching the white cloth, she tossed it onto the table and pressed her hands to the small of her back. An array of colors on the fancy hand towel caught his attention. A small wooden hoop clasped over the white fabric, the circular portion of cloth stretched tight. A threaded needle hung from a half-finished yellow blossom amid a cluster of brightly colored flowers.

"You sew," he said, looking closer at the intricate bouquet embroidered on the dish towel.

"I do." She picked up a covered basket from the floor beside her chair. Flipping up the lid, she tossed the towel over a rainbow of thread.

"Did you stitch the flowers on the shirt you're wearing?"

She glanced down and seemed surprised by the red blossoms draping down from her shoulders. "Yeah."

"It's pretty."

Her face scrunched with a frown. "Still storming?" she asked, glancing toward the unmistakable sounds of a grueling wind battering the trees outside.

"I'd say so. Boots and I were just headed out. Why don't you curl up in that warm bed? There's bound to be fresh snow. Soon as I shovel out to the woodpile, I'll relight the stove."

Maggie hadn't stopped assessing her cabin, the bed he'd made up, the pail of ashes sitting before the stove. He'd found his hat, the brown Stetson pulled low on his brow. He wore his thick coat. The bottoms of his trousers were tucked into the tall shaft of his boots. Apparently he'd been up and around for quite some time—and she hadn't woken up?

"I'll be back with some wood as soon I finish the shoveling."

Ready to be rid of him, she waved him off. "Go. Shovel's in the corner by the—"

He was already lifting the bar, shovel in hand. He opened the door to a gust of wind. Snow rolled in onto the floor, which was to be expected. Maggie reached for her blanket, shivering as she cinched the quilt tight around her shoulders.

Boots barked, but didn't bound out the door as he usually did.

"Sonuvagun," Garret muttered. "That's a lot of snow."

Curious about both their odd reactions to a bit of snow-drift, Maggie stepped forward. *A bit of snowdrift* was actually closer to five feet. Nearly snowed in, the high point almost reached the stone overhang.

"The wind just builds it up against the cabin."

Garret eased out and knocked back the soft powder. To Maggie's surprise, he hit a solid four feet of snowbank. He glanced back at her but Maggie's gaze was locked on the blur of white whipping beyond the break, a blizzard that would swallow anyone who ventured too far out.

She couldn't send him out in that.

Boots kept barking at the wall of white blocking his path.

"Stop your griping, old man," Garret said to his dog. "I'll get you out."

Boots quieted but stayed at his heels as Garret shoveled out a narrow path. The moment he eased to the side his dog jumped through the narrow channel.

"Looks like I'll be getting a late start."

Maggie tightened her hold on the blanket to clamp out the cold. "You can't leave today."

"I can manage," he said, shoveling at the frozen ground.

"Yesterday you could hardly stand."

He straightened and looked back at her. "Do you want me gone or not?"

"I want you gone, *not frozen.* I didn't spend three days keeping you alive just to send you back out in the middle of a blizzard."

"Believe me, I'm just as anxious to get back to my ranch as you are to see me off."

"It's already well past sunup. It will be noon by the time I'm dug out and we get you outfitted and ready to go. Even in clear weather it'd take a full day for you to reach your ranch." She shook her head. "You'll have to wait."

His jaws flexed, his eyes narrowed slightly and Maggie was reminded she spoke to a man of considerable size and strength. And she was demanding he stay? Fear nettled beneath her skin. She'd lost her mind.

"I'll start digging you out and see how it goes."

Boots stuck his head in, his sharp barks rattling through the cabin.

"Would you stop shouting at me," Garret said with exasperation. "I can't squeeze through a rabbit hole!" Boots moved back and kept barking as Garret dug at the thick snow pack. "All your yapping isn't helping," he grumbled, which Boots answered with another series of barks.

Maggie was surprised to find herself grinning as she watched them. The way he talked to Boots, as though talking to a person, had been something she'd always found endearing about him. His wide shoulders shifted in fluid motions as he cleared the doorway with impossible speed, shoveling away snow in minutes that would have taken her half the day. She envied his strength.

He turned back and dragged the flat shovel across the floor, clearing out the hard-packed snow that had slid inside. "I'll bring in some wood as soon as I uncover the woodpile. You go on and get some sleep," he said, nodding toward the bed before shutting the door.

Sleep? With him tromping around outside her cabin?

He sure seemed spry this morning for a man who could barely stand the day before. Amazing what a good meal could do. Maggie dried the floor and went to check the stove. She wasn't pleased to find he'd cleared out all the hot coals, leaving the stove completely cold. She knew better than to let the fire die out during a storm. The way it was snowing, she'd have to go up top and dig out the stovepipe before she could light a fire. The mere thought made her shiver.

Garret came in with an armload of wood as she shrugged into her coat. He dumped the wood into the box, his hands slamming down on his hips as he regarded her for a silent moment.

"What's wrong?"

"I let the fire die down, which means the pipe likely snowed over. I'll have to clear it before I build a fire." She refrained from telling him she never removed all the hot coals from the stove in the dead of winter.

He turned, his gaze following the pipe up through her ceiling. "I'll take care of it," he said, tugging his collar up as he headed for the door. *"Stay inside."*

The door slammed and she bristled at his parting words. Who was he to be giving her orders?

Biting out a curse, she took off her coat and went back to the stove. As she filled it with kindling and wood, she could hear the scraping sounds coming from up above. The very idea of him knowing her location filled her with unease.

"All clear." His deep voice carried through the pipe with crystal clarity and caused an annoying stir of ripples in her belly.

If food was what it took to keep him strong, she'd keep cooking until he was gone.

Garret had hoped to get a lay of the land, but could hardly see more than five yards in front of him. Through the distortion of snowflakes none of the surrounding white ridges looked familiar. In this storm, eight miles from his ranch might as well have been a hundred.

Chilled to the bone, he went back to clearing snow from around the woodpile stacked along the front of her cabin, or so it appeared. Wood slats wedged into the mouth of a cave. Even with a wide storage chest built up to one side of the false front for added support and the woodpile stacked on the other side, the upkeep had to be constant. He'd uncovered a large kettle a few yards out she likely used for laundry.

He shook his head, hardly able to believe a man had left his woman in a place like this. A miner should know only trappers, outlaws and renegade Indians frequented these mountains—even they sought more hospitable ground over winter.

Pulling back the heavy tarpaulin covering the woodpile, he collected a few more pieces to take inside. She'd at least stay warm until the end of winter. Hopefully she'd hunkered down in that bed while he uncovered her yard. Despite all his labor, fresh snow continued to pile up, the steady snowfall showing no sign of slowing. Just as Grace had said, he wouldn't be going anywhere today.

"Come on, Boots. Let's head in."

He opened the door to a welcoming burst of heat and a mouthwatering scent that made his stomach roar with hunger. His gaze locked on a steaming pile of golden biscuits at the center of the table.

"Breakfast is ready."

He whipped his gaze toward the all-too-inviting view of Grace lifting a kettle from the stove. Apron strings created a tidy white bow just above the gentle swell of her backside…a shapely backside that had him appreciating her buckskin britches.

Don't go there, he silently warned, forcing his gaze up to a second white bow securing the silky black hair she'd brushed into a single ponytail. Boots bumped up beside her. Soaked from his morning run, he was about to shake water all over Grace's cabin.

"Boots."

His dog froze—so did Grace, her eyes popping wide as he rushed toward them.

Garret grabbed the dog's blanket from the corner and draped it over him, briskly drying his wet fur. "Miss Grace doesn't take kindly to a wet floor."

Or sudden moves from stray cowpunchers, he thought, noting how her slender body had shuddered before she had dragged in a deep breath. She grabbed up the mugs and hurried to the table.

The moment he released Boots his dog shot to the bowl of broken biscuits and meat Grace had placed in his corner. He turned and she stepped back, practically pressing her back to the door.

"I filled the basin with warm water so you could wash up."

He spotted a fresh towel beside the water-filled basin and realized the pleasing scent of spring mingled with the aroma of breakfast. Glancing back at Grace he noted the fresh shine of her skin. He reached for the buttons on his coat and she instantly fluttered past the foot of her bed, anticipating his move toward the door to hang his jacket.

Her wariness of him stung at his pride—not that he blamed her.

By the time he finished scrubbing up she was rummaging through her shelves, conveniently giving him plenty of clearance to get to the table. His plate had already been served, a stack of broken biscuits smothered with chunks of venison and white gravy. He collected the linen napkin from beside his plate, noting the tiny pink flowers across the bottom as he draped it over his thigh.

She hadn't set a place for herself. Already back at the stove, she obviously didn't have plans to join him at the table, so he dug in. Just as the heavenly aroma had hinted, her biscuits and gravy were the best to pass his lips since he'd lived in his sister's home.

Maggie glanced up from mixing a fresh batch of biscuits as a low, rumbling groan sounded behind her. Garret sat with his eyes closed as he chewed. The coarse stubble along his jaw from a couple of days ago had become smooth fibers with another day of growth. She missed being able to stroke his face, his skin.

I don't need to be petting on any man, she silently scolded.

His tongue skimmed over his full lips and tingles danced across Maggie's skin, awakening the memory of his soft mouth pressed to hers, the shocking surge of pleasing sensations stirred by his seeking tongue. His blond lashes lifted and Maggie forced her gaze back to her task.

He didn't mean to kiss me. No man in his right mind would.

Anger burned away the reverie.

"Grace, that was the best breakfast I've ever had."

She started dropping biscuits into the pan with extra force. "It's not hard to please a starving man."

He stepped beside her holding his empty plate, and Maggie wondered how he could spend his morning shoveling snow and still smell of wood smoke and musk.

"You're a great cook. But I thought you'd be sleeping."

"And I'd hoped you'd be leaving."

Realizing the rudeness of her words, she looked up. His blue-green eyes sparked with amusement. Of course he'd find her amusing, and not at all ladylike.

Damn it!

"Thank you," he said, his steady gaze holding hers.

Be normal. She forced a smile. "You're welcome."

There, that hadn't been so hard.

His lips shifted slightly, and the heat blossoming inside Maggie warned her that nothing was going to be easy in his presence.

"Grace, would you mind returning the rest of my gear? If I can't head out today I'd like to at least get ready and my revolver likely needs cleaning. You can hold on to the bullets."

Cleaning the gun would keep him busy and *stationary.* "All right," she said, wiping her hands on her apron—yet another item sacrificed from her winter bartering supply. "I've stored them outside."

"In the box against the house?"

Her breath stalled. She hadn't even thought about him digging out the storage chest.

"It was locked," he said.

Oh, thank God.

"If you want to give me the key—"

"No," she said, ushering him back as she moved toward the shelf. "Excuse me."

He stepped back as she reached for a cup near the top shelf. She dumped out the slender key. "Wait here," she said before pulling on her coat.

"Mind if I refill my tea?"

"Tea canister is above the stove. Help yourself." She slipped outside and shut the door firmly behind her.

What had she been thinking to let him come out here with a shovel? She dropped to her knees before the storage box and brushed the fresh powder from the lid. She lifted the cold lock and tugged it open without use of the key. The temperamental thing wouldn't always open and she'd gotten used to leaving it unlocked. A partially closed lock was enough to keep out critters. The tap of a shovel would have clicked it open and all her effort would have been wasted. Just as Ira had told her, a safe place wasn't something that lasted—it was something to be found. With folks crowding her every turn, it was getting harder to find peace, even in the wild.

She glanced at the door, making sure Garret didn't take a mind to join her as she opened the latch and lifted the lid on her old livelihood. Hinges creaked as the odor of bear hide rolled out into the whip of wind. She pushed the thick brown pelt aside, uncovering traps and snares and various tools. She'd also tucked her rifle inside for good measure. With her shotgun inside for protection, she didn't want to chance Garret recognizing the Winchester carbine she'd had that day in town. Folks didn't tend to look too closely at her, but she didn't doubt Garret had noticed her rifle.

She tugged his chaps and holster out from the far end. Setting the holster aside, she sniffed the buffalo hide, making sure they hadn't absorbed Mad Mag's odors. Wasn't nothing compared to the stench that old coat could give off in the warmth of spring.

"You ever smell a b'ar?" Ira had said to her when she'd first complained about his foul odor. *"They don't smell invitin' for a reason."*

She sure missed him at times. And he'd been right of course. Folks didn't come within six feet of her. The few her coat didn't discourage, her rifle did.

All but Garret. He'd actually touched her. Her eyes burned at the thought of him knowing she'd been the one standing beside him that day.

"Stay in there," she said, tucking in the telltale signs of Mad Mag before clamping down the lid.

She had him fooled. One more day and he'd be gone.

Chapter Six

Garret stood at the open door. His muscles flexed beneath his shirt as he gripped the door frame overhead and stared out at steady snowfall. Maggie could feel the restless tension rolling off him from her spot on the bed. The entire day he'd been a mess of pent-up energy. The task she'd hoped would keep him busy all day had taken him an hour.

The backpack she'd given him sat beside the door, filled with the salted venison and biscuits she'd packed, now topped by his holster and polished gun. He'd since reshoveled the yard and brought in more wood than she'd use in a week. They'd shared a surprisingly silent evening meal and she actually found herself missing the sound of his voice. He'd taken his dog outside for a while afterward, and while Boots now slept in the corner, Garret clearly hadn't worn himself out.

His shoulders flexed, bunching beneath his shirt, and Maggie's thoughts drifted to the varying textures of his body, hard muscles, coarse hair and warm, smooth skin.

A sharp sting in her finger brought her gaze back to her needlework. Blood swelled from a pinhole on her index finger, the newest among many already dotting her finger. Trying to stitch with such distractions in the room was plain hazardous. Biting back a curse, she stuck her finger in her mouth before she bled on the white apron.

A burst of cold wind swirled inside, putting a chill in her skin.

"Do you really think you can stare down the storm?"

He glanced over his shoulder, his green eyes aglow with frustration. "Four days, Grace, and hardly a reprieve?"

"You slept through the reprieve. And now you're wasting my wood by trying to melt snow."

His lips twitched with the start of a grin, and Maggie realized she'd snapped at him again. Knowing he found such humor in her sharp tongue increased her annoyance.

He shut the door, a hard sigh breaking from his chest. "All that snow makes me nervous."

She didn't have to guess why. She'd weathered her share of harsh winters, but nothing so powerful as the late-winter freeze a few years back. It had taken her a few days to dig out and a week before she'd trekked out to the rim. The blizzard had blown clear across the plains, smothering those grasslands and freezing man and cattle alike.

"This type of storm isn't uncommon for this elevation," she said, wanting to ease his worry. "Your place likely hasn't gotten a foot of snow, if any at all. Your pacing and staring hasn't helped to clear the weather."

He dragged the chair toward the stove and dropped onto the hard surface. "Storm or not, I'm heading out at first light."

Maggie looked up as he shoved his hands through his tousled hair, which only seemed to emphasize the span of his chest, the thickness of his arms. His short beard added to his rugged appearance. He looked like a man who could take on a storm.

"How do you stand it? You just hibernate up here all winter?"

"I keep busy."

He glanced around the room. "In this small space?"

"I'm used to being snowed in. I venture out and hunt on clear days. I have to keep the fire going and food on my table. And I sew."

Garret eased back in the chair, his gaze moving over the tiny woman sitting near the head of her bed, her legs stretched out before her, her sewing basket tucked close beside her. She appeared relaxed, focused on her stitching, but he knew she was subtly watching him. She fluttered around him like a little bird, always managing to keep a few feet between them. No small feat considering the tight space of her cave. She wasn't obvious in her evasion, which intrigued him. He moved in, she glided back, fluttering to safer ground.

"You do real fine needlework," he said, leaning in to look at the tiny pink roses spaced across what appeared to be an apron.

She glanced up, a smile curving her lips before she looked back at the cloth in her hands. "It passes the time."

Her smile hinted at her growing ease with him. Lamplight glinted on the needle she pulled through the fabric. As she repeated the process it was her hands that stole his attention. He leaned in, looking closer at the array of scarring on her tender skin.

My God. Every finger bared a white mark of some previous injury. Surely that bitty needle didn't inflict such wounds. Her man likely had her holed up in a mine somewhere. Part of him hoped her husband had left her a widow instead of abandoning her. The fact that she was too embarrassed to tell him her full name suggested otherwise. He didn't doubt she'd been mistreated. Beneath all her apprehension was a gentle and giving woman. He wished she'd tell him her husband's name so he could find him and beat the living hell out of him.

"You've got a real talent and a mess of patience to sew such tiny things. You must have a hundred little pink flowers on that apron."

"There about." She met his inquisitive stare over her needlework. "Maybe you ought to give it a try? I could show you how to darn socks."

He enjoyed sarcasm. She had knack for answering his questions without telling him a damn thing about herself—other than she had a quick mind and a stubborn nature. "I'm game if you are. That is, unless you have a deck of cards?"

"No."

"Checker board?"

"With whom would I play checkers? My shadow?"

Garret grinned, liking how she'd said that. Seemed to him most folks dropped a swear word or two when their guard was down. Even his sister had been known to slip on occasion despite her efforts to keep a clean mouth in front of her youngens. Yet the more relaxed Grace seemed around him, the more pristine her word choice became. Which told him she'd most likely been raised in a strict and fancy household.

"How long have you lived up here, Grace?"

"Long enough to know you can't fight the weather."

"I'm not trying to pry," he hedged.

"Uh-huh," she countered, her disbelieving eyes briefly meeting his gaze. "Must be why you ask so many questions."

"I'm going a little stir-crazy, Grace. I hate being away from my ranch and not knowing...anything. For all I know, my ranch is under siege. One of my ranch hands, his folks were burned out of their place last year—burned their house and barn to the ground. They lost everything."

"Did they catch the raiders?"

"His own neighbor." Garret shook his head. As if the freeze hadn't been bad enough, desperation had turned folks plumb crazy. "Those hangings haven't slowed the number of rustlers springing up all over these hills, hitting ranchers still trying to recover from the freeze."

"That's the nature of folks. *Vultures.* Attracted by the weak and the dying."

The disdain in her voice sprang a new crop of questions in Garret's mind. Not that she'd answer a single one. His gaze moved over the fabric that had held her attention over the past couple of hours.

"I suppose I'm interrupting your production."

"Yes, in fact. Because of you I've missed out on nearly a week of work."

"So thread me a needle."

Her blue eyes rounded. "You're not serious."

He seriously enjoyed her reaction. He liked those big blue eyes looking up at him. "Why not? You labored over me. I'm not above doing needlework."

"Quit it," she said, a smile breaking through her scowl.

"I'm serious. I need something to keep my mind busy."

He stood and eased onto the mattress beside her, trapping her between her sewing basket and the headboard. Expecting her to take flight or reach for the knife at her hip, she surprised him by resuming her stitching. Though her hands were none too steady. He didn't have to wonder why she preferred life without her man—he'd hurt her. Of that he had no doubt. Anger tensed his muscles at the thought of any man raising a hand against her tender body.

"Let me help you, Grace."

"You'll waste my thread," she said, a quiver in her voice.

"You think I'm just a clumsy cowpoke, don't you?" he accused.

Her heart skittering from the sudden closeness, Maggie risked a glance at the man sitting beside her. Garret Daines was far from clumsy—and neither was she, unless he was nearby. She'd never known anyone like him. Good-natured, hardworking, *and charming as sin.* "I don't want—"

"Have I told you that I have eight nieces?" he asked, delivering that bit of information as though it pained him. "They've taken great pride in teaching their uncle the finer points of tea parties and needlepoint. I'll have you know I can knit a fine scarf—*while under proper guidance.*"

She could just picture him surrounded by eight little Morgan girls, the image widening her smile.

"I've never stitched flowers," he said, leaning over, his shoulder brushing hers as he looked at her design. "But I'm not afraid to try somethin' new."

Maggie swallowed hard. She doubted Garret feared much of anything. And yet he wasn't a hard man. She wasn't afraid of him, that admission alone was enough to terrify her. She knew more about Garret than she wanted to admit to herself.

"I want to help you out," he said. "It's the least I can do when you saved my life."

After the way his big hands had moved so gently over her body, she didn't doubt those callused fingers could likely handle a needle.

"Okay."

Stunned by her quick acceptance, Garret watched her scamper off the bed and over to her trunk.

Well, hell.

He likely couldn't stitch anything resembling a flower—he'd just enjoyed sitting by her. She shocked him again by reclaiming her spot on the bed, her eyes bright with a smile. Lingering on her blue eyes conjured images he had no right remembering.

He watched as she placed a small hoop beneath a fresh white dish towel and clamped another hoop over the top of the fabric, trapping the towel between the two, the circular portion of cloth stretched tight and ready for stitching.

"Any particular design you'd like to sew?"

The clear amusement in her sweet expression made him smile. She didn't truly expect him to sew a decent flower any more than he did. But, hell, to keep her smiling, he'd give it a shot.

"You choose."

She plucked a pencil from her sewing basket and began drawing at the center of the tight circle.

"You don't draw your designs."

"I do if I'm trying something new or if it's a large pattern. There you go," she said, passing his project over.

Garret held up the circle and frowned. The faint criss-crossed lines at the center didn't resemble any flower he'd ever seen.

"What is it?"

Grace looked up from her basket, a needle protruding from her lips, and his smile was back.

"You're holding it upside down. It's your brand."

He turned the hoop and gooseflesh prickled across his

skin. Sure enough, the lines across the circle created an off-kilter *L* leaning over a slanted *J*. His gaze strayed back to the woman busily pulling brown thread through a needle.

How the hell did she know his brand? Had her man been a rancher? Knowing she wouldn't answer his questions, he held his tongue—and nearly swallowed it as she scooted up beside him, taking the cloth from his hands.

"You want to start at the bottom," she said, placing his hand on the hoop as she drove the needle up from underneath. "Up, then back," she said.

Garret tried not to notice the gentle brush of her breast against his arm as he breathed in her intoxicating floral scent.

"Each stitch should be the same size. See?" She smiled and held the needle out to him.

He didn't see much beyond the sparkling blue eyes of a mighty sweet woman. "Thank you, Grace."

She stiffened, as though just realizing she was practically on his lap. "Just…follow the lines," she said, sliding back against the headboard. She shifted her basket into the space between them.

He studied the few stitches she'd done for him. He'd already violated her, and here she was starting to trust him and all he could think about during her lesson were the perfect breasts he'd had no right touching, or kissing.

Oh hell.

Forcing himself to focus on the cloth, he gauged the length of stitches she'd started and he poked the needle through to the backside. Trying to get the tip to come back up at the base of the stitch took a dozen attempts. Beside him, Grace's needle moved in and out in a steady rhythm.

"Do you really think anyone will want to buy a dish towel with my brand on it?"

"Well, no. But I'm hoping it will keep you quiet for a while."

Laughter leaped from his chest and echoed off the surrounding walls. How a woman could speak her mind with such quick honesty yet manage to hold so many secrets truly amazed him.

His finger knocked the needle through before lining up the next stitch. "Damn."

"Problem?"

"How do I fix this?" he asked, turning the cloth to show her the thread hanging a half-inch from its target.

She plucked the towel from his hand and expertly guided the needle back through, freeing the thread. "There."

"Once again, my saving Grace."

He enjoyed the soft pink in her cheeks as she went back to her own stitching. He managed a few more passes, pleased to find he'd nearly completed the first leg in the *L*. He didn't mind the easy silence between them, but his curiosity was like a coal burning in his mind.

"Why haven't we met before?"

"We likely have, and you just didn't pay me any notice."

"Not possible," he said. "I would have noticed you, Grace."

She stiffened, her hand pausing midstitch. "Well, *you didn't*."

"We've met?" he asked, his shock apparent.

"I've seen you, is all. Why don't you have a wife?"

The question stunned him as much as her admission. It was the first question she'd asked about him, and likely the only question he'd rather not answer.

"I did for a short time."

She looked up, her eyes wide with surprise. "Oh. I'm sorry."

She obviously misunderstood, and he was tempted to let it go at that. Wasn't easy for a man to admit his wife had left him after the worst eight months of his life—and likely the worst eight months of hers.

"She's not dead. She's just…gone."

Slender black eyebrows pinched inward. "Gone where?"

"Back to Texas."

"She left you?"

Her shocked expression nearly made up for the pinch in his pride. "She did."

"Were you…mean to her?"

"Do I strike you as man who'd mistreat his wife?"

"Well…no. But people aren't always what they seem."

He couldn't argue that. Amanda Billings certainly seemed to embody everything he'd imagined a perfect wife would be, and not the sort of woman a man bedded before he married. Problem was, outside of the bedroom they hadn't had a whole lot to say to one another. Didn't help that her lady attendant had run off with one of his ranch hands a few weeks after they'd married, leaving her on a ranch full of men with only her cook and housekeeper for company during the day. Good God, but he didn't know a woman could shed so many tears. He'd flat run out of ways to console her.

"Maybe it was cruel to expect Amanda to find happiness with me on a ranch in the middle of Wyoming wilderness. I sure couldn't keep her happy and she hated living in Wyoming."

"Then why did she marry a Wyoming rancher?"

"Same reason I married a Southern belle from Texas. We didn't know any better." His experience with fancy women likely matched Amanda's experience with dusty cowpokes.

He could count on one hand the number of times he'd seen his sister cry—one of those times being the day he had announced his engagement. Her disapproval of his marriage had been like salt on a festering wound. He still hadn't told her about the divorce—he hadn't told anyone.

"Did you like being married to a Southern belle from Texas?"

"I didn't mind it, but we weren't well suited. She'd been raised to shine in polite society, schooled in proper etiquette and polite conversation. Her skills were wasted on me and I couldn't give her the amount of attention she needed. When most of my stock was dead or dying I was too busy to think of much else—and Amanda was too busy packing her bags to care."

"Eighty-seven was a hard winter and an even harder spring."

It had been sheer hell, which Amanda hadn't wanted any part of. He couldn't say he blamed her.

"Seems like that would be a time when having a wife around would be useful," Grace said, turning back to her task.

"I'll be honest with you. When she told me she was going home, I was mostly relieved." It had been a wonder to him that he could share his bed with a woman and feel so utterly alone. "It's a hard thing to be responsible for a woman's unhappiness."

"I don't know that most men worry about their wives' happiness."

Considering Grace's situation, he could understand why she'd think as much. "Those men must not have had sisters."

Maggie glanced up, ready to protest that comment. She knew for certain having a sister didn't stoke a man's compassion toward women. The sheer misery in Garret's expression stalled her words. Sister or not, he'd been hurt by his wife's displeasure.

"Your wife wasn't the only one spooked by such a harsh winter," she said. "Plenty of folks packed up and moved on after the thaw. Maybe she'll come back now that grasses have returned."

His slanted grin surprised her, and had her hoping his Southern belle of a wife had gotten lost in Texas.

"You want to know a secret?" he asked, leaning toward her.

"No." Just sitting beside him was far more personal than anything she'd experienced in a good long while—other than the kisses he hadn't meant to give her.

The reminder stung.

"I suppose it's not really a secret," he said. "I figure most folks know she's not coming back. But the truth of it is, Amanda and I were divorced last spring."

"What does that mean?"

"We were legally unmarried."

Unmarried? What woman in her right man would want to unmarry Garret? The man was capable, clean, dreadfully good-looking and his kisses weren't something a woman would dread.

"I didn't know there was such a thing," she admitted.

"Me, neither. Guess there isn't anything left in this world a lawyer can't undo. I don't suppose you want to tell me what happened to your husband?"

"You'd be correct on that account." She couldn't rightly call Ira her husband, but she knew most folks assumed he had been. Not that she minded. Ira had been a good man. On the rare days he had bathed, she wouldn't have minded if he'd been her man. She'd even asked him on more than one occasion. Close to seventeen years of age, she'd started noticing the babies with their mothers when they'd traded with a local tribe. Over the next few years she'd been consumed by a powerful longing for a child, a little life all of her own to care for and keep her company.

Ira had been furious the first night she'd asked him to give her a baby. She couldn't see why he shouldn't give her one, unless he was too old. That question had set off his temper right quick. He'd stormed off swearing a blue streak and shouting that he wouldn't be back.

But he'd come back weeks later with piles of hides for tanning and supplies he knew she'd need. She hadn't given up on her request, but his answer was always the same, that she didn't know what she asked of him, and there should be something more than friendship between a woman and a man to be making babies. The moment he started suggesting she search out a brave or a white man she stopped listening. Wasn't anyone she'd trust to be near her and he knew it. She'd been mad that he'd deny her the one thing she'd truly wanted. Not until his death did she know he shared her disappointment.

She'd skinned out the bear that mauled him. She'd heard the skirmish. By the time she'd reached Ira he'd killed the bear and was covered in rivers of red. She'd never seen so much blood. She'd been frantic to stop the bleeding and all the man could talk about was her. He'd likely spoken more words to her in those horrifying moments than in the seven years they'd been together. But it was his last words that haunted her.

I'm sorry, Maggie. You'd have been a good mother.

It was the only time she'd known him to be wrong. Over the years she'd realized her yearning for a baby had been the selfish dreams of a child. It wasn't that Ira hadn't cared for her—she knew he had. He hadn't wanted to tell her the plain truth; no child deserved to have Mad Mag as a mother.

"I didn't mean to upset you."

Garret's voice startled her from her thoughts.

"No matter who he is, I won't think any less of you, Grace."

Yes, he would. How could he not? It was the nature of folks to shun what wasn't familiar to them.

"Do you think he's coming back?"

"Oh, I don't think so."

"Then you've got no reason to stay up here. Crafty as you are with a needle, you could find work in any town. I bet you'd be a real star at one of them lady sewing parties."

There wasn't a lady within a hundred miles who'd sew with the likes of her.

"You can't be much over twenty. Hardly an old maid."

Was he blind? So she'd brushed her hair and put on a flowery shirt…she was still a wild woman in britches and well past the age of courting. There wasn't a town that would accept her, old maid or otherwise. Which suited her fine. "I'm well beyond twenty and have been choosing my own way since long before you were dressing yourself."

His expression darkened. "That's rot. You're young enough that you could remarry and have a family."

He didn't know the first thing about her or her failures as a woman. Her daddy had insisted she learn the *delicate arts of a lady,* but she'd since learned that it didn't take a delicate lady to stitch pretty flowers. Her life before Ira had been a *lie.* He'd taught her to depend on no one but herself. She didn't sit around and bellyache over her lot in life. She made an honest living. She worked hard.

"I think you'd find—"

"I think you should *shut the hell up!*" Her voice shouted back at her from the stone ceiling and startled Boots from his sleep. "What makes you think I give two wits about what you or anyone else thinks of me?"

The caution in his expression made her wish she could suck her defensive words back into her mouth. "You're right. I was prying. I apologize."

Heat stung her cheeks. "I shouldn't have sworn at you." He couldn't know how his foolish suggestions had hurt her. There wasn't a man who'd want her and she'd long since let go of her yearning for a child.

"You don't have to tiptoe around me, Grace. Wasn't my place to make assumptions about your life. If my yammering is wearing on you, you're more than welcome to tell me to shut the hell up."

Good Lord, but he was sweet. Maggie couldn't help but smile. "You don't yammer. You may not believe it, but I was raised to be polite."

"I was raised by my shouting and swearing older sister," he said with a grin. "I don't offend easily, sweetheart. And you did save my life. I can't think of anything more polite than that."

Maggie stared up at his gentle gaze, not having heard anything beyond *sweetheart*. It occurred to her that she may have been intrigued by Garret from a distance, but up close, he was devastating. The sincerity in his eyes made her yearn for things she shouldn't. He made her want to be the woman he'd kissed and called beautiful. His lack of intent didn't erase the memory of his kiss or the sweet ravaging of sensation she'd felt while in his arms.

Boots scratched at the door.

Garret cleared his throat and looked away. He drew a

deep breath as though suddenly winded and set his stitching aside before pushing to his feet. "You ready for a walk?"

Maggie expelled a hard breath, trying to release the wild stir of sensations as she watched him shrug into his coat.

Tomorrow he'll be gone and none of this will matter.

She picked up his dish towel and was surprised to find he'd nearly completed the outline. Not the straightest or most even stitches, but decent. *For a man.*

"Be damned," Garret said, having pulled the door open to a bright night sky. "It finally stopped snowing."

She tucked the towel into her basket and joined him at the door. Her breath hit the crisp air in a puff of white. The storm had dissipated, but the cold hadn't. She crossed her arms to block the chill as she watched Boots run beyond the clearing Garret had shoveled, all but disappearing into the deep bank. Moonlight glistened against snow, silhouetting the rim of mountains surrounding her cove. Her stomach clenched at the thought of Garret walking through the gap beyond the forest of trees.

He's going to find out who I really am. It's time to move on anyhow.

Chapter Seven

A minty scent hung in the air as Garret stepped inside. Grace stood at the pantry, tucking a slender canister onto the shelf. *Tooth powder.*

"Did you just brush your teeth?"

"Yes," she said, clutching a quilt around her shoulders as she looked up at him. "I should have offered you a toothbrush. I have a small supply and you seem to be one of the few men I've known who'd use one."

"That I do. I used some of your baking soda before you woke."

Her pretty white teeth flashed behind her smile as he went to the stove. He stoked the fire and added another log. He turned to find Grace sitting in the chair by the table. Her moccasin-covered feet propped on the chest, her sewing basket on the table beside her. She paid him no mind as she pulled green thread through the cloth.

If she intended to sleep at the table again, she was in for a fight. She'd already worn herself down taking care of him. The woman needed some solid sleep before she ended up sick.

"You're sleeping in the bed tonight, Grace."

Her needle paused as she glanced up at him.

"I've put you out for long enough."

"I'm fine right here."

"Like hell. You're going to get sick if you don't get some rest. You'd be warmer here in the bed."

"You're the one with a long walk ahead of you tomorrow."

"All right, then. We'll share the bed."

She gaped at him before her eyes narrowed. "We tried that once."

"I wouldn't knowingly disrespect you. I swear you can trust me."

"I'll be fine right here. *Go to sleep, Garret.*"

Her haughty tone snapped the last shred of Garret's patience. Just because her man had treated her with neglect didn't mean he'd follow suit. He'd weather her rage to keep her warm.

"You're getting a good night's sleep," he said, watching her eyes round as he plucked the cloth from her hands then scooped her slight weight into his arms.

"Put me—"

He dumped her onto the bed. "Scoot," he ordered, and piled into bed beside her.

"I won't—"

"Yes, you will." He latched his arm around her middle as she moved to leap toward the foot of the bed. He dragged her down and locked her against his chest. "The only warm place in this cabin is in this bed. Might as well hunker down because you're sleeping right here."

She shoved at his arm and tried to surge up. "If you think I'm going to—"

"I'm going to make sure you do," he said, shifting on top of her. "You've been taking care of me for days."

"Get...off...me," she said through gritted teeth.

"I won't hurt you, Grace."

"If I thought you'd hurt me you'd have bled out by now!"

Her shouted words eased some of his tension. Fully aware of her blade pressed to his hip, he hadn't been certain she wouldn't try to gut him. The woman was a mind-bending combination of compassion and defensiveness.

"If I feared you," she said in a milder tone, "you wouldn't be in my cabin, much less my bed."

"So relax," he said, easing his hold and shifting onto his side. "I'm not fevered out of my mind. I'm not going to try anything."

Her eyes flinched. "How reassuring." She twisted onto her side, but not before he saw the moisture hazing her eyes.

Damnation. He meant to reassure her. "Grace, don't think for a moment I'd have to be to want you."

She didn't respond.

"You're a real fine woman."

"If you don't pipe down, I'm getting up."

The last thing he needed to do was to elaborate on an attraction he'd been fighting to hide. He tugged up the blankets and turned onto his side, putting his back to hers. Not the most comfortable position, but certainly the safest.

"Good night, Grace."

Trapped beneath the covers, the warmth of his back pressed against hers, Maggie didn't answer. So much for his *gentle nature.* Staring at a spot of light cast by a lantern, she felt like a sardine packed into one of those tin cans. The stone wall sent her breath right back into her face.

She shifted her shoulders, trying to find a more comfortable spot, but it was no use. Garret's big body forced her to lie straight as a fence post. She couldn't deny her body's craving for sleep. She ached to curl up, to curve her legs, to really feel his warmth against her. If she had to lie beside him, she might as well be comfortable.

"Garret?" she said, pushing up.

"What?" He sounded wide-awake and just as irritable.

"I'm not comfortable."

He muttered a few words beneath his breath before saying, "You can have the bed."

"No," she said, reaching over him before he could toss the blankets back. "That's not what I meant. We fit in this bed when we weren't back to back."

His eyebrows shot up, the surprise in his expression nearly making her smile. The heat of his side penetrating her shirt made her eager to snuggle against him.

"I didn't think you'd want—"

"Just lie back," she said, her voice surprisingly gruff.

He stared at her a moment then eased against the pillow. "All right."

The stiff blade at her hip hindering her plans, she released her belt and looped the beaded leather over the bedpost. Burrowing back beneath the covers, she shifted partially over Garret, settling her head against his shoulder. His shirt wasn't as soft as his skin had been—but he felt nice all the same.

She marveled at the heat of his body as the tension in her muscles melted away. Warmth shimmered inside her, soothing her chill far more efficiently than any blanket ever had. She stroked his chest, her fingers burning to feel the direct heat of his skin.

Staggered by Grace's display of trust, Garret stared at

the ebony crown of her head and struggled to breathe. Her hand brushed over his shirt, her fingertips slipping just inside his open collar. The slight brush of skin turned his sleeping solution into sheer punishment. Did she really think their clothes made all that much difference when they were twined together so intimately?

Apparently so, he thought as she yawned, her firm breasts brushing against his chest. If she moved her thigh a tad higher...

Holy hell.

"Okay?" she asked, seeming snug as a bug and sounding half-asleep.

"Sure." He forced the word past his desire-constricted throat.

She didn't suffer any such affliction, her body completely relaxed against his. *She's just exhausted.* Or incredibly naive. Or perhaps she meant to torture him.

He tugged the heavy blankets up over her shoulders, knowing full well she didn't have a clue as to how deeply her innocent movements burned him to the quick. He had to remind himself that Grace didn't want him in her home and couldn't wait to kick him on down the mountain.

Her hand moved again, sliding clear down to his waistband. Her fingers found a gap at the bottom of his shirt and burrowed inside. His breath hitched as fingertips trailed across his belly, leaving sparks beneath his skin.

"Grace?"

"What?" she asked, sounding sleepy, her husky voice adding to the wild stir of his blood.

"Your hand is in my shirt," he said, as if she was somehow unaware of her hand stroking him as though he were a big tabby cat.

"You're so warm."

His hand flattened hers, holding her palm to the place where his heart thumped wildly. He shifted to his side, the sudden move dumping her onto the pillow beside him.

She tried to pull her hand away. "If you don't like my touch—"

"I more than like it! *You're setting me on fire.*"

"I am?"

He could hardly believe the surprise in her expression. She didn't have any idea what her touch was doing to him. "It's damn hard to have your hands on me when I've been fighting the urge to kiss you all day."

Sapphire-blue eyes widened. "You wanted to kiss me?"

"I figured that much was obvious."

"Not to me. No one's ever wanted to kiss me before."

Not wanted to kiss her? "Not even your husband?"

Her expression soured. "No. He wasn't a tender sort of man."

Garret had guessed that much, but he couldn't have guessed the kiss she'd given him a few days ago had been her first. Guilt festered inside him as he recalled just how fully and all the places he'd kissed her. "I must have shocked you, waking you up the way I did."

"You did." Her slow smile filled him with the urge to relearn the textures of her mouth. "But I've had worse surprises. Like coons in the pantry, a skunk in my cabin—

Garret couldn't fight his laughter. She tensed and tried to push away from him—not appreciating his humor.

He grabbed her hands. "Don't get mad," he said, brushing his lips over her fingertips. She trembled against him. "I'm just happy to hear kissing me ranked above skunks in your cabin."

Her fingers curved around his as her smoldering blue eyes lingered on his mouth. "Can't imagine your wife would have objected to kissing."

"I haven't had a wife in nearly three years, Grace. You're the first woman I've kissed in a long while."

She drew a deep breath and slowly released it, the minty scent tempting him.

"You didn't really kiss me," she said. "You thought you were dreaming."

"It was a good dream." Watching her eyes widen, he leaned in, pausing a breath away from her lips. "Grace, would you like to be kissed?"

Her hand slid into his hair and tugged him to her lips—incredibly soft lips that parted beneath his, welcoming the deep kiss he hadn't stopped thinking about. The desire he'd been trying to suppress burst to life as she kissed him back without hesitation, her cool, minty tongue stroking against his. For being half out of his mind with fever when he'd kissed her last, his memory of her generous mouth and alluring tongue sure hadn't dimmed. His hands remembered the path they'd followed, the curve of her hip, swell of her backside, the firm, resilient flesh of her thigh still hidden beneath soft buckskin.

Her moan was captured inside his mouth as his hand began a slow ascent up her body until her breast filled his palm. Layers of wool and cotton didn't hide the tight peak rising to his touch.

She whimpered against his mouth, her short nails biting into his shoulders.

Unsure of her response, he pulled back.

"Grace, if you want me to—"

"I do," she said, her breath ragged as she pulled him back to her lips. *"I want you."*

She took possession of his mouth, his mind. Every stroke of her mint-tinged tongue pulled him deeper into a rush of passion exceeding anything he could have conjured in a dream. She arched against him, her breast pressing into his palm, seeking more of his touch. He groaned as she shifted beneath him, her thighs sliding over his hips as she pulled him more fully on top of her. The contact was like a jolt of lightning straight into his veins. Hunger roared through him, shaking him.

Returning her fervent kiss, he caressed her fully, but it wasn't enough. He sought the buttons on her shirt but she combated his attempt. He moved back just as her hands stole inside the shirt she'd discreetly unbuttoned. Watching her eyes burn with pleasure as she combed her fingers over his chest enchanted him. She shoved the fabric toward his shoulders.

"Get this off."

He definitely loved that demanding tone. Unable to resist, he recaptured her mouth, his hips shifting against hers as he drew her flushed lower lip between his teeth. She moaned, her body flexing against him, shuddering from the rhythmic caress of his hips. She was like a flower blooming beneath his touch. He ached to give her the pleasure she'd been denied.

"Kissing you," he breathed against her mouth, "holding you…it's like discovering spring." He leaned back to comply with her wishes to remove his shirt.

Maggie couldn't deny the feelings he awakened inside her were akin to springtime. Watching sculpted ripples move in the lamplight stirred a wave of flutters low in her belly, like a thousand rose petals opening at once. Every flex of muscle doubled her need to feel him press against all the parts of her body aching for his touch. She reached up, smoothing her hand across the contrast of his pale hair and deep bronze of his skin. Her fingertips traced a thin, darkening trail down his belly to the waistband of his trousers.

He groaned and moved over her. "You're amazing."

"It's you." She'd never felt this way before. The mere thought of pressing her skin to his made her shiver all over. To have his gentle hands on her body again…

She tugged at her wool undershirt but his hands stopped her.

"Let me."

Maggie stared up at the warm green eyes intent on hers as he caressed her waist while making a slow ascent. She trembled as he brushed the sides of her breasts, his gentle fingers searching into the sleeves of her shirt, caressing and lifting the fabric away from her body.

"You're soft as a spring blossom."

Maggie knew she wasn't, and tensed at the sudden thought of Garret seeing her body in the bright light, exposing years of hard-learned lessons with hair-trigger traps and unruly critters.

"*Garret—*" Her shirts enveloped her as he pulled them up.

"*Grace.*" Her hands caught over her head in a tangle of fabric, making her completely vulnerable, powerless against his roving gaze. Gasping for breath, she watched as he noted every imperfection.

Her eyes hazed. Before she could protest, his mouth was on her, dusting her body with kisses, showering her with tenderness. The thrilling caress of his lips melted away her apprehension as heat swirled inside her.

His lips brushed the tip of one breast and then the other, sparking tendrils of new sensation.

"I like that," she said, the words escaping her lips.

He smiled against her breast and the coils tightened.

"Me, too," he whispered, his tongue grazing the tight, tingling peak before drawing her into the warm, wonderful wetness of his mouth.

Her back arched. She fought the fabric from her hand and plunged her fingers into his hair. His roving hands overwhelmed her as he caressed and molded, pushing away clothing until she felt his fingers caressing every inch of her skin.

He kissed a slow trail to her other breast, the hands stroking her thighs adding to the wild strumming of her pulse. She cried out as his mouth closed over her, welcoming the brightness, the beauty of being wanted, *cherished.*

His hand grazed the juncture between her thighs where an ache flared into an unquenchable need. She pressed her feet into the mattress, her legs quivering with tension as she strained against the pressure of his hand. His long finger stroked her shockingly sensitive flesh, each gentle glide startling her with a sting of pleasure.

She'd die if he kept on. She needed more of him. Breath escaped her as he suckled and stroked, each new burst of color and sensation bringing a deeper yearning.

"Garret!"

His weight settled over her and Maggie reveled in the feel of his skin against hers, her hands feasting on the corded muscles of his back as he kissed her. She twisted against him, sliding her fingers just beneath his waistband, trembling from the volatile combination of intriguing textures, the hair on his chest, his smooth, firm backside. He broke the kiss and pulled away from her.

Stunned by his sudden retreat, she sat up, ready to haul

him back against her. He stood and stripped off his trousers in a few deft movements.

Maggie's breath stalled at the full sight of him. Her Viking, powerful, beautiful—ready to conquer. She suddenly felt very small, dainty even.

The mattress sank beneath his knee, and Maggie swallowed hard, her body flooded by a rush of anticipation and apprehension at the thought of lying with him.

"Grace?"

She shivered, the gruffness of his voice stirring the wonderful sensations he'd conjured with his mouth and his hands. He tugged at the tie holding her hair and she felt the loose strands spread across her shoulders.

"Beautiful," he said, his arms circling her as he eased her back.

She reached for him, her hands framing his handsome face, stroking his short beard. She couldn't have known the "something more" Ira had told her about was a kind of spring in winter, melting away the ugliness of life. Nothing mattered but this man dusting her with gentle kisses as though she truly were the delicate woman of his dreams.

Desire gripping his body, Garret settled over Grace. The friction of her skin against his burned through the last strand of his control. Taking her mouth in a hard kiss he pushed home with a single thrust. Her pleasing moan didn't go any further than his mouth as her welcoming warmth surrounded him. He held her pressed to the bed, the tight sheath of her body about to undo him.

Her hands stroked down his back until her fingers closed over his backside. Her hips shifted, seeking, caressing him so completely he groaned against his body's unbearable demand for release. *Not yet.*

Grace shoved against his shoulders. "Am I...*hurting you?*"

The alarm in her voice broke through the wild surge of sensation. How could she think she'd hurt him when he'd never felt anything so incredible as her generous heat? The combination of passion and concern in her bright blue eyes answered his question, reminding him of the abuse he knew she'd endured. That she had opened her trust to him, her body, moved him beyond physical pleasure.

"No," he said, brushing his lips over hers. He rocked against her and she trembled, her eyes widening with surprise. "No more than I'm hurting you."

Focused on the desire brightening her eyes, he repeated the slow, deliberate caress. Her thighs moved higher on his hips, silently asking for more of him, and he gave it to her, every thrust deeper, harder as pleasure expanded between them.

Her head tipped back as she rose to meet him. He drove harder until the velvet grip of her body clenched around him. Her cries of completion didn't go any further than his mouth as he sank into her a final time, giving himself over to the sharp, shocking pulses of his own release.

Spent and panting, he locked his arms around her and shifted onto his side. He brushed a soft kiss against her cheek, his hand following the curve of her body.

My dream lover.

Releasing a long sigh of sheer satisfaction, he settled back on the bed. He smiled as she followed him, pressing her damp skin firmly against his side. Her arm tightened around his waist.

Maggie breathed in Garret's musky scent and snuggled closer. Her head resting on the cushion of his arm, she marveled at the security she felt at being wrapped in his strong embrace. She'd never felt anything like it…peaceful, free, like the scattered white fluff of a dandelion floating on a warm breeze.

His gentle fingers traced her spine. The light tingling touch made her shiver.

"Are you cold?" he asked.

She didn't think she'd ever be cold again. He was like a warm spring sun burning away the snow, leaving color and life in his wake.

"Grace?"

"No," she said, brushing her lips over his chest. "I'm not cold."

His fingers slid beneath her chin, tilting her face up to meet the tender caress of his lips. "You sure I'm not dreaming?" he asked, his eyes searching hers.

"No." She smiled. She may have wondered what it would be like to be held by him, to be truly kissed by him. But she never dreamed she'd be lying with him like this, skin to skin, nothing between them but the wild beating of their hearts. She reached up sliding her fingers into his thick white hair. She could still feel the abrasion on his scalp where he'd been struck. The memory of his blood-matted hair sent a shiver of cold fear twisting through her heart.

"When you slept so long after your fever broke, I was afraid you wouldn't wake up."

"While I was kissing you, I was afraid I *would* wake up and you'd dissolve with the dream. I'm glad I woke up, Grace. You put any dream I've ever had to shame."

She smiled and he shifted over her, dusting kisses down her neck, adding tingles to the lure of his words. She stretched beneath him, loving the feel of his body brushing against hers.

"My saving Grace," he whispered. His teeth grazed lightly against her skin, raking the embers he'd left smoldering in her blood. She smoothed her hands over his hips to the firm swell of his backside. He groaned and she realized she wasn't the only one trembling. The warm male flesh pressed against her thigh grew hard, increasing the tantalizing stir of her blood.

"You should sleep," she said, knowing he had a long trek tomorrow.

"Are you tired?"

How could she be tired when she felt renewed, revived. "No, but *you* will be come sunrise."

"I've been resting for days," he said, his mouth seeking hers.

For the first time in her life, tomorrow would come too soon. Until it did, she intended to embrace every thrilling moment.

Chapter Eight

"Time to go, Daines."

Garret woke to Grace's voice and his clothes being heaped onto his chest.

"The sun's up."

Bright light blinded him before the door slammed shut.

"What the hell?" He sat up wondering when he'd drifted off and how Grace had managed to slip from his arms without waking him. He'd spent the last few hours before sunrise watching her sleep, studying her pretty face and the tender scarred skin that filled his mind with a thousand questions. The thought of her suffering such abuse enraged him.

A teapot whistled on the stove. A skillet sat beside the steaming pot, the cast iron filled with some biscuits Grace had baked the day before.

She'd been up for a while, clearly anxious for his send-off. And he had reason to get home. Sorting through the clothes on his lap, he started pulling them on, reminding himself all the while that his partner could be in trouble, his ranch under attack. He had to get down this mountain *today*.

He was fully dressed before he lifted the squealing pot

and filled a mug. His stomach grumbled at the scent of the herbal tea. He picked up a warm biscuit and noticed the salted venison she'd tucked into the soft center. He shoved one into his mouth and wished he had a cup of his usual strong morning coffee.

A canteen hung from the corner of her pantry, another item she'd set out for him. The woman was efficient. And a damn fine cook, he thought, eating another fluffy meat-filled biscuit before filling the canteen. He quickly made up the bed before starting toward the door. A white strip on the floor near the foot of the bed caught his gaze. He crouched down, picking up the tie he'd pulled from Grace's hair. Desire flared at the memory of those waves of black fanning out behind her shoulders, her blue eyes aglow with passion as she reached for him.

For all her fire last night, she'd obviously awakened with a burning desire to see him gone. He placed the fabric on the table holding his hat and gunbelt. The backpack he'd prepared the day before was gone. He turned and searched the small dank space. He didn't spot his pack anywhere within the rough rock walls. His gaze stopped on one of Grace's fancy stitched towels that didn't fit this rough-cut cave any better than the polished wood floor.

She doesn't belong up here. He didn't understand why she'd keep herself hidden on this mountain.

Donning the rest of his gear, he tugged his hat low and opened the door to the blinding glare of sunlight reflecting off the snow. His backpack sat propped against the woodpile along with a pair of large snowshoes. His gaze moved over the tarpaulins covering her firewood—enough to last her the rest of winter. She must have been swinging an ax through the spring, summer and fall to build up such an impressive pile. He'd seen the calluses on her slender hands, had felt them against his skin as she turned his world to fire.

Leaving her up here, so far into the wilderness…it wasn't right. He turned, his eyes adjusting to the brightness as he took in a clear view of the tall white mountain peaks creating a cove of serene beauty around a forest of dusted pines. A breathtaking contrast of white against the pristine sky, not a single cloud marring the bright blue. He supposed he could see her drawn to such a tranquil place—which didn't do a damn thing to ease his apprehension about leaving her here.

Spotting her tracks leading into the trees, he started toward the woods. So far as he could tell, she held no desire to leave. One night in her bed didn't give him a right to demand anything of her.

Boots barked and he spotted them walking back through the trees, following the path they'd treaded. Grace stepped into the clearing, a light breeze tugging at her loose hair, and his body responded to the memory of that silken mass brushing against his chest while she had kissed him.

Cool your fire. When it came to women he had a bad habit of falling fast and landing in rubble. He wasn't looking to repeat any such mistakes. Grace watched him with a good degree of caution as she approached. Her tense expression didn't reveal any of her passion from the night before—none of which discouraged his burning desire to kiss her. Caution had never been a strong voice in his mind.

She stopped in front of him. "Snowpack is thick but—"

He slid his hand into the loose silk of her hair, ending her words in a gasp as his fingers caressed the back of her neck.

"Good morning," he said, and pressed his mouth to hers.

Maggie's initial instinct to fight him melted the moment he touched her. The past half hour of convincing herself she'd reestablished her defenses against him dissolved beneath the tender caress of his lips. Her arms entwined around his neck and she welcomed the easy comfort of being in his arms, the slow, soothing rhythm of his deep kiss. He released her too soon, stepping back, a satisfied grin tipping his lips.

Smug, she thought, while fighting a smile. She'd worried he'd see her differently in the harsh light of day. She hadn't bothered to bind her hair. Her coat covered her warm buckskin tunic. He was leaving and she had no reason to continue the facade. But as Garret's gaze roamed over her, his eyes warm, appreciative, she didn't feel like a deranged mountain woman. She felt…*desirable.*

"You two go for a walk?" he asked.

"To the rim just beyond the gap." She motioned to the trees behind her then crouched down to remove her snowshoes.

Garret searched the rim of stone visible above the trees and couldn't make out a break. "I wondered how I was going to get out of this crater."

"My tracks will lead you to a break in the cliffs. The snowpack is thick. You'd find yourself waist-deep at some points without the snowshoes. The ledge leading off the rim is narrower than the snow leads to believe, so keep to the cliff."

She glanced down at his dog panting beside her.

"Have you thought about how Boots will manage?" she asked.

"Yeah. It'll be a struggle for both of us. But I can't wait any longer."

"He's worn-out after a fifteen-minute run through that

dense powder. You won't reach your ranch before nightfall with Boots."

He knelt and rubbed behind Boots's shaggy black ear. "You tired, old man?"

"He's welcome to stay with me."

Garret looked up in sharp surprise.

"I thought it over during the walk back. I can send Boots on to your ranch as soon as the thaw sets in."

Leave his dog? Garret didn't like the idea of leaving Boots behind any more than he wanted to leave Grace.

"He won't make it, Garret. You'd have to carry him part of the way and that will slow you down."

His dog panted hard from the laborious run through the snow, but his tail wagged as he looked up at Grace. Boots was sporting, but he wasn't a young pup. And Grace was right—he needed to arrive with enough daylight to scout his ranch for trouble.

"Somehow I don't think you'd mind a few more weeks with Grace." Knowing he'd get to see her when she returned Boots eased his trepidation about leaving her up here alone. "All right," he said. "This won't be an easy trek."

"If I thought it would be easy I'd blindfold you until you rounded the mountainside."

"*Blindfold* me?"

Grace's stone-serious expression kept him from laughing at the thought of her strapping a blindfold on him. She stood beside him with her arms wrapped tight around her middle as though holding in a bundle of nerves.

"The only reason you've never noticed me on this mountainside is because I don't want to be seen," she said distinctly. "The one time I had visitors at my old cabin, I moved. Took me a whole spring and most of summer just to resettle."

Garret glanced back at the cabin front, hearing the implications that she hadn't been abandoned anytime recently as he'd assumed. She'd built this place on her own? He couldn't imagine the kind of fear that would drive her to seek shelter way up in this wild country.

"I like to be left alone," she said, her expression hard.

"I won't come pester you, Grace, and I won't breathe a word."

"You've been gone for five days and I'm sure you've been missed. I don't expect you to lie. Once you get out to the rim you'll know right where you're at and how close I am to your ranch. It's not a great distance when you know where you're headed."

The sadness in her voice increased his reluctance to leave. Her white-knuckled grip on her snowshoes strengthened his urge to hold her. The thought of her hiding out up here, alone and afraid—he couldn't just leave.

"Honey, why don't you come with me?"

"You can follow my tracks," she said. "Honestly, once you're beyond the gap, you'll have a clear view of your ranch in the valley below."

"I meant come home with me. To stay at my place."

She took a few steps back, her startled expression far from accepting. "W-why would I do that?"

"I owe you my life. I have plenty of room at my place."

"You don't owe me anything. I'm well suited here."

"Grace, you have a nice cave, but it's a cave. This is no way to live."

"My *cave* kept you sheltered and warm for nearly a week. Remember that when you're back in your fancy house."

"I'm not putting you down." He reached for her, but she moved beyond his touch.

"You're not putting me anywhere!" she spat.

"I'm not saying you'd stay in my bed—hell, I'm not trying to take advantage of you. I'm offering help."

"I don't need help. When did I ask you for anything?"

"I owe you my life, Grace."

His concern filled her with a deep yearning to be the delicate woman he saw in her. Whoever he thought she was, he was going to be disappointed. There wasn't a damn thing delicate about her. She had wondered what it would be like to be held by him, and now she knew.

Mind blowing—she'd have to be out of her mind to allow herself to become so vulnerable.

"I can take care of myself, Garret. Whether I stay here or move on, it's not your business."

"I'm offering an invitation. Not an order. Nothing but an open door."

"A *trapdoor*. I'm not so naive. I had a grand house once, full of expensive finery and servants, for all the good it did me."

Garret snatched at the first real hints she'd given him about her life. He'd already guessed as much—he wanted to know more. The stern set of her jaw and chill in her gaze suggested she wouldn't be offering. She had a strength he admired, a deep sense of compassion she tried to hide and more passion than he'd ever known in a woman.

"You're a good woman, Grace. You deserve better than this."

"If I wanted better, I'd get it myself. You've got no call to worry over me. I've been taking care of myself for years."

"How long have you been living alone up here?"

"You're going to run out of daylight if you don't get going."

"Grace—"

"If there's trouble at your ranch, you don't want to arrive late."

The reminder ended his protest. He had no idea what he'd be walking into. This wasn't the time to bring a guest home. "Are you sure you don't mind housing and feeding Boots for a few more weeks?" he asked, kneeling to pet his companion. "I've already cut down on your food supply."

"I have plenty."

"All right." He straightened, his gaze intent on hers. "My offer stands."

"I know where you live."

His smile was gentle, reassuring—and increased the ache swelling in Maggie's chest. He stepped toward her and she couldn't keep from reaching for him, from meeting the caress of his lips. The gentle kiss only increased the sense of loss expanding through her soul.

"Thank you," he said, brushing another soft kiss over her lips. "For everything."

Maggie had to force herself to release him. "I like living a quiet life," she said, needing the reminder. "I don't want—"

"I gave my word to leave you be. I'll keep it. Whether I want to or not. You can trust me, Grace."

To her horror, tears burned at her eyes. Thankfully he knelt down to bind the snowshoes.

She cleared her throat. "I hope everything is well at your ranch."

"Me, too."

"Come on, Boots," she called.

Garret looked up as his dog ran past, following Grace

into the cabin. The door slammed shut as he straightened, followed by the sound of the bar being dropped into place.

Lifting his backpack, he noticed the butt of her shotgun protruding from a long pouch sewn along the side of the canvas pack. He wasn't going to take her only decent weapon.

"Grace?" he called out.

"I have a rifle," she shouted back. "Get moving, and *be careful*."

He scowled and shifted the pack onto his shoulders. He'd likely appreciate her intuition and meticulous preparations had he not been leaving her behind.

He'd find a way to repay her.

Sticking to shadows cast by the sun setting behind him, Garret crouched near the fence of an outer pasture. Lanterns brightened the windows of his two-story Victorian-style house. No one milled about in the yard or surrounding paddocks. Odd for this time of evening. His men were usually finishing up with evening chores.

He shifted the shotgun to his left hand and hopped the first fence. Keeping low, he approached the east side of the bunkhouse. He couldn't hear any conversation from his rowdy crew coming from inside. As he reached the end of the long building, he spotted a crowd gathered on a small hillside fifty yards from his back door.

Looking closer he recognized his crew standing with men from the Morgan ranch. None of the dozen or so men huddled together wore a hat. Kuhana's long black braids trailed down his back. Beside him Everett's short brown hair flipped in the wind. He searched the group for Duce's shaggy red mop. Clint, a tall, wiry cowpuncher, shifted and he spotted reverend John Keats standing before the men circling a plot of land.

Oh, no.

He started toward the hill. His gaze shot back to the men with their heads bowed, hats in hand. His sister stood on the far side, her long, lithe form wedged between two blond, broad-shouldered men, her husband, Tucker Morgan, and his twin brother, Chance. He still didn't see Duce.

His throat tightening, the burning in his gut intensified.

Skylar looked up, his sister's glistening eyes widening at the sight of him closing in on them.

"Garret!" She broke away from the others and set into a full run. A green skirt flashed beneath her long gray coat with every rapid stride. Garret dropped his shotgun and let the pack slide from his shoulders to the ground. Opening his arms, he caught his sister as she leaped at him.

"Oh, thank God," she cried, clutching him in a fierce grip.

He brushed her fallen blond hair away from her tear-streaked face. "I'm okay, sis."

She pressed her face to his coat and sobbed. He'd never seen his usually stoic sister so distressed. He looked up at the approaching Morgans, their expressions identically mournful.

Tucker put a hand on his wife's shoulder and tugged a brown Stetson over his blond hair. "You had us worried," he said to Garret.

"You've been up in the high country," Chance said, glancing at the snowshoes tied to his backpack.

"Yeah. The storm. I was snowed in."

Skylar sniffed and eased back. Like a mother who'd just found her missing child, she smoothed her hands over his whiskered face.

"I'm okay," he assured her, her grief-stricken expression tearing at his heart.

She managed a trembling smile.

"Only your horse returned the day after you and Duce rode out," said Chance. "A couple of your men came to our ranch."

"We've been here for four days," Tucker told him, "dividing up terrain and riding out as high as we could manage with the snow. Your sister was ready to shovel her way into those mountains."

"I'm just grateful you're well." Skylar grabbed him for another tight squeeze.

"Sorry I worried you." Garret returned her firm hug. "I had to wait out the storm." He looked again toward his ranch hands beginning to amble toward them, and the mound of fresh dirt now visible in the distance. "Tell me that's not a grave."

Fresh tears hazed his sister's blue eyes.

"We found Duce and his horse yesterday," Tucker said, his arm sliding around Skylar. "A couple of miles shy of the snow line. He'd been dead a few days."

They'd been attacked. He hadn't reached Duce in time. He shut his eyes, willing himself to remember something, anything about his attackers. It was no use. The last he could recall was staring down at muddy tracks being washed out by the rain.

"How'd he die?" he said to Tucker, steeling himself for details.

"Hard to say. He was broken up real bad."

"He'd been dragged," said Chance. "No way to tell how he got hung up in the stirrup."

The thought of Duce suffering such a violent death ripped through his shock. Rage burned inside him. "He was killed by whoever knocked me out. The ranch hasn't had any other trouble?"

"Nothing aside from searching for you," said Tucker.

"You were attacked?" Skylar asked, alarm straining her voice.

"When Duce didn't ride in I went looking for him. Someone must have drawn him up into that high country. When the rain began washing out his tracks I had to dismount to find them. That's the last I recall before being pulled from the snow."

"Any idea about who hit you?" Tucker asked. "Have you been having trouble with rustlers?"

"We noticed all your men ride armed," said Chance.

"Anyone with a herd fights to keep it," he said, knowing the Morgans didn't share the same struggles on their horse ranch in a neighboring valley.

"Why haven't you said anything?" asked Tucker.

"There isn't a rancher in these hills who hasn't had trouble. What I don't understand is why Duce would have been riding up the mountain. We weren't keeping stock in that high country. Something drew Duce up there."

"Where's Boots?" asked Chance.

"I left him with, uh…the woman who helped me," he said, keeping his voice low, mindful of the approaching men.

"Man, are we glad to see you!" Everett, a fourteen-year-old cowhand he'd taken in last spring rushed up and smacked his shoulder. "We thought you must have froze up there on that mountain."

"Not I," Kuhana said, his hard amber eyes narrowed as he scowled at his young co-worker. "I know you live."

"Where you been for five days?" asked Clint, nudging his way into the crowd of men gathering around him.

"Snowed in." He shifted his focus to an older man standing off to the side. Reverend Keats waited patiently, a bible in his frail hand. He'd known the retired preacher for quite a few years. He'd been a regular guest in his sister's house. "Reverend Keats. Did I miss the service?"

"No, my boy. I've only read a few verses. Now that you've returned, Duce can rest in peace."

Drawing a deep breath, he started toward a reality he wasn't ready to face.

The sun had been down for hours by the time Garret left the bunkhouse. Discussing local ranchers and possible motives with his men hadn't led to anything solid. The few shots of whiskey he'd consumed hadn't done anything to ease the weight bearing down on his chest and his mind. He paused at the base of the back step, his gaze drawn to the cross they'd fashioned, the carved wood barely visible in the darkness.

Duce's death didn't seem real. Even as he'd sat on the benches talking to his men, he kept expecting to hear Duce join in with one of his wisecracks, to see his red hair when he looked around the room.

Exhausted, he turned back to the house—a house that had never really felt like his home. Without Duce for company, he'd likely be better off staying in the bunkhouse. The moment he stepped through the back door, his sister's presence was apparent in the polished wood floor and scrubbed surfaces across his large kitchen. Even the pink wallpaper seemed brighter. He'd hoped the ugly stuff would fade over time but the original owner clearly spent a fortune on durable wall covering.

Chance and Tucker sat across from each other at the table centered in the room. Skylar stood at the stove on the far side of the kitchen. The sizzle and aroma coming from the frying pan reminded him that he hadn't eaten anything since the bread and venison Grace had packed for him.

He sat at the end of his scuffed kitchen table and wished he was back in the warm serenity of Grace's cabin. His gaze moved over the plates and platters already spaced across the clean, dull surface. Unlike his sister's home, bachelors maintained his house. Not a single surface shone unless one of them spilled something and took the time to wipe it up, inadvertently creating a clean spot. He and Duce had tried hiring a housekeeper, but they couldn't find any willing to stay on a ranch full of men in the middle of Wyoming wilderness.

His gut churned with renewed anger as sorrow rolled over him. "We got to find who did this."

Chance's side-glance reflected the raw anger twisting through Garret. He gave a slight nod of agreement.

"He had a will." Chance pushed a platter of fried potatoes his way. "He left his portion of the ranch to you."

Garret didn't give a damn about any shares in the ranch. Duce had been more of an older brother to him than a business partner. Unlike the other riders in his father's outfit, Duce had been willing to give a ten-year-old the time of day, offering pointers and advice instead of berating his lack of skill. Even Skylar had liked him, and that was saying a lot. Back then his older sister didn't warm to anyone. Duce had been different—he'd been family.

"Was there anything in his will about sending his belongings to a relative?"

"Nope. Guess he didn't have any other family. Besides you, three ladies are mentioned by first names only. Five hundred dollars is to go to each of them."

Garret chuckled despite the grief weighing on his soul. "Daisy, Tulip and Maxine?"

A smile curved the other man's lips. "I take it you'll know where to deliver their, uh, tokens of Duce's affection?"

His sister glanced over her shoulder, her stern gaze making him feel like a kid caught with his hand in the cookie jar.

"I couldn't point them out," he admitted, "but he talked about *his girls* at the Gilded Lady often enough."

Skylar placed a plate of fried steaks on the table and sat beside her husband. "Speaking of ladies, who's the woman you mentioned earlier? You said she helped you?"

Garret was surprised they'd waited so long to ask him, but then, this was the first time he'd been alone with the three people he trusted most.

"Grace. I'd be dead if she hadn't hauled me from the snow and dragged me up to her cabin."

"Grace?" said Chance, his eyebrows arched in question.

"Yeah."

"You can be straight with us, kid. The only woman I know who'd live up on that mountain is Maggie Danvers. I've been wondering if she had moved into those northern ranges."

"You been shacked up this past week with *Mad Mag?*" asked Tucker.

"No," Garret said with a grimace. "I've been within smelling distance of that trapper woman." Grace was as fresh and clean as a spring rain. "Grace is clean."

"So is Maggie when she's not trying to repel folks."

"Not the same woman," Garret insisted. "Grace can't be older than—"

"Twenty-five or so," said Chance. "Short little thing with black hair and piercing blue eyes. Quick mind, sharp tongue. She wears a long blade sheathed at her hip and a white fur coat over winter. Blends with the snow. Light as she is on her feet, you'd lose her in a patch of aspen."

Garret's stomach dropped at Chance's thorough description of "Grace."

"Same woman?"

"I can't believe it. I mean, I might have thought it for a split second, but…she didn't have anything in her cabin to lead me to think she was a trapper."

"You didn't get a look at her hands?"

Chills pricked across his skin. "I did."

"Her skill might have been slow coming but she mastered her craft. I've seen that woman wield a blade with a refined finesse to make any man mind his footing while in her company."

His mind refused to absorb that soft, compassionate Grace could be *Mad Mag*.

"Don't feel duped, kid." Chance slapped him on the shoulder.

The nickname grinded on his nerves.

"Maggie makes sure people see what she wants them to see."

"I'd be worried about your hound if I were you," said Tucker as he cut into his steak. "Poor Boots might be skinned out by spring."

Low chuckles drew his gaze to the others sitting at the table. Even his sister fought a smile.

He'd heard all the Mad Mag rumors and legends, but they'd actually *met* her. How could they not want to help her? They'd known Grace was on that mountain, and they hadn't told him?

"She wouldn't hurt Boots. She saved my life."

"He's teasing," Skylar said, casting a reproachful glare at her husband. "Cora told me how Maggie helped her on the day of her wedding. "

"All of you knew she lived up there?" he demanded, outrage building inside him. "And none of you offered to help her?"

"Help her with what?" asked Chance. "Maggie's one of the most inhospitable people I've ever met. She don't take kindly to favors."

Last time I had unexpected visitors I moved... "You've known she was up there all these years? Why hasn't anyone ever told me she lived so close to my ranch?"

"Not for me to tell," Chance said, and took a bite of his steak.

He couldn't believe his ears. They knew and had just turned a blind eye?

"Besides," Chance added, "she abandoned her place on the ridge between our two valleys years ago and I wasn't sure where she'd relocated. Star still shows up in my north pasture for winter housing, so I figured she hadn't gone too far."

"You sold her Star," he said, recalling now what Duce had told him that day in town.

"Maggie expressed an interest in the mare when she helped Cora Mae. She's saved my hide more than once. Not that our run-ins have made Mag the least bit cordial. She flat don't like people."

"Exactly how long have you known her?"

Chance gave him a measuring stare, likely put off by his short tone. "I came upon her and her man years ago on my first ride into our valley."

Maggie Danvers...*wife* of Ira Danvers. His mind somersaulted over the recollection. "You've met Ira Danvers?"

Reluctant to answer that question, Chance Morgan stared at Garret. His shaggy state and bloodshot eyes resembled more of a mountain man than a cattle rancher. On the one occasion Chance had met Ira Danvers, the grizzly-size trapper had been dead for several days. He'd no sooner spotted the body when he'd been knocked to his knees and had Mag's knife pressed to his throat. Had he tried to reach for that knife, he had no doubt he'd have died. It was his offer to finish the grave she'd started that finally convinced her to release him.

Chance's first glimpse of Mag had been an unsettling sight; her hair a mess of black tangles, her coat smudged with blood and mud. She'd been struggling to dig a grave in frozen ground. Her eyes cold and expression viscous, she appeared as wild as the scavengers she'd been fighting off for days.

He'd helped her bury her man and she'd guided him into his valley he'd been trying to find for a week, a disconcerting alliance to say the least. She'd sworn him to silence about Ira—an oath he hadn't broken, not even to his wife. Wasn't his secret to tell and he respected Mag's privacy. Rumors of Ira still inhabiting those mountains was another level of protection for her—one she needed. If Mag wanted Garret to know about her dead husband, she'd have told him.

"I've met him. Not surprised they weren't together. I've run into Maggie on occasion, though she's never been what I'd call *friendly*. Must have been a precarious week for you."

Garret could hardly believe her deception. No wonder she'd been in such an almighty hurry to be rid of him.

My God. He'd committed adultery.

"She couldn't have been too rough with you," said Chance, "for you to think she's some little flower in need of shelter."

Tucker choked on a laugh and Garret glanced up at identical grins. Their visible humor was another blow.

She'd made him care about her, and she'd used him. She knew damn well what she was doing, shoving her hand up his shirt like she had.

The realization turned his stomach. Garret shoved away from the table and headed for the back door.

"Garret?" Skylar called after him. "You haven't eaten anything."

"I need some air."

His history with women had been nothing but a joke. If they caught wind that even Mad Mag had kicked him from her bed, the ribbing would be endless.

She'd been so damn convincing.

Maggie Danvers.

Not only had she duped him, but she still had his dog!

He walked toward the hillside where his best friend lay beneath the ground. He crouched at the edge of the upturned dirt and reached out, touching the broken earth.

"You'd get a kick out of this one."

He stared at the tethered feathers twisting in the wind Kuhana had tied to the cross. One-sided attractions seemed to be his curse in life. Twice he'd given his heart to a woman, and twice she'd handed it right back. It wasn't a lesson he needed to learn a third time.

He had bigger issues to be fretting over than a promiscuous mountain shrew. His partner had been killed. The moment he found out which cattle-grubbing bastard was responsible for Duce's death, there'd be hell to pay.

Chapter Nine

He ought to cut the damn thing down.

Reclined against a pile of satiny pink pillows, Garret stared at the dusty lace canopy above his large four-poster bed. Rays of light pierced through lace curtains in the window, announcing the dawn of anther spring day. The increasing glow of daybreak burned shadows away from a suffocating concoction of frilly lace, pink satin and dried flowers. Widow Jameson's new husband had been a smart man to cart off his wife, leaving behind the fancy furnishings of her oversize Victorian dollhouse.

He'd once thought his future wife would enjoy such ladylike surroundings and he wasn't usually in the house long enough to be bothered by all the feminine frills. In the past two months sleep hadn't come easy. Dreams of Grace merged into nightmares about Mad Mag, his mind melding rumors with memories of the passionate woman he'd come to know.

No one's ever wanted to kiss me before.

The woman he'd met in town wouldn't have welcomed any such advances.

Nor had the defensive woman who'd emerged from the storm, he reminded himself. She'd done all she could to avoid him in that tiny cave. He'd been the one who'd dumped her into bed with him, despite her protests. He'd been the one who'd given her the kisses they'd both been craving.

While he had tamed the mountain shrew, Duce lay dead. That knowledge tore at his conscience. He'd spent several days with the sheriff in Bitterroot Springs, a man overwhelmed by the violence running rampage across the county. The lawman had too much ground to cover, every cattleman was a suspect and no one had been brought to justice.

With the spring drive closing in and his time constrained, he'd resorted to hiring his own investigating attorney. An expense that had amused his crew and resulted in more questions, more worry and too many sleepless nights of staring at the useless fancy weave above his bed.

His muscles bunched, anger boiling, he surged up and swung his feet to the floor. He stood and grabbed the pile of clothes he'd tossed onto a pink-and-white-striped settee the night before. In the past few days he'd ridden through the northern pasture, surveying his stock, but he'd wanted to ride up that mountain.

Stuffing his shirttails into his pants, he strode toward the window. If he could see across the miles, he'd be looking right into her hideaway. The snowline had receded to the highest peaks. And yet his elusive mountain woman hadn't surfaced. As much as he wanted to ride into that high country and flush her out, he'd promised to leave her be.

Cursing that bit of stupidity, he shifted his gaze to the long, patchy roof across the yard, a bold reminder that he was the sole owner of his ranch and wasn't free to simply ride range. The barn roof was about to collapse. He and

Duce had talked about doing the needed repairs in early fall but had put it off. Rains would be coming soon and he couldn't risk the loss of grain. None of his men wanted to spend a day out of their saddle any more than he did. Everett was sure to grumble at the news that he'd be on the roof today instead of riding out with the others.

He headed for the stairs. His boots clapped on the wood floor, each step echoing through the silence of the empty house, an emptiness that choked him. Spending most of his life on a cattle trail or at his sister's house, he lived in constant noise and commotion. It wasn't a wonder Amanda had run and not looked back.

Just enough sunlight spilled into his kitchen to reveal weeks of neglect. Lighting the overhead lamps would only draw attention to a layer of dust, an array of dirty coffee mugs stacked beside the basin he never got around to filling with dishwater. Hard to make much progress in a place he tended to avoid. Now that the spring crew had been hired meals were served in the bunkhouse.

He stepped up to the stove, missing the scent of bacon and coffee, the buzz of conversation—*life.* A few months back every man on the ranch would have piled into his kitchen for Duce's mean flapjacks. Early mornings were the only time Duce stood at the stove, a cheroot clamped in his teeth, spatula in hand. The cast-iron monstrosity was big enough to grill ten flapjacks at once. His two-pound hotcakes would weigh down a man's gut clear till nightfall.

Garret lifted the coffee kettle from the cold range and gave the contents a swish. *A quarter pot.* After lighting the stove he scoured the side table for his shaving supplies. Didn't make sense to haul water up to his room when no one cared if he shaved at the kitchen pump.

By the time the back door squeaked open, Garret stood beside the stove with a cup of the lukewarm coffee in his hand, his toothbrush stuck in his mouth.

Kuhana stepped inside. A sleek black feather tucked under the band of his high-domed hat gleamed against the morning brightness. The satiny texture reminded Garret of Grace's ebony hair. Kuhana's tawny face creased with a scowl as he glanced around the darkened room before spotting him at the stove.

"You are late," he said, stepping inside.

Garret gave his teeth another pass with the toothbrush before spitting into the basin. "Last I checked I owned this place. I'd say you're early."

His Indian friend eyed him warily. "Then you pay us to wait."

Everett stomped in behind him. "Hey, boss. We helping the crew on the south side today?"

Not ready to kill his youthful eagerness by announcing the roofing task, he avoided the question and reached for his coat draped over the back of a kitchen chair. "Everyone in a hurry this morning?"

"This place is a mess," Everett said, his gaze raking across the dirty floor and cluttered tables. "You ought to get your sister to come for a visit."

The last thing he needed was his older sister picking up after him and meddling in his business. "I'll get to it later tonight."

Kuhana grunted. "You need wife."

"I've got all the complications I can handle."

Sweat dripping in his eyes, Garret sat back on his heels and swiped his arm across his brow as Everett continued to hammer nails. He shifted his hat over his damp hair and blinked up at the midday sun. A rooftop was not the best place to be at high noon on a hot spring day. Fresh, sweet scents of spring permeated the air as busy birds chattered around them. His gaze was drawn back to the mountain.

He couldn't take a breath without thinking about the scent of her skin, the taste of her kiss, the sting of her deception.

I'm not going to wait much longer.

He stood, his gaze skating across miles of green hills spotted by splashes of gold and blue. A herd in the distance darkened the land like a shadow over the thick grasses. Having been raised in the saddle, he'd seen just about all the terrain the States had to offer, and none of them compared to this rich expanse of wilderness and blue sky— a beauty that used to soothe his restless spirit.

"You worried that trapper ain't bringin' Boots back?"

Garret looked over at Everett watching him from a few feet away. He hadn't told his crew more than the basics. A trapper had helped him out and was keeping Boots until the spring thaw.

"Last few weeks you're always lookin' at that western range," he said.

"Boots will turn up." He wouldn't drive stock without his dog. "We're making good time," he said, nodding at the section of roof they'd finished. Everett hadn't put up the fuss he'd expected and had set to the task with a skill that surprised him. "We'll be done by this evening. You've had some experience with roofing."

"Yeah." The corners of his mouth turned down. The instant sadness in his expression added a childlike quality to his brown eyes. "My pa and me roofed our barn just weeks before it burned."

Garret felt for him. The boy's family was another victim of the panic following the freeze, rancher turning against rancher. Their neighbor saw fit to torch the homestead. After fighting each other, both ranchers had lost their land to new money moving into the area, those who sought to capitalize off the tragedy of longtime residents. He'd hired Everett as a favor to his folks. At fourteen he was a decent ranch hand and a hard worker, but he was still a boy who missed his family.

"You'll get to see your folks in another month, once we reach the stockyard."

Fighting moisture from his eyes, Everett gave a nod as he looked away.

"Why don't you head on into the bunkhouse and find us something to eat."

He didn't hesitate. His boots tapped rapidly across the steep slope to the top rung of the ladder. "Bacon and toast all right?" he asked as he descended.

"Sounds good."

He hoped he'd done the right thing by bringing the kid out here. Barns were still being burned and ranchers lynched or run off their land. Two years since the freeze and tensions continued to rise. Everett's father now worked a mining job to support his five younger children, and spent his days deep underground.

Garret shuddered at the thought.

They'd have to bury me first. He lived for ranching, driving herd. His livelihood was his life.

He walked to the next bundle of cut planks. He released the rope and began spacing out the shingles. Over the clatter of wood and chirping birds, he swore he heard a faint bark.

About to drop another board, he paused.

A series of faint barks carried back on the southern breeze. *It's about time!*

Straightening, he turned, looking toward miles of open range in the lowlands. She was trying to sneak him in through the south end. His gaze honed in on the line of dark foliage marking the nearest river, the only real coverage to be found in those open hills. She had to be following the river.

He wasn't about to let her slip through his land without talking to him.

He was down the ladder and mounting his saddled horse in seconds.

"Hey, Everett," he called out as he rode the brown and white mare past the bunkhouse. "I'll be right back."

A half mile out he reined in, easing his horse into a slow, silent trot, the mare's hoofbeats drowned out by the steady rush of the swollen river. He rode along the outside edge of the trees and scrub, peering through the low, dense branches. He wanted to call his dog, to flush them from the brush, but he knew if he did that she'd take flight. They couldn't be far.

A sharp bark from just ahead confirmed that notion.

Garret dismounted, leaving his horse as he pushed past the thick brush, stepping into the blend of light and shadows.

"Damn it, Boots."

Her low voice grated over him, prickling his skin, heightening his anticipation.

"Stop following me. You know your way home from here."

He eased past another veil of low branches. The sight of her kneeling in a patch of sunlight to pet his dog slammed his heart against his chest.

"I took off the muzzle so you could *go home,* not chase

after me," she said, her voice strained with frustration. *And affection,* he thought, watching her set her rifle aside to embrace his dog. He recognized the well-worn Smith & Wesson, the gun she'd held to Strafford's chest. Something else she'd hidden from him.

She sniffed as she sat back on her heels, a shudder in her breath suggesting he'd find her eyes wet with tears. The wide brim of a familiar tan hat hid her face and the loose black hair touching the base of her shoulders. Buckskin covered the rest of her. The dark fur coat any man in this area would recognize was tied to the outside of her large backpack.

Mad Mag.

She's not crazy, his mind shot back. *She's sneaky as hell and sharp as a tack.*

"Don't make me be mean," she said, pushing Boots away. "Just go on," she urged, pointing in his direction. *"Go home!"*

His dog turned and ran right to him. She looked up, her glistening blue eyes popping wide at the sight of him. She lunged up, but the weight of her pack dragged her back down and she fell to her knees.

Boots pounced up, his front paws landed against his thigh.

"Hey, boy," he greeted, petting his dog as he stared into the startled blue eyes looking back at him. She didn't so much as blink. Slowly she picked up her rifle and subtly shifted the shoulder straps of her large backpack as she stood. She took a step back, her delicate features tense, her posture defensive.

Didn't matter that he knew her name was Maggie or that she wore the garb of Mad Mag…all he could see was *Grace.*

A married woman, he had to remind himself.

"Afternoon," he offered.

"Garret." She lifted her chin a few notches, standing her ground. But she wanted to run. He could tell by her quick side-glance.

Lucky for him, her pack appeared to double her weight, keeping her grounded. Fear darkened her eyes. The fear of a woman caught in a lie.

I don't expect you to lie to your family.

And yet she couldn't be troubled to tell him the truth. She'd sent him off, knowing he'd look a fool in front of the two men who'd never see him as a grown man.

Not trusting his tongue, he turned his gaze on his dog.

"Looks like she took good care of you." He'd make sure Boots got some extra scraps from the table for giving him the chance to sneak up on their mistress.

A twig snapped, drawing his gaze back to *Grace.* "Leaving so soon?"

She stared at him as though waiting for him to explode, to demand answers he damn well deserved. But he was a patient man. He'd let her stew on her curiosity just as he'd stewed for more than two months.

"You look good, Grace."

Surprise showed in her eyes and he had to fight a grin.

"Are you back to being your silent self, or do you not have anything to say to me?"

"I didn't expect to see you."

She had an odd habit of stating the obvious and leaving the rest to his imagination. "I have your shotgun. My horse is just beyond the trees." He turned away, wondering if she'd follow him or run. She wouldn't get far.

"Come on, Boots."

Maggie watched him duck beneath the low braches and step out into the open sunlight. Uncertainty kept her rooted in place when she likely should have run. She'd seen anger in his eyes when he'd first looked at her.

He whistled and Maggie spotted the moving patches of brown and white, his horse walking along the other side of the trees and scrub. She couldn't just stand here in the brush like a frightened rabbit. Facing his anger couldn't be worse than the past weeks of heartache and worry.

As she stepped into the open he pulled her gun from a scabbard beside his saddle. His ivory shirt and the pale hair beneath his hat made him stand out like a beacon in the afternoon sun. He looked back and smiled at her, and Maggie's heart skipped a few beats. He strode toward her, all stealth and brawn, far more handsome than she remembered. His clean-shaven jaw was no less appealing than his short beard had been. She couldn't close her eyes during the past two months without seeing those rugged features. His voice haunted her dreams.

"Here you go," he said, handing her the long gun.

"Thank you." She lifted the straps from her shoulders and let her pack hit the ground at her heels. She shoved the gun into the sleeve sewn into the side, beside the brown fur coat she'd strapped to the outside. Garret watched her, the brim of his hat shading his eyes, his expression uncommonly vague.

He had to know.

"You sure took your sweet time in coming off that mountain. I was starting to think you'd decided to keep Boots for your own."

"I was tempted," she said, wondering where his anger had gone. "He's a good dog."

"The best, and a vital part of my crew. Boots does the work of two riders. A few more days and I'd have come for him."

"We've been slow moving and we took a longer route."

"I noticed. When did you start down?"

"Four days ago," she said, taking another step back, anxious to be on her way. "The south side has more coverage."

"Also made it real easy to avoid me," he said.

"Well…I tried," she said, figuring there was no point in lying to him.

"Why?"

The question was more of a demand.

The sound of an approaching horse stole her attention. She stepped back into the shadows of the shrubs behind her. Garret followed her gaze.

"It's Everett," he said as the horse and rider topped a nearby hillside. "One of my ranch hands."

Didn't make any difference to her who the man worked for—she didn't know him. She wasn't in the habit of allowing anyone to be near her. Plenty of men had tried to catch her, even before there was a bounty on her head.

"Everett's a good kid," Garret said, moving in beside her. "He's no threat to you."

She didn't look away from the rider closing in on them. His eyes widened when he spotted her near the trees. His gaze shifted between her, Garret and the dog standing between them as he reined in.

"I, uh…thought I heard Boots barking."

"You did. Everett Perish, this is Mrs. Danvers."

Her gaze whipped toward Garret. *Mrs. Danvers?* No one had ever addressed her by Ira's last name.

"Ain't you Mad Mag?"

"Everett."

The young man stiffened at the harsh tone of Garret's voice.

"Apologize to Mrs. Danvers."

"I apologize," Everett obediently replied. His twisted expression showed he wasn't rightly sure what he was apologizing for. "I didn't mean no offense."

"None taken," she said, though she didn't attempt a hospitable expression.

"I left your supper on the stove," he said to Garret.

"I appreciate it. If you've eaten go ahead and get started on the next section of roofing."

"Yes, sir." He briefly met her gaze as he tugged on the brim of his hat. "Ma'am." He turned his horse and made a fast retreat.

"That wasn't necessary," she said to Garret. "He didn't say anything that's not true."

"Your name isn't Mad Mag. It's *Mrs*. Maggie Danvers."

"As with most gossip, you're only half right."

"You're married," he said with bold accusation.

"I've never married. I was kept. Hell of a difference if you ask me." A difference he'd shown her in such a short time.

His expression softened. "Are you still?"

"Am I still what?"

"Are you still *kept?*"

Caution pricked at her skin. Only one person on this earth knew the truth about Ira. It appeared Chance Morgan had kept his word.

"Well, are you?" Garret demanded.

She couldn't lie to him. "Ira's dead."

"I'm sorry," he said, though his expression showed clear relief. "When did he die?"

"Seven years back."

His eyes flared. "You've lived alone up there for seven years?"

"Why does that surprise you?"

"Why wouldn't it? You had to be so young. How old are you?"

"Same age as you, I suppose."

A single blond eyebrow quirked up.

"Old enough."

His lips hinted at a smile. "I swear, if you ever gave me a direct answer I'd likely have heart failure."

"I'm twenty-seven. How old are you?"

"You can't be the one with all the secrets. How did Ira die?"

"Bear. Caught him by surprise. Ira was strong, but he wasn't a young man."

"You weren't much more than a child. How did you end up with him?"

"I was…in trouble. He helped me."

"Where's your family."

"Dead," she said, knowing her father had been the only person who'd ever truly cared about her, and the only one she considered family.

"You must have a last name."

"I don't." She gave up her last name when she'd been given away.

"I don't even know what to call you," he said, his hushed tone jabbing at her conscience.

"I didn't lie to you, not really. My name is Margaret Grace. Most call me Maggie. Or Mag. Mad Mag to some," she said with a shrug. "I suppose Maggie would do. Or Grace. Hell, I don't care."

"I think I'll call you Magpie."

"A *bird?*"

"It's a compliment," he assured her, the smile she'd come

to love making her weak in the knees. "Why don't you come on up to the bunkhouse and have dinner with me?"

Maggie stared at him in disbelief. She'd just admitted to being Mad Mag and he was inviting her to his ranch?

"You walked a long way to get here. You've got to be hungry."

She was, but not hungry enough to be lured up to his ranch.

"Thank you, but, no."

"Why not? The rest of my men won't be back on the ranch until nightfall. You already met Everett."

"I can't. I've got—"

"I'd appreciate the company. It's been too long since I had anything to look forward to."

"Dinner with me is hardly something to look forward to."

"Can't think of anything I'd enjoy more."

Sensation swirled low in her belly. "If you're looking to repeat what happened that last night, I'm not—"

"I'm inviting you to supper," he said, irritation darkening his eyes, "not my bed. You're headed to my sister's place, aren't you?"

She hesitated. She'd never thought of Morgan's ranch as his sister's place. "Yes."

"After we eat I'll lend you my horse."

"I can manage on my own."

"You'll manage better in a saddle. It's only an hour ride through the canyon passes on horseback."

"Wouldn't be right," she said, shaking her head.

"You kept my dog for over two months. I don't see how sharing my supper and borrowing a horse could be improper. Besides, we're friends."

"I don't have friends."

"Only 'cause you haven't met the right people."

Maggie nearly smiled. "You think you're the right people?"

"Yes, ma'am. I know I am."

His confidence and easy charm impossible to resist, a smile worked its way across her lips.

Not waiting for her reply, he lifted her backpack, shifting the heavy weight onto his shoulder. "What do you have stuffed in here?"

"A winter's worth of work."

"No wonder it took you four days to get down here. This pack must weigh more than you." He hoisted her supplies toward his saddle, draped the straps over the saddle horn and Maggie realized she was being railroaded.

"Garret, I haven't—"

"At least walk back to the ranch with me." He grabbed his horse by the reins and held his hand out to her.

Staring at his open palm brought back the memory of the last time she'd taken the hand of another.

You old enough, Margaret Grace?

She could still feel Ira's big, rough fingers closing over hers. She couldn't have guessed where taking his hand would lead her.

Run, Maggie.

She had, blindly following him into her new life. Some days, like today, it seemed she'd never stopped running. Wasn't anything she could do but trudge forward—it was too damn painful to look back.

"Maggie?"

She looked up at Garret's handsome face. His smile gentle, his green eyes seeming so disarming, she wondered where taking his hand would lead. The fact that he could still look at her with affection in his eyes truly amazed her.

"Why aren't you put off by me?"

"Why should I be?"

She could only glance down.

"A bit of buckskin doesn't hide the fact that you're pretty as a magpie. I've also seen you wearing nothing but a smile while I kissed every inch of soft skin hidden beneath those clothes."

Heat rushed to her face. "How improper of you to say so."

Garret chuckled. "Propriety has never carried much weight in the Daines family. Hard work and honesty, now those are qualities to live by."

She'd noticed that about him.

"I can also be a gentleman," he said, stepping close and capturing her hand in his. "If I try real hard."

Her skin tingled at the sudden contact, the jolt of sensation taking the air from her lungs, but she didn't pull away. As he led her toward his ranch in the distance she strived to suck in a deep, calming breath. Boots trotted along beside them.

That mangy mongrel had gotten her into this.

"I can't stay. I don't want your ranch hand getting any notions about us."

"Right. You being a woman who avoids scandal and all."

She pulled her hand from his. "*I do.* I'm not known for being social."

Garret wanted to snatch her hand right back but she tucked them away, folding her arms as she walked beside him. Her face hidden beneath the wide brim of her hat, he could only see the stubborn set of her jaw and loose, black hair. No more than he'd seen of her that day in town. Her heavy bearskin coat hadn't given any indication of the delicate woman beneath. She'd been guarded by enough stench and grime to keep him from looking any closer.

"Darlin', no one around these parts knows you at all."

"I intend to keep it that way."

Garret knew at least one man had been close enough to Maggie to know she wasn't what she seemed. "Chance mentioned he housed your mare over winter. That's a long spell to be without a horse."

"I don't mind walking. I miss the company, but Star also makes me more visible."

"I noticed her right off when I saw you in Bitterroot Springs. I was told Chance had sold Star to Ira. I'm curious as to how he'd do that when Ira's been dead for nine years."

"Morgan was being helpful."

"He knew about Ira?"

"He's the only one who knows for certain. He helped me bury him."

Old jealousy reared at the thought of Chance harboring her secrets, forging a relationship with another woman Garret had a mind to pursue. To be so close to her, Chance had to know the rumors of Mad Mag were unjust.

"He helped you bury your man and then abandoned you?"

Maggie looked up, her expression creased with confusion. "I wasn't his to abandon. It was bad enough he'd approached me without my notice. If I hadn't needed help with the grave, I likely would have shot him on sight. And he knew it. When we parted ways he was as glad to be rid of my presence as I was to be rid of his."

"Chance must think highly of you to sell you his favorite horse."

"I doubt that. More likely he was feeling guilty after

running off his bride. I guess she had second thoughts about marrying him. She took a mind to trek over the mountain and Chance was grateful to get her back unharmed."

Garret remembered that day quite well and didn't care to reflect on his foolishness. He hadn't known about Maggie's involvement. The notion that anyone could be so close to her and not be struck by such delicate beauty and a vibrant spirit was a sheer wonder to him.

"A few weeks later I found Star in my yard with a note that said he'd house her over winter if needed. I was leery to accept the offer and he likely thinks me rude and un-grateful. I don't really care what he thinks so long as he keeps his word and his distance."

Seemed to Garret that Chance could have been a tad more elaborate about his involvement with Maggie. A mention of Ira's passing would have eased his torment of the past two months, and his maddening urge to drag her from those mountains and demand some explanation. He supposed Chance's silence was his meager way of protecting her.

"Did you know they put a warrant out for your arrest after your scuffle in Bitterroot?"

"Yeah. I saw the posters last fall."

"Men like Strafford tend to bully those they don't believe will shove back. Guess he learned his lesson."

"Men like him never learn," she said, her voice rough with anger. She looked up, her gaze accusing. "His death would have been a favor to gentle society. Why did you stop me?"

It was still hard for him believe it had been Grace standing beside him that day—or rather, *Maggie*. He recalled her hands shaking on the rifle as she held the barrel to Strafford's chest. She'd knocked him out cold. If she had pulled that trigger she'd have been charged with murder.

"Because that mob would have caught you and you'd have hanged."

"You didn't know me. Why should you care if I hanged?"

"I knew enough. You were alone and you weren't seeking trouble."

"I might have turned my gun on *you*."

"That thought did cross my mind. As you said, you're not known for being social. I was more worried about an innocent woman coming to harm because of an arrogant jackass like Strafford."

Her slow smile surprised him, and brightened her blue eyes. "You're not like most people."

"Sure I am."

She shook her head. "No one else would have stepped a foot into that alley. There must have been more than thirty men on that boardwalk, all of them watching as he came after me. Yet I'm the one being hunted for a crime, forced to find trade farther north."

He hadn't thought about the warrant preventing her from bartering her needlework.

Maggie slowed to a stop at the edge of the tall grass, her gaze pensive as she looked across the front yard. Everett hammered shingles on the far side of the barn, his hat barely visible beyond the highest point.

"No one else is on the ranch."

"I can't stay, Garret." She glanced past him as though gauging the distance to the river. "Give me my pack and I'll—"

"You're taking my horse," he said, his arm moving around her shoulders, tucking her against his side as he continued past a large chicken coop beside the barn and on toward the bunkhouse.

Trapped beneath the weight of Garret's arm, Maggie's heart pounded erratically. As they moved closer, the massive house at the center of his ranch seemed to rise up, stretching taller than the mountains, looming over her like a castle with its tall peaks, glass windows and imported walls—not so unlike her childhood home. The comparison brought the threat of memories she didn't want to contemplate. Dread pooled in her belly and her steps began to drag. A short distance beyond the house a lone cross marked a grave site. New grass grew from recently worked dirt. She glanced up at Garret and found him watching her.

"Duce didn't make it off the mountain," he said, a hardness coming into his eyes.

"Your friend with the red hair?" she asked, recalling the man who'd been with him the night he'd helped her.

"Yeah," he said, grief clear in his expression. "He was killed by whoever attacked me."

"I'm sorry."

His arm tightened around her shoulders, the strength of his embrace increasing the stir of awareness swirling inside her. "I'd have ended up in a grave right beside him if you hadn't hauled me from the snow."

Awareness sweltered into burning need—the need to hold him, to feel his arms around her. So tempted to wrap her arm around his waist, to return the reassurances he offered, she looked away, her gaze moving over the quiet ranch. Beyond the buildings and expanse of fencing another ten miles of green hills led to the mountains marking the western horizon. The only place she truly felt safe.

"Did you find out who attacked you?" she asked.

"Not yet," he said, stopping beside the bunkhouse. "But I will."

Maggie stepped away from the weight of his arm.

"You can take the trail just beyond those corrals," he said, motioning beyond the bunkhouse as he turned to the backpack hanging from his saddle. "Takes you through a pass that leads right to my sister's place."

"I can get to the Morgan ranch without using a marked trail."

Expecting him to hand her the pack, he shocked her by walking off with both her canteens. He shuffled up the steps to the longhouse.

"What are you—?"

"I'll just fill your canteens. Come on in."

He disappeared inside, leaving the door open behind him. Boots followed him, leaving her alone in the yard.

Damn it! She glanced across the quiet grounds and tried to tamp down the sudden flare of panic. He'd led her into the open and now he just left?

Birds chirped in the tall trees spaced around the yard.

Not enough trees.

As she waited the chirping and chatter seemed to grow louder, as did the beat of her pulse. Didn't matter that the only man on the ranch was the one watching her from the barn roof. She didn't like being here. Beyond the perimeter of Garret's ranch the only shelter was the tall grass stretching over miles of hills, the river a quarter mile to the south.

Her gaze stopped on the lone grave beyond the house— a reminder of how ruthless men could be, killing for no other reason than greed.

Just like Nathan.

Chilled by the thought, she rubbed her hands over her arms. Garret was fortunate that his land didn't border any of Nathan's ranges. Not that Nathan was the only threat in the area. Rustlers and marauders had been plaguing these rangelands long before her brother had arrived.

She glanced again at the open doorway. She supposed she should count herself lucky that he hadn't gone into his fancy house.

Biting out a curse, she started for the steps.

Chapter Ten

Garret sensed her hovering in the doorway behind him. He'd blatantly used her gear like a trail of breadcrumbs to lure her into the bunkhouse. Twisting the cap onto the second canteen, he glanced at the meal Everett had prepared, ready to bribe her any way he could.

I'm not trying to catch her. He just wasn't ready to let her flutter off just yet. He wanted to know more about the woman who'd saved his life and kept her own hidden.

The fact that she wasn't married was a damn good start.

He slid the strap over his shoulder and picked up the plate. He turned to find Maggie a few steps inside, her distress apparent, her complexion white as a bed linen.

"Maggie?"

"Smells in here," she said, touching a hand to her stomach.

"It's the bacon grease." His gaze locked on her flat belly. "Do you not like bacon?"

"I used to. Been a long time since I've had any." She swallowed as though combating a bout of nausea. His sister had birthed enough babies over the past eight years for him to know an upset stomach could be an early sign of breeding. They'd only been together the one night. In the eight months his wife had shared his bed she hadn't gotten pregnant.

"It also smells of tobacco," she said, fanning the stagnant air.

"Smells like a bunkhouse." He stopped a few feet away from her and slid his plate onto a table. "Can't be worse than the bundle of fur hanging from my saddle."

Her lips shifted slightly. "It's not far off," she conceded, glancing briefly at his supper.

"Maybe you just need to eat something." He grabbed a fold of bread and strode toward her. "It's past noon."

She shook her head. "I'm okay. I need to get going."

"You look half-starved and ready to pass out."

"I've been eating plenty," she protested. "I've put on weight."

"Have you? Hard to tell beneath all that loose buckskin." Her belt and blade defined her narrow waist, the rest of her alluring curves masked by the gathered folds of the large tunic. Knowing she wasn't wed gave him the freedom to explore sensual memories he'd been trying to repress for weeks. Desire flared as he embraced the image of her flushed skin, her impassioned responses to his touch, his kisses.

Despite her harsh glare, her cheeks brightened to a soft pink.

Mad Mag blushing beneath his appreciative gaze. Just as all the rumors hinted, she was wild and resilient. He also knew what hid beneath all that buckskin and attitude—a gentle heart and a fierce lover.

Grinning, he held up his sandwich. "Want a bite?"

"I want my canteens."

He lifted the straps and draped them over her shoulder. "There you go."

"Thanks." she said, taking a step back. She turned, making a dash for the door.

"Magpie?"

The endearment stopped her. He waited for her to look back.

Maggie was slow to meet Garret's gaze, the emotion she saw there binding her as tightly as any rope.

"Are you pregnant?"

The question hit her like a blow. *"No."*

"You'd tell me if you were, wouldn't you?"

The distrust in his gaze stung. "I haven't lied to you, Garret."

"You weren't wholly honest with me, either. I've spent the past two months believing I'd slept with a married woman."

"And I told you I've never been married to anyone."

Anger firmed his features. "That old trapper took advantage of you."

"Ira *saved* me."

"He also hurt you." It wasn't a question.

Maggie couldn't deny that life with Ira had tested her endurance. "He didn't coddle or dote. He expected me to learn the trade and to fend for myself. And I was grateful for the schooling. I couldn't have enjoyed these last years alone if he hadn't taught me how to survive out here."

"Hard lessons for a young girl." His gaze moved over her, pausing on her hands and all the hidden places where he knew scars lay beneath. The compassion in his eyes pricked at her temper.

"Stop looking at me like that! Ira wasn't gentle, but he wasn't a cruel man."

"He must have done *something* to keep you tucked away in those mountains all these years, to have you flinching at my every move. How long did you live with him?"

"Five winters, but it's not how you think. I wasn't afraid of Ira, not once I understood him."

"That he'd give you protection if you shared his bed."

"No!" she said, startled by his misunderstanding. "He never touched me. Not once! He told people we were married so they'd leave me alone."

"So, you and he didn't—"

"Never. I told you I'd never been kissed. Not until *you*."

"Kissed. I assumed you'd been bedded."

She shook her head. Garret's blatant shock increased the heat burning into her cheeks.

"You were *untouched?*"

"It's not like I'm a young girl, Garret."

"An innocent woman all the same," he protested. "Why? Why did you let me?"

"I didn't plan it! You started kissing me and I…I liked it. I liked *you*."

Garret moved toward her. Relieved as he was to know she hadn't been abused by Ira, he suddenly worried he may have hurt her—a worry banished by the memory of her body arched beneath his, her warm blue eyes revealing the undeniable pleasure shared between them in the hours they'd spent making love. She'd been a more-than-willing participant, her passion exceeding anything he'd ever experienced. He assumed he'd been the first to give her real pleasure, but never imagined he'd been her first, the only man to love her.

He couldn't fight his grin.

"I have to go," she said, taking a sliding step back. "Thanks for the water."

"I'll walk you out," he said, heading her off in the doorway.

"No need." She tried to slip past him.

"A gentleman always walks a lady out."

Wedged beside him in the doorway, she stiffened. Her chin jetted up as she glared at him. "I'm not a lady."

"*Yes, you are.* You're as much a lady as any I've ever known."

"You'd be the first to think so."

Garret smiled, damn pleased by that discovery. "I like being first."

Her expression softened, and he didn't hesitate to seize the opportunity. He kissed her, a gentle brush of lips, followed by another. And another.

She leaned in, her lips parting beneath his. The first touch of her tongue and Garret dropped his supper to the floor and closed his arms around her. Maggie's fervent kiss filled him with something he needed more than food—passion...*hope.* Her tongue returned every touch, every stroke. He tightened his hold, lifting her against him.

She whimpered against his mouth and folded her arms around his neck, pulling him to her. Desire roared as she clung to him, kissing him with reckless abandon. Her touch, her taste, the demand of her tight embrace burned away the emptiness inside him, filling him with a deep sense of satisfaction.

Maggie pulled back, ending the kiss as quickly as it had escalated. She bumped against the door frame, gasping for breath.

"You shouldn't...have done that."

Garret would have laughed if she'd left any breath in his lungs. She hadn't hidden the fact that she'd wanted that kiss just as badly as he had.

Boots moved between them, nibbling up the last of the bacon Garret had tossed aside.

"Can't see why not," he admitted. "I think I've made it fairly clear that I fancy you."

Her eyes widened before she tugged her hat low, hiding her pretty, blushing face. "I'm leaving."

She dashed across the porch.

"I promised you my horse," he said, catching up with her.

"I don't need it."

"It's ten miles to my sister's ranch. Twice that if you follow the river."

"Which is why I need to get moving." She reached for the pack still hanging from his saddle.

Not about to let her walk, Garret plucked her backpack from her grasp.

Her expression fierce, she slammed her hands onto her hips, drawing his gaze to the long blade she wore there. The barrel of her rifle was visible just behind her shoulder and he knew too well she could be a lethal force when reckoned with. A man who didn't know the tender woman beneath her scowl would likely be quaking in his boots. Garret felt a kind of admiration for her that made his heart ache.

"Anyone ever tell you that you have a stubborn streak a mile wide?"

"No."

"Another first," he said, giving her a wink.

"Garret—"

"You're taking my horse, sweetheart. Feel free to stand there and fume while I tie down your gear and raise the stirrups."

"You don't understand. I'd really rather walk."

The distress in her voice made him look up from

securing the rancid bundle to the back of his saddle. "You can leave her with Chance."

"Which means I'd have to talk to him. Aside from bringing home an occasional frozen cowboy, I strive to avoid such situations."

"Am I part of a vast collection?"

"No! I can assure you I don't go around the mountain looking for cowboys to take home."

"Good to know," he said, smiling at her expression of sheer agitation. Even with her temper flared, he'd never been more attracted to a woman. Every moment in her company reaffirmed a notion he'd been trying to deny for two months.

He was crazy about her. And just like Amanda, she took to his ranch the way a cat takes to water. Unlike his ex-wife, Maggie appreciated the land—it was the people she feared.

"About time you started to recognize friend from foe. There's not a man on the Morgan Ranch who'd be a threat to you, least of all Chance." He recalled Chance's mention of her moving into the northern ranges. "Did you move because of Chance and Cora Mae?"

She gave a slight nod.

"You had to know the Morgans weren't a threat to you."

"Anyone knowing where I live is a threat. Word spreads and these hills aren't what they used to be. When we worked the rivers we'd travel for weeks on end without seeing another soul. Ira told me these hills would fill with settlers once they ran off the Indians, that I should go north. I didn't want to believe him. But he was right, *like always.*"

Ira may not have abused her, but the man's reclusive nature had definitely fueled her fear of people.

"Maggie, there's no reason you couldn't settle somewhere around here."

She averted her gaze, the pain he saw there ripping at his heart. "My trouble in Bitterroot suggests otherwise."

"You don't want to go. You love these hills and ranges as much as I do."

She drew a ragged breath, her features firming. "I want to be left alone."

"You won't have to see Chance," he said as he finished the second stirrup. "Leave her in any pasture. They'll recognize her and get her back to me."

She didn't look any more convinced as he stepped back so she could mount up.

"All ready for you, darlin'."

"And you think *I'm* stubborn?"

He only smiled.

She crouched down and Boots rushed into her open arms. "See ya, Boots."

"He's liable to start missing you. You're welcome to come by and visit him anytime. You're always welcome here, Maggie."

Her gaze moved over his ranch as she straightened, and came to rest on Duce's grave site. "I've never understood why folks take the risk. Living in the open."

"Honey, most would say you're the one taking the risk by living up in that wild country alone."

"Up there I know the harmless critters from the ones that would kill me. Down here, you can't tell."

"No matter where you go, you won't find a place that doesn't have danger lurking somewhere. It wasn't a man that killed Ira."

"I know that better than you!"

"You think he would have lived differently to avoid that bear?"

"No. If you knew Ira, you'd know he didn't belong out of those mountains. Folks were likely grateful he chose to stay in them."

"I feel the same way about these hills. When you love where you live, what you do, the people in your life…it's worth the risk. Something worth fighting for."

"To you, maybe. Ira didn't believe in any such thing. He thought a man standing still was nothing but a target. He didn't understand my need for a cabin, to stay in one place. The two years we wintered apart he seemed surprised to find me well when he came back."

"You stayed anyway? Alone?"

"I don't mind solitude. Winters aren't too bad so long as you prepare. The rest of the year I'm surrounded by all I need. But not anymore. It's not safe."

Garret hated seeing the fear that drove her to push him away. "Is that really what *you* think? Or is that Ira's influence?"

Maggie didn't know anymore. Standing here with him was making her head spin and her heart ache. "I gotta go," she said.

He took a step back and waved a hand toward the mountains. "Then, go."

She mounted his horse and noticed he'd tucked her old shotgun into the side scabbard. "Thanks," she said, refusing to look at him as she tugged on the reins, guiding his spotted mare toward the western rise of mountains.

Garret watched her go, wondering what he could have said differently to ease her fear.

"See you around," he called after her.

"I doubt it. You ranchers are mostly blind."

She glanced back, her bowed lips all he could see beneath that wide brim—which was enough to stir his pulse.

Once she rode past the house, the mare broke into a run. His dog charged after them as though he intended to go with her.

"Boots!"

He stopped at the edge of the yard, his two-toned eyes glancing back at him.

"Get over here."

He ran back to his side and barked at their departing magpie. As she descended over a rise his bark turned to a howl.

"I know the feeling, boy. I'd like to chase after her, too."

Nothing but misery came from holding a woman who didn't want to stay. And yet, he'd felt the yearning in her kiss, her reluctance to let go of him.

He'd have to convince her he was worth the risk.

Her horse wasn't where she should be.

Maggie sat at the mouth of the high canyon pass, her telescope moving over the green valley below. Star should be waiting for her in that northeast pasture, as she had been for the past six years.

The only horse within a mile was a saddled roan. A man worked on wire fencing a few yards away from his mount. She could just make out the tufts of golden hair beneath the brim of his dark hat.

Morgan.

Was he waiting for her? Had something happened to Star?

Apprehension nettled beneath her skin. Garret's mustang shifted beneath her, the spry mare ready to descend into the narrow valley.

"Easy," she soothed, tugging at the reins, scanning open hills and deep folds of countryside for other riders. She'd had all the surprise confrontations she could handle for one day. She didn't know what Garret had been trying to prove, kissing her the way he had.

For all her worry that he'd shun her once he knew the truth, she now wished he had. Every mile she'd put between them only increased the ache in her chest and hadn't done anything to dim the feel of his arms closed tightly around her, the scent of sawdust on his skin.

She needed to get her horse and move on.

Satisfied all was clear, she started down. By the time she reached the rise of grass marking a northern paddock, Morgan had long since spotted her and had been watching her approach as he worked on the fencing. Setting his equipment aside, he pulled off his heavy gloves and straightened.

"Hey, Mag," he greeted as she reined in a few yards away.

She dismounted on the opposite side of the fence. "Where's Star?"

"I wondered when you'd show up," he said, striding toward her as though he hadn't heard her question. "You're later than usual."

"Only by a week or two. Where's my horse?"

"I figured Star could use a few extra days to fatten up on oats in the barn. I wanted to thank you for helping Garret like you did."

"By withholding my horse?" she demanded.

"I'll get you your horse," he assured her. "We had quite a scare when he didn't come off that mountain. We're all indebted to you, Maggie."

"Is that so? Then how about you stop wasting my time and go fetch my mare?"

Morgan didn't rush off, as he should have. His stance wide, he shifted his hat over his golden-blond hair, his green eyes raking over her with nerve-racking interest.

"You're looking unusually fresh this afternoon, for being so far from home."

She tensed, annoyed by his bold observation. Wasn't any business of his if she chose to keep the grime off her.

"That's Garret's mare. You must have returned Boots."

Maggie didn't answer. Conversation had never been part of their bargain.

"And here I thought the kid might have improved your social skills."

"What *kid?*" she said, rattled by a second mention of children and the thought of Garret revealing all that happened in her cabin.

"Garret."

"He's hardly a kid. Last I checked Garret was a full-grown cattle rancher with man-size troubles."

"That he is," Chance agreed with a nod. "The rest of us were wondering how such an experienced rancher could end up knocked out in the snow and his partner left dead."

"I don't know. Garret had been unconscious for nearly a day when I found him."

Morgan's eyes widened with surprise. "He didn't tell us that."

"He couldn't remember the attack when he woke. I never saw his partner."

"Strange that he hasn't had any trouble since. Why wouldn't they have gone after his cattle while he was subdued on the mountain?"

Did he expect her to have answers? "You'd have to ask Garret."

"He didn't say anything to you about—"

"Morgan, I make it a point to not get involved in other people's business. If you have questions for Garret, you know where to find him. Now are you going to fetch my horse or not?"

"Sure, Mag." He started toward his mount grazing a few yards off. He reached for his saddle, then paused. "You're welcome to come with me. Skylar has been anxious to thank the woman who saved her brother."

Go with him? To his *house?*

What had Garret told them to have Morgan behaving so cordial toward her? Whatever he'd said, he'd obviously ruined her reputation.

"Just because I didn't let a man freeze to death doesn't mean I'm willing to cozy up and break bread on every damn ranch I come across! If our bargain is done, you just say so! There isn't a place I can't get to by walking!"

Chance held up his hands. "No call to get riled. One saddled mare coming right up." He mounted his horse and started toward the cluster of buildings a few miles to the south.

"Be quick about it!" she shouted after him. "I ain't got all day to be sitting in these open hills like a duck on a pond!"

He reined in. "No one's going to bother you on my ranch."

"I bet Virgil Thompson thought the same thing. A rope still found its way around his thick neck last fall and left him dangling from one of his own trees."

Morgan touched a hand to the red bandana tied at his throat, likely recalling the noose she'd dug from his skin some years back after the old foreman of the Lazy J had taken a mind to hang him.

"I heard about that," he said. "Thompson and two of his men."

Maggie hadn't been near Thompson's homestead the night of his death, but she knew who'd been stealing his cattle. Ol' Thompson had likely made the same discovery.

"Just so you know, I won't be bringing Star back in the fall. These mountains are getting too crowded."

"Heard about your trouble in Bitterroot Springs."

"You and everyone else."

"Where will you go?"

"Wherever I please. Once you fetch my horse, that is."

One side of his mouth kicked up in a grin. "I'll be right back."

"You got fifteen minutes, Morgan."

"How the hell did Garret survive a week with you?"

"Carefully."

Morgan's deep laugh echoed back as he rode toward his ranch.

She hadn't been careful enough.

Her heart aching fit to burst, Maggie led Garret's mare to an outcrop of trees and settled in the shade. This morning she'd nearly convinced herself that she'd gotten over the loss.

She leaned back, sinking into the tall green blades. Above her a blue sky shined though the branches. Chirping black birds fluttered around in the canopy of leaves.

A bit of buckskin don't hide the fact that you're pretty as a magpie.

She shut her eyes—which only served to sharpen his image in her mind, the sound of his voice, the surge of thrilling warmth she felt at just being near him.

Once she got Star back, she wouldn't miss him so badly.

* * *

Garret laid down the last shingle in his row and reached around only to discover Everett had hauled the nails up to the next level. In the past couple of hours they'd worked in steady silence and had finally reached the last section. A few more rows and they'd be done.

"Toss down a tack. You snuck off with that bucket again."

"No sneakier than you." Everett's grin slid clear across his face.

"What are you smiling about?"

"Why didn't you tell us she was the trapper that helped you?"

"What difference does it make?"

His bony shoulders shifted. "I'd imagine a whole lot. I saw you."

"You saw me where?" he asked, tacking down the shingle.

"In the doorway." His wide grin returned. "With *Mrs. Danvers*."

Garret stood, confirming the straight shot view to the porch of the bunkhouse. "You breathe a word to anyone," he said, glaring at Everett, "and I will beat the living tar out of you."

"I won't say nothin'," he said, losing his smile. "Can't say I blame you for not wanting folks to know."

The boy's attempt at understanding snapped at Garret's temper.

"Don't go making assumptions, Everett. I won't have her talked about with disrespect on my ranch. You hear me?"

"Yes, sir," he said, and quickly turned back to his task.

Boots barked from down below. Garret glanced back to see his dog take off like a shot across the yard. Movement farther out caught his eye. Approaching riders fanned out over a distant hillside. Their faces obscured, Garret stood and looked closer.

Masked riders. Canvas draped beneath their brims with holes cut for the eyes. There was no doubt as to where they were headed. He counted eight riders as they descended the hillside, the outside riders banking hard to the north and south.

This can't be good.

"Garret?" Everett froze midswing, the hammer still in the air, his wide gaze on one of the masked men trying to sneak over the rise.

"We gotta move." He slipped the hammer through his belt loop and followed Everett to the ladder.

"They'll burn you out," Everett said, his voice trembling. He stepped back, his eyes wide with panic.

Garret grabbed the rifle propped against the barn and took Everett by the arm, hauling him toward his saddled horse. He wasn't about to chance the boy living through such a hell a second time.

"Ride to the Morgans. Tell the first man you see we've got trouble."

"But the others—"

"Are working too far out to do us any good. Those men have fanned out. No telling how many there are. Now git!"

Everett didn't argue. He swung into his saddle. "I can make it there in thirty minutes," he shouted as he set off toward the western rise.

An hour too long, Garret thought as he made his way back to the front yard. They hadn't topped the next rise. He couldn't see his dog in the tall grass but he could hear him.

"Boots! Heel!"

Black fur flashed through the dense green. Still barking,

Boots ran back. Reaching his side, his dog turned to stand guard, the hair down his neck standing on end. As was the hair on Garret's neck. Something about armed men hiding their faces behind flour sacks led him to believe they didn't have talking in mind. Garret had waited too long for answers and preferred an enemy he could see. He backed toward the chicken coop, taking cover.

"Got to be patient, old man. Let them come to us."

Five riders topped the last rise, which meant at least three others were sneaking around to surround the ranch.

Boots's bark became a low growl as the masked men made a steady approach. He fought the urge to start shooting, picking off as many as he could. He'd only draw return fire from more directions that he could cover. These men didn't ride for any struggling rancher and with cattle barons controlling the law, a bloodbath on his land could still earn him a noose. His best chance was to stall them as best he could.

The moment they cleared the grass at the edge of his yard he murmured, *"Git'em,* Boots."

His dog bolted into action, darting for the riders, his bark at full blast as he made tight circles between the horses, nipping at their legs and haunches. The animals reared, stamping as Boots rushed them back. Two dumped their riders. Shouts filled the air, the men tried to control their mounts and dodge hooves.

"Call him off, Daines!" one shouted, struggling to control his mount.

Not a voice he recognized.

Another rider raised his rifle, taking aim at Boots. Garret sighted the man's hand and fired. The bastard's shout and fall from his saddle was hardly noticed by the others in all the chaos. One masked man dropped to his belly. Two others ran after the horses Boots chased farther into the tall grasses.

Spotting movement beyond the barn, Garret dropped back and pressed tight against the barn door as he turned his focus to the figure crouched on the far side of the hog pen. Scouting the open ground around the house and bunks for any others, he edged his way to the north side.

The intruder straightened to find Garret standing over him. His eyes flared wide behind the ivory cloth just before Garret cracked the butt of his rifle against his skull. The man dropped like a sack of oats.

Paybacks are hell.

"Hold it right there, Daines."

Not likely. He turned and barely dodged a fist. He swung, his knuckles slamming into the canvas-covered face with a satisfying crack.

Spotting a second man coming up on the right, Garret pulled the hammer from his belt and sent it spinning while fighting off his companion. A cry of pain assured him he hit his target as a blow to the gut sent the man before him crumpling to the ground. A fist clipped his chin as the brawl shifted to another target.

Each time he knocked a man back, another sack-covered face appeared before him. Delivering two punches for everyone he received, Garret moved against the wave of men. Boots growled and barked from somewhere behind him. A man's scream was punctuated by a gunshot. His dog yelped.

Garret whipped around to see Boots lying on the ground, blood pooling beneath him. Something struck the back of his head, the ring of pain sending him to his knees. A dozen hands slammed him down, pinning him against the dirt. Garret looked up at Boots and was relieved by the slightest movement of fur.

"That dog was a goddamn nuisance!" shouted one of his captors.

Garret twisted against the weight bearing down on him. "He knows that scarecrows belong in cornfields. What's your business here?"

A hand slammed his face into the dirt. "I owe this one a bullet!"

"Not yet," argued another.

"Should we stand him up?"

"Hell no!" another man shouted. "Hold 'im down!"

The pressure on his back increased, the heel of a boot digging into to his spine. Garret fought the hold on his hair and looked up at the man striding toward him. His gaze focused on a small circular brand burned into the lower flair of the man's chaps—*Circle S*. It was a practice among loyal foremen to wear the brand of their employer—which gave Garret the answer he'd been seeking for nearly three months.

The man stopped a few feet away and lifted his flour sack just high enough to reveal a dark mustache as he spit out a mouthful of blood and at least one tooth.

"Goddamn, he scraps like a bear!"

His weary crew closed in behind him, all of them nursing wounds and bleeding beneath their flour sacks.

"Where's the second man?" he asked, pulling his flour sack back into place.

"Found fresh horse tracks leading toward the cliffs. No one's here but Daines."

"Yer man deserted you." The masked foreman with a deep Southern drawl took another step toward him. "Might as well cool yer fire. We got ya beat. If I were you, I wouldn't bank on makin' it to the stockyards next month."

"Then you must intend to bury me." Nothing less would keep him from driving his stock.

"You should have stayed on the mountain with yer haggard lady friend."

Rage rolling through him at the man's admission. *"You killed Duce."*

"Things might have gone differ'ntly if he chose to be helpful. Seems we wasted our time with the wrong man. Now where can we find Mad Mag?"

They're after Maggie? His gaze moved over the eight masked men waiting for his answer. "All of you are after one little mountain woman?" Rather drastic measures to collect a five-hundred-dollar bounty, especially to be dispersed among a large band of men. Strafford had to be behind this.

"Told you he knew her," said a man holding him down.

Garret wrenched against the pressure on his back and the hold on his arms. "You won't find a man in these hills who doesn't know of her. Why in hell would that mountain woman be here?"

The Circle S foreman crouched down, his unfamiliar blue eyes snapping with anger. "No need fer you to die today. We know she was here. She was spotted comin' off the mountain and we tracked her here. She had yer dog, Daines."

"I thought I lost him on the mountain until he showed up today. Figured he just decided to come home."

"She helpin' you steal cattle? You do know the penalty for rustlin'?"

"You know damn well I haven't stolen any cattle."

"Someone has been," he said, a smile coming into his

eyes. "Who's to say she's not leadin' 'em straight to you? You bes' hope the missing stock ain't wearin' a Lazy J brand when they turn up."

Garret didn't take that threat lightly. Men had been wrongfully hanged due to such malicious tactics.

"Mad Mag has made herself a real nuisance, releasin' stock and vandalizin' ranches. You have a hand in that, too, or you just got a hankerin' for haggard old women?"

"Strafford's ego must be awful damn fragile. Folks of Bitterroot might like to know their new mayor has hired a bunch of masked raiders to handle his dirty work."

The man's boot slammed against his jaw, knocking dirt into his eyes as pain exploded through his face.

"Pull him up."

The moment his boots touched the ground a fist pounded into his abdomen, the blow knocking the breath from his lungs.

"The only tellin' you'll be doin' is where we can find Mad Mag."

Thank God she'd taken his horse. Hopefully she'd stay on the west side of those mountains. "Go to hell," he wheezed.

"Take him into the barn." He glanced around the yard before turning to the men standing behind him. "We're gonna need some rope."

Chapter Eleven

They came up out of nowhere, horses splashing through a shallow stretch of river.

Maggie moved back, quickly guiding Star into the shelter of late-afternoon shade amid the dense trees and scrub. She clamped over her mare's muzzle to keep her quiet as the riders rumbled past.

Outlaws. Wasn't any other reason to risk a horse riding through a rocky riverbed.

"We should have killed him," one called over the clatter of hooves and splashing water.

"Ain't sure we didn't," another shouted. The splash of water distorted their conversation as they rumbled past.

"Shot his dog."

The words carried back on the river.

Maggie shifted, trying to get a look at the horses, a glimpse of a face, but couldn't make out much beyond a bit of horsehide before they rode out of view.

She waited until all she heard were the sounds of the river then stepped from the foliage and led Star back to the river's edge. Someone had received an unpleasant visit.

The comment about the dog played in her mind, stirring a deeper unease.

Most ranches had dogs. Garret's ranch was the closest.

Her gaze was drawn toward the bright sky to the west. She'd followed the river beyond his ranch over a half hour ago, and without so much as a side-glance to see if he stood on the roof. She now wished she'd taken the time to scout out his presence.

Must have been more than a half a dozen riders splashing through the river. At noon Garret had only one worker on his ranch. Not a good time for an ambush.

Biting out a curse, she shifted into her saddle. She wouldn't be able to bed down unless she at least scouted from a distance.

Just a quick look. Once she saw him or Boots she could leave without notice.

Thirty minutes later she stood beyond the line of trees. The low sun lit up the empty rooftops of his ranch. She rode over the next small rise and pulled out her telescope. No lamps glowed from inside either dwelling. So far as she could see no one stirred. She steadied the scope on the barn roof for a few minutes but didn't detect any movement on the far side. She sat back in her saddle, apprehension turning her belly to fire.

Two men and a dog should be somewhere in sight. The house and the bunks would be dark and needing lamplight this late in the day. His herds were too far out to be riding out at this hour.

Something's not right.

She kicked her heels against Star. Approaching the yard, she pulled her rifle from the scabbard. Star's slow, plodding steps echoed across the quiet grounds as she rode close to the bunks, nearing Garret's house. A dark spot shifted beyond the porch.

Maggie reined in and raised her rifle. Boots limped out from beyond the front steps, his black fur matted with dried blood.

Maggie slung her gun over her shoulder and grabbed a canteen. She dismounted and pulled a towel from her saddlebag. Boots whined beside her.

Where's Garret?

Constantly watching the area around her, she knelt beside Boots and poured some water over the matting of blood and dirt. Fresh blood welled from a hole in his shoulder. Boots whined as she prodded the wound. "Easy, boy," she whispered. The bullet had passed through. Quickly securing the towel beneath his front leg and around his shoulder, she scooped him up. She hurried up the steps to the porch and set Boots on a bench beside Garret's front door. She turned to look back across the quiet shadows and various buildings beyond the yard.

"Garret!"

Something rattled in the direction of the barn.

"Stay," she said to Boots, and moved as swiftly and silently as she could across the yard. Her rifle in her hands, she pushed against one of the double doors. The heavy wood creaked. She inched through the small gap into the musty shadows. Near the center of the barn, Garret's pale hair stood out in the dim light. Coils of rope bound his arms across the top of the gate where his arms stretched wide, his legs folded beneath him.

"Garret?" she said, her strained voice barely a whisper.

He lifted his head. The sight of his battered face knocked the breath from her lungs. His eyes were nearly swollen shut and blood was…*everywhere.*

He muttered a curse, chin lowering back to his chest.

"Garret." Tears burned her eyes as she knelt before him. His arms strapped tight beneath the rope and blood covering his shirt, she didn't know where to touch him. "Who did this?"

"Covered faces," he said in a ragged breath. "They shot Boots."

"I found him. He's okay." She reached blindly for her blade. "I'll cut you down."

"Left arm first. My shoulder, I think it's broke."

She cut away the spiral of rope along his arm. The bone at his shoulder appeared to be poking up beneath his shirt. His arm rolled from the top of the gate as the rope fell away. He grunted as she eased the limp limb against his side.

Using her body to hold him up, she pressed firmly against him as she cut the rope holding his right arm. His swollen lips pressed against her neck.

"You smell like heaven," he breathed against her skin.

"You look like hell," she said, hoping his frisky move meant he wasn't hurting as badly as he appeared.

His other arm fell forward and his weight knocked her back. She landed on her butt, her arms banded around his chest. It took all her strength to ease him to the side before she fell on top of him. He groaned and hooked his right arm around her, holding her against him.

"We gotta stop meetin' like this, Magpie," he said in a weak voice. "You lookin' pretty as springtime. Me on death's door."

She eased back. Fresh tears hazed her vision at the full sight of him. She'd never seen such a battered face. The bones in his left shoulder pitched up, creating a rise beneath his shirt.

"You are *not* on death's door."

"Am, too," he insisted. "Better strip me nekkid and have your way with me. Do it quick."

"Garret!"

His swollen lips shifted in what could have been a grin. "Worked last time."

"They've knocked you senseless."

He shifted, attempting to sit up but only managed a deep moan before settling back on the dirt and straw. "Just lay here with me," he said in a pant. "I'll get up in a minute. You sure Boots is all right?"

"Yes. And you shouldn't try to move. Your shoulder is broken. God only knows what the rest of you looks like."

"Shh," he whispered. "I'm trying to impress my girl."

He'd suffered far too many blows to the head. "I'm not your girl."

He peered up at her through the swollen slit of one eye. "You will be."

She tensed, the confidence behind those three words sending a combination of fear and longing shooting through her.

A rumble from outside caught her attention. She eased up to listen. "Horses approaching from the south." She looked back at Garret. "Your ranch hands?"

"Too early."

Maggie grabbed her rifle and stood. "Don't move," she whispered.

"Mag—"

"Shh!" She hurried into the stall and lifted the latch on the window. Using the barrel of her rifle, she eased open the wood shutter.

A band of riders swarmed in from the south pasture,

guns drawn. Chance Morgan and his brother rode at the center. Relief shook her as they thundered into the yard.

Thank God.

"Garret!" shouted one of the Morgans. His brother's bellowing voice followed like an echo.

"He's in here!"

Garret groaned and made an attempt to rise.

"Don't move," she ordered, rushing back to him. "It's the Morgans."

"I'm all right," he insisted.

She dropped back to her knees and placed a hand on his chest. "Please don't move, Garret."

He muttered a swear word, and his body relaxed beneath her palms.

Both barn doors swung wide. The Morgan brothers stepped inside.

"He's in a bad way," she said, not caring which was Chance.

"Maggie?"

Chance Morgan followed his brother into the dim light of the barn and could hardly believe the scene before him. A teary-eyed Mag kneeling over Garret—at least he thought it was Garret beneath all the blood and bruises.

Her gaze moved past him and all emotion drained from her face, her narrowed eyes seeming to glaze with frost. She straightened. Her hand closed over the hilt of her knife.

Suddenly aware of the murmuring voices, he turned to the men filing into the doorway behind him. "The rest of you cover the grounds, search the buildings and alert Garret's crew. Find out which way the raiders went."

"East along the south river," Maggie said as Tucker crouched beside Garret. "They have an hour lead."

His foreman gave a nod and stepped out.

Chance joined his brother and knelt across from Maggie. "Holy hell, kid. You took a wallop." If his gut was half as bruised as his face, he was in some serious pain.

"Anything broke?" asked Tucker.

"Oh, yeah," Garret said in a shallow breath.

"His left shoulder doesn't look right," Maggie said, sniffing back tears, forcing Chance to give her a second glance. Mag had never struck him as a woman prone to cry in any situation.

"Let's check out that shoulder." Before he could touch Garret, Maggie's hands moved over the row of buttons and brushed open Garret's shirt with shocking familiarity.

The kid's one-eyed glare told Chance voicing that shock would cost him strips off his hide.

She pressed back the edge of the shirt and Garret sucked in a hard breath.

"I'll cut the sleeve," she said, drawing her blade.

"Try not to draw more blood," Garret said, his voice weak.

"I ought to just skin you," she scolded, her blade parting the fabric over his shoulder. "For making me fret so."

"Thank you, Maggie," Chance said, and tried to ease in.

She continued to hover over Garret, her hostile expression and the long blade in her hand making him more than a little tense. He spared a glance at his brother. Tucker watched the mountain woman with equal caution.

"We'll need some room," Chance told her.

She sat back and Tucker closed his hands over the rise in Garret's shoulder. Garret groaned through clenched teeth. Maggie eased closer, watching intently as his brother felt the wound.

"Good news is it's not broke," said Tucker.

"Dislocated," Chance said. "Looks like Mitch's shoulder did after that bronc tossed him last year."

"Bad news is, it's gotta go back."

Chance's gut burned with the knowledge of what had to be done. Mitch had screamed through the process and promptly passed out the second his shoulder popped into place. "A cinch strap?"

"That should do it. Sit him up."

"This is going to hurt," Chance warned.

"Ain't much…that don't," said Garret.

A shout ripped from his lungs as Chance and Tucker curled him forward.

"How are your knees?" asked Tucker.

"Better than the rest of me." Sweat beaded on his bruised brow, his eye glazing with pain as they shifted him up.

Tucker leaned back to check his shoulder blade.

Garret fisted the front of Chance's shirt with his good arm and dragged him to eye level. *"Take Maggie out,"* he whispered through gritted teeth.

Chance held his demanding gaze for a long moment, then looked up at Maggie standing a few feet away, her lower lip clenched beneath her teeth.

"Hey, Mag? Why don't you go on out and wait for us?"

"If I can help—"

"We've done this before. It's not pleasant." Chance nodded toward the open doors.

Her worried gaze moved between him and Garret before she took a step toward the open doorway. "All right. I'll be right outside."

The moment her footsteps left the barn, the pain Garret had been trying to hold back etched across his features.

"Someone's sweet on Mad Mag," Chance murmured, a grin stretching his lips.

"I think I've…got her wooed," Garret said in a pant.

Chance's and Tucker's laughter drowned out Garret's groans as they moved him into position, curving a leather strap over his shoulder.

"You've got gumption, kid," Chance said. His feet braced, his hold tight, he looked up at Tucker. "Ready?"

"God, no," Garret groaned.

Tucker gave a nod.

"Sorry about this," Chance murmured, just before Garret's scream shook the rafters, echoed by the pop of his shoulder snapping back into place.

So far as Chance could tell, no air rushed back into Garret's lungs.

"Breathe," he said, easing him down to the ground.

Hurting clear to the roots of his teeth, Garret wasn't sure death wouldn't have been the best option. He sucked in air as the blinding pain subsided, leaving a nauseated ache pulsing through his body. If the barn would stop spinning, he might be able to save himself from total humiliation.

"Come on, Garret," Chance prodded. "Say something."

"Hurts…too much."

"Who did this?"

He blinked his good eye, trying to clear his blurred vision. "Covered their faces. They ride for Circle S."

"Who's Circle S?"

A wave of nausea forced his eye shut. *Good God.* He hurt.

"Strafford, isn't it? He was at our last two colt sales."

"Oh, yeah." The sharp kick in his tone identified Tucker. "The tall feller in the shiny suits. Isn't that the one Mag knocked out last spring?"

"Yeah," Garret said, wishing they wouldn't talk so loud. Maggie was sure to be back at any moment. "They were looking for Maggie." The thought of them coming back tempted him to ask Chance to take her to the Morgan Ranch, out of harm's way. He had no right to ask any such thing. "Wanted to know where she lived."

"Does Mag know this?" asked Chance.

"No. Don't want her to know. Not yet." He didn't know how she'd react to the news that he'd been attacked on her account. Maggie could be as fierce as she was tender, and at the present moment he was in no shape to look after her if she took a mind to retaliate.

"I suppose we ought to stand him up," said Tucker.

Garret moaned at the thought.

"Your ribs don't look much better than your face," said Chance. "You got bruise upon bruise."

Garret didn't have to see the purple flesh to feel the ache.

"How do you feel otherwise?"

A sweat broke out over his body at the mere thought of standing. It hurt to breathe. Hurt even more to talk. His pride ached worst of all—his girl having to be the one to cut him down and Chance and Tucker coming to his aid.

"If it weren't for visions of magpies, I'd just have you shoot me."

"Magpies, huh?"

"Up you go," said Tucker, sliding his arm under his injured shoulder. Chance lifted on his right side. Pain lanced his shoulder. Garret didn't even try to help them, allowing them to lift his limp weight. Once on his feet, he held his left arm steady against his aching middle.

Tucker grimaced at him. "Sure hope your lady friend

wasn't interested in you for your good looks. Your face is mighty colorful."

"She can't resist…my boyish charm."

"At least they didn't damage your sense of humor."

Peering through the narrow slit of one eye, he spotted Maggie standing just inside the door, her arms crossed stiffly over her chest, her cheeks flushed to a pretty pink.

"There's my girl." He stepped away from the Morgan support. His attempt at a smile was answered by a glare.

Stubborn.

Another step and the barn began to spin. "Chance…I'm gonna be sick."

An arm braced across his shoulders and he was turned away from Maggie's startled gaze.

"Grab a bucket," said Morgan.

"Out you go, Mag!" the other shouted, and Garret felt a true appreciation for their help.

"But—"

"Now!"

Maggie jumped at Chance's booming voice. Furious at her brash dismissal she turned and stomped back into the darkening yard where another fifteen or so brutish men waited. They hovered at a distance, not one of them daring to say a word to her.

Men and their stubborn pride! She didn't need to be shielded!

She went back to the porch to sit with Boots and found him on his feet and about to descend the steps.

"Boots, *stay!*"

The dog halted, his front paws on the first step. She hurried up to the wide porch and gently lifted him. He whimpered as she set him back onto the bench.

"You need to stay still and out of the dirt," she said, sitting beside him.

He laid his head on her lap and her affection for this dog and his owner rushed to the surface. She cared for them in a way she'd not cared for anything or anyone. After two months with Boots, he felt like her own. Garret had left an imprint on her heart after only a few days.

"Leave you two alone for half a day and all hell breaks loose." She checked both sides of the blood-stained towel she'd tied around his wounds. Thankfully the bullet had missed the bone.

The moment she saw movement by the barn she eased Boots aside.

"Stay."

"Ma'am?"

A tall cowboy stood at the base of the steps. A smile twitched beneath his wide brown mustache. "Name's Mitch. Boots and I been friends a long time. I'll sit with him."

"All right."

"Is he hurt bad?" he asked, coming up the steps.

"He was shot through the shoulder. There's no lead. It should heal."

"We keep a salve in the barn for cuts and such on the livestock. I'll be sure to use some on him."

"I'd appreciate it."

Boots sat up as though to follow her but Mitch took her spot and urged him back down. "Easy, boy," he soothed. "She's not goin' far. Takin' a bullet for Garret, you're gonna be the hero in the bunkhouse tonight."

Maggie's focus was on Garret slowly walking across the yard. Chance held his arm over his shoulders, which was likely all that kept Garret on his feet.

"How is he?"

"He didn't throw up any blood," said Chance. "About as good as we can hope for at this point."

"I'll hitch the wagon," Tucker suggested. "No way he'll tolerate the ride in a saddle."

"Not going," Garret said, his voice hoarse.

"We're taking you home. Skylar will have you whipped back into shape—"

"I *am* home."

"It's not safe," said Chance. "Those marauders could come back and torch the place. The shape you're in, you wouldn't even make it out of the house."

"If my place goes, I'll go with it."

"No piece of land is worth your life," said Tucker.

"Amen," agreed Chance.

"My crew will be in soon."

"A bunch of cowpokes won't want to play nursemaid."

Garret's bruised jaw clenched and Maggie surmised what the Morgans hadn't yet determined. Garret was staying put.

"I could stick around," she said, "keep an eye on him."

Identical expressions gaped at her.

"I don't need a nanny," Garret said through clenched teeth.

"Earlier today you were nearly begging for my company."

"Wouldn't be…proper."

"*Now* you're worried about being proper?" She moved in beside him and helped to support his injured arm. "I'll try not to cry when they kick me out of the quilting bee."

"I'm starting to see why he's so smitten," Tucker muttered to his brother. Both brothers grinned.

How could they smile when Garret couldn't even stand?

"Can we get him into the house now?"

"Yes, ma'am," they said in unison.

Tucker rushed ahead toward the porch.

"Boss? You all right?"

The young rider she'd met this afternoon broke away from the group. His smooth face didn't have so much as a scratch.

"You!"

Everett lunged back, bumping into the man behind him.

"Where were you when Garret was getting the life beat out of him?"

Everett looked at the men standing beside her. "She gonna hurt me?"

"Hard to say," said Chance. "Mag?"

"I want to know why Garret looks like hell worked over and this derelict doesn't have a scratch on him?"

"We were on the roof when we spotted the riders," said Everett. "He told me to go for help."

"And you left him here to face a whole band of men alone?"

"I…" His gaze moved frantically between the three of them. "I did what he told me to do."

"You did good," Garret said.

Maggie huffed her disapproval.

"Go clean up the roofing supplies. When the men ride in, make sure all our branding irons are accounted for."

"Yes, sir." Everett backed away, keeping his wary gaze on Maggie.

"Maggie."

She shifted her angry glare to Garret.

"Wasn't his fault."

"You need to lie down," she said, keeping her opinion to herself. She wouldn't have left him. She moved her arm around his waist to steady him as they climbed the steps.

Tucker stood at the open door. "You want me to get him?" he asked as they stepped into the dark entryway.

"No." She kept Garret's arm tucked against his side as Chance led him toward a staircase just beyond the foyer. As they crowded onto the stairwell, she knew three broad-shouldered men wouldn't have fit in such a narrow space.

"Which room?" Tucker asked.

"End of the hall," Garret answered.

Light blossomed in the room up ahead. Maggie wedged in through the doorway and felt as though she'd stepped into her childhood bedroom. She blinked, not sure she believed her eyes.

Pink satin wallpaper lined the walls. A massive four-poster bed, complete with a lace canopy, dominated the room. But the spindly carved vanity and wardrobes along the walls spoke of femininity, as did the lace curtains and rose painted lamps. She'd once had a room of such privilege and comfort, the memory adding to the chaos welling inside her.

Chance chuckled as they lowered Garret onto the mattress.

"Now isn't this sweet," he said, stepping back to take in the lace canopy and floral swags. "A room fit for a princess."

"Takes a real man...to pull it off," Garret said in a shallow breath, and collapsed against the pink bed coverings.

Both brothers laughed as they helped to prop him up against a stack of fancy satin pillows.

Maggie pushed past Chance. "Are you going to tease," she snapped, casting a reproachful glare over shoulder, "or make yourself useful?"

"I'll be right back," Tucker said, and left the room.

Garret's fingers combated her attempt to remove the rest of his shirt.

"Maggie, I can—"

"You are going to sit still!" she raged, her vision blurred by unshed tears. "Or I will cut the rest of that shirt off you!"

He captured her trembling hand and held it to his chest. "Honey, I'm all right," he said softly. "Just bruised."

He could have been killed. She couldn't stop the rush of tears. "You look like you've tangled with a bear. I should know."

"Come'ere," he whispered, pulling her against his warmth, and Maggie couldn't resist his comfort.

Chance watched in stunned silence as Garret held Maggie close, consoling her fear, calming her tattered nerves. He'd known Mag for seven years, but obviously he didn't really know her at all.

She straightened a moment later, drawing a deep breath as she wiped her eyes.

"Maggie, could you warm some water to clean his cuts? There's a pump in the kitchen downstairs."

"Okay."

Tucker stepped into the room as Maggie went out. He shut the door behind her and held up a brown bottle.

"Let's get you liquored up."

Garret had downed a quarter bottle of whiskey by the time they had him stripped and back into bed. They'd fashioned a sling for his arm from a spare bed linen and secured it around his neck. Strafford's crew had done their damnedest to stomp the kid into the ground. It was hard to look at him, his face and abdomen a mess of purple and black lumps. Ropes had left a spiral of bruising along his arms.

Judging by the shape of his bloody knuckles, he'd torn up a few raiders before they got him tied down. There wasn't anything else Chance could do but pray he didn't have any internal bleeding. Only time would tell.

"Strafford has gone to a lot of trouble to find Maggie," Chance said as he sat on the stool in front of the vanity. "Seems to me, if she's in danger, she has a right to know. Any particular reason you're not telling her?"

"She'll think it's her fault." Garret's slow speech told him the booze had taken effect. "And I'm in no shape to keep her from going after Strafford."

"You think she would?"

"Might have noticed…my gal's a bit of a firecracker."

"That she is, but I've never known Mag to seek out trouble. What does she have to do with Strafford?"

"I'm not sure. Send for my attorney. He's supposed to be looking into Strafford and some of the other new ranchers. The man in the chaps, he mentioned Duce. Said he wouldn't cooperate when they asked him about Maggie."

"They killed Duce because they thought he had something to do with Mag?"

"They figure we've been protecting her, helping her. Said she's been vandalizing Strafford's ranch."

"Has she?"

Garret tried to peer up at him through his good eye. "I don't know. She laid him out quick that day in town. Upset as she is, I don't want her to get a notion to go after him. I'm in no shape to protect her."

"You do realize you're talking about Mad Mag?" asked Tucker. "Seems to me she can defend herself just fine."

"So can my sister," Garret retorted, anger firming his tone. "She had to for years. Does that mean you want Skylar facing down gunmen alone?"

Tucker gave a solemn nod. "I see your point."

"And her name is *Maggie.* How could y'all not see? She's soft and sweet as a rosebud."

"Don't look at me," said Tucker, holding his hands up. "I never met the woman until today."

"I'm thinking Maggie gave you more than shelter from the storm up on that mountain."

"Watch it," Garret warned in a growl.

"All right," Chance said, appreciating the kid's discretion and respect for a woman Chance had long admired; a woman he didn't recognize in Garret's presence.

By the time Maggie made it upstairs with a pot of warm water the room wreaked of whiskey. Garret was tucked in bed, his arm bound and his swollen eyes closed. Dried blood marred his skin and hair.

"He'll likely be out for a while," said Tucker.

"If I'd taken a beating like that," said Chance, rising from a small bench, "I'd be praying for sleep. We've got to head back. Garret's crew should be in anytime and I'll leave a few of our men. I'd stick around but Cora Mae is due to have a baby. She was having pains when we left."

"I meant what I said. I can watch over him for a couple of days."

"Magpie?" His black-and-blue eyelids fluttered. He started to push up.

"I'm here," she said, sliding the bowl onto the night table as she sat on the bed beside him. She dunked a rag into the warm water and lightly swabbed his jaw. "Just lie still."

"So damn pretty," he murmured, reaching up to caress her cheek.

"You're drunk." Noting his lack of inhibition did little to keep a blush from scorching her face.

"Want to hold you."

"Hush," she said, placing the damp cloth over his face to keep him quiet. She glanced at the men standing behind them.

Both brothers grinned at her.

"Did you have to give him the whole bottle?"

"Wasn't more than a quarter," Tucker said, hooking his thumb toward the bureau.

"Garret's not much of a drinker," said Chance. "I do believe he's announced intentions to court you, Mag."

"A man full of whiskey will say just about anything. If you want to help Garret, follow the tracks and find out who did this to him."

"We sent out riders," Chance said, wondering at Garret's decision to keep information from her. "You can bet we'll be looking into it. We told him we'd send for his attorney."

"What good will an attorney do?"

"Garret spent a few weeks trying to find the ones responsible for Duce's murder and is convinced someone on the Cattlemen's Association is responsible. Someone's terrorizing the smaller ranchers and driving them out. Either the local law is stumped or they're turning a blind eye. Garret hired a man to gather information on the new ranchers in the area, anything to help him narrow his search. We'll send for the man he hired and see what he's uncovered."

"Don't fret if you hear someone on the porch," said Tucker. "Mitch said he'll be keeping watch. We sure appreciate all your help."

Maggie flushed and gave a slight nod.

"Night, Maggie," Chance said, and followed his brother to the door. "Keep him alive for us." A smile curved his lips before he disappeared into the hall.

What have I gotten myself into?

"Magpie?" Garret said from beneath the cloth.

Heaving a sigh, she sat beside him and raised the damp rag. "You behave," she said, and rinsed the cloth. He remained silent as she gently swabbed each cut on his face and rinsed the dried blood from his hair. Best she could figure most of the blood had come from a cut just above his eyebrow.

"Thanks, Maggie." He lifted his arm, inviting her to slide in beside him.

"I don't want to hurt you."

His arm closed around her waist, hitching her breath. He pulled her close. The instant warmth of his body seeped beneath her clothes, easing the ache in her tired muscles.

"Holding you...is worth every bruise."

The lump in her throat made it hard to breathe. "If I find out you set this up just to get me into your bed, you're a dead man."

His shoulders shook, his silent laughter ending in a groan.

"Sorry," she breathed, touching her lips to his temple.

"No worries, Magpie," he whispered, pulling her closer. "I feel better already. That's saying a lot."

She relaxed against his shoulder, her fingers dusting lightly over the bruises on his chest.

I need to be making a poultice, not lying in this bed.

She hadn't liked standing in his large kitchen and had a hard time figuring out which of the many fireboxes to use on the massive stove. The thought of venturing back through the eerie shadows of his fancy house sent a chill across her skin. She preferred the warm security of lying in Garret's arms.

All the more reason to keep her distance.

She eased back and his hold tightened.

"Stay with me," he whispered, and her resolve melted.

"I'm just taking off my moccasins." She unlaced the tall boots and removed her belt, setting them on the floor beside the bed. Closing her mind against the rush of reasons why she shouldn't, she slid beneath the blanket, allowing him to guide her against his good shoulder.

Just for a little while.

He sighed as she settled against him, and Maggie savored the rare luxury of being held.

Chapter Twelve

Glass shattered against the wall, forcing the group of mercenaries to flinch away from a spray of glistening shards.

"It's one woman!"

Nathan Strafford slammed a bottle of bourbon onto his desk. The brown streaks trailing down the office wall behind his men screamed of the mess they were making of his newly forged political ground. "I didn't tell you to start a ranch war—I told you to bring me Mad Mag!"

"You told us to do what was necessary to track her down," Smith defended. "We followed her to the Lazy J."

"Then where is she?"

His foreman's jaw twitched, the movement emphasizing a bruised mouth and swollen lips beneath his dark mustache. Gideon Smith, a man he entrusted with his life and his future, wasn't often on the receiving end of a fist. Every man in the room nursed an injury of some kind: bandaged arms, busted lips and black eyes.

"You told me she had no allies! That you'd have no trouble bringing *one woman to heel*. Yet you come into my office in the middle of the night looking like a pack of kicked puppies to tell me she's eluded you yet again."

"She ain't no ordinary woman," said a man standing in the back, his sniveling excuse increasing Nathan's rage.

"The hell she's not! I'm paying an outrageous amount of money to hire seasoned mercenaries. If you can't handle the job—"

"We can handle it," Smith interjected. "Daines is working with her. He must be. He covered for her in Bitterroot and we know for certain she was on his ranch today."

Garret Daines was not a complication he needed. No other ranch his size could meet the Association's shipping penalties, yet Daines had passed over a bank note without so much as a flinch. He'd then helped in his humiliation. And Nathan had since discovered that Daines was more than a small-time cattleman. He'd stirred up a ruckus in Bitterroot Springs after his partner's death and his family tie to the Morgan Ranch was enough to make any man think twice before crossing him.

"How many dead?"

"Larson is dead. He fell from his saddle on the ride back. A piece of his skull was bashed in. Guess the swellin' killed him." Smith shrugged, and Nathan felt his patience wearing thin, the vein ticking in his neck close to bursting.

"I meant the number of Daines's men, *not ours!*"

"It was just Daines. The only other man on the ranch deserted him before we closed in."

His gaze moved over the battered crew. "Are you telling me Garret Daines beat the lot of you like a bunch of school-yard bullies?"

"He also turned his rabid dog on us," said Cabot, a

broad-built man of tall stature, his forearm bound by a bloody cloth. "Good riddance to the both of 'em!"

"Daines's place is built on a rise," said Smith. "There was no way to sneak up undetected. We wore the hoods and rode in hard to surround the ranch. He and his dog got the jump on us but we got him under control."

"And Mad Mag?"

"She'd come and gone by the time we reached the ranch. He wouldn't admit to workin' with her, but he has to be. He knew we rode for you, and she had his dog. Would also explain why she had a Morgan horse last fall. She's been afoot since. As you well know, that woman don't leave a trail or we'd have caught her by now. Only reason we traced her to the Lazy J is because she had the dog with her. We didn't find no prints leadin' away from the ranch. Nothin' but the tracks of his man that road out."

"Which way did he ride?"

"West."

"Straight to the Morgans," Nathan seethed. "Exactly why I told you to lay off Daines!"

Disgusted by their incompetence, he slammed into his chair and turned toward the darkened window. His reflection glared back at him, but it was her black hair and laughing blue eyes he saw.

Margaret Grace. She was taunting him. Like always.

He could still hear little-girl giggles, the maddening blend of piano recitals and his father's praise echoing through the foyer halls, all of it grinding on his nerves. He'd waited too long to claim what was rightfully his. The moment she'd looked up in that alley, he knew he had trouble on his hands.

She'd taken him by surprise. He hadn't expected her to

be alive, much less in this part of Wyoming. He'd meant to bury her fourteen years ago, but the trapper had run off with her in haste. Nathan had been certain she wouldn't last a week of such ill use.

He'd come too far, had worked too hard. He was on the verge of having the political career his father should have paved for him. She wouldn't ruin this for him.

"You will finish this job, Mr. Smith," he said, turning back to his overpaid crew. "Or your men will hang for the murder and cattle rustling that's been going on around here."

A roar of protests broke across the room. Smith merely smiled, the sheer delight in his eyes reminding Nathan of why he'd been drawn to him in the first place. The man was void of fear and thrived under pressure. He was one of only a few men whose company Nathan had ever truly appreciated.

"Don't go gettin' skittish on me now," Smith said as he strode to the desk. He leaned in and braced his hands wide on the edge. "You wanted your ranging doubled. We doubled it and cleaned out the stragglers."

Nathan reclined in his chair. "I didn't order you to kill every rancher who got in your way."

"I didn't see you hangin' crepe, neither. Why are you expendin' so much effort on Mag? I'll admit she was a serious pain in the ass last fall, but as you keep sayin', she's just one woman. How, *exactly,* is she such a threat to this operation?"

"Don't overstep your bounds, Gideon. I'm the one giving orders and asking questions."

Anger narrowed his foreman's eyes, and Nathan realized his error. Gideon Smith wasn't a man to be cowed before his men and Nathan knew better than to address him by his first name while in the presence of others. But damn it, he hadn't expected to be disappointed!

"By what you just said," Smith growled, "we're the ones with our necks on the line. My men don't face no risk without me. You want to issue threats, you'll have to offer reassurances. Better yet, I'd say my men deserve some combat pay. Little somethin' to soothe their injuries and…*unease*."

Nathan conceded with a slight nod, certain a refusal wouldn't be accepted. "Fifty dollars will be added to your wages."

"Fair enough." Smith straightened and turned to the men waiting anxiously behind him. "Y'all can head to the bunkhouse. And pick up the glass on yer way out. I'm not wakin' my lil' señorita."

His crew didn't hesitate, each man crouching to pick up the broken pieces before shuffling out the double doors. It was that kind of control that made Smith such an asset to Nathan's ambitions. His eyes still alive with anger, he sat on the chair opposite Nathan and opened the cigar box on his desk. He clipped the ends then leaned back and propped his boots on the corner of the desk, a spur scraping the mahogany as he crossed his ankles.

"Comfortable?" Nathan asked, watching his lips as he lit a cigar.

"Not quite." He pulled the cigar from his mouth. "You try to dress me down in front of my men again, Nate, and you'll be paying in more than wages."

"I admit I lost my temper, but I *am* your employer."

"I *let you* pay me! You wouldn't have a foothold on this county if not for me. I'm not one of yer goddamn cow-punchers and I refuse to be spoken to as such. Call me Gideon in front of my men again and I will knock your teeth out."

Hard and ruthless as Gideon was, Nathan knew he also liked to be dominated—a combination that appealed to him as nothing else ever had. He'd never known another who matched him on every level: strength, ambition, desire. Fire and lead pooled in his groin at the mere thought.

Gideon glared through a cloud of smoke unfurling from his mouth, and Nathan supposed he'd guessed the direction of his thoughts. His boots hit the floor as he shifted forward.

"*I'm being serious!* You know damn well I kill folks for talkin' to me in such a fashion—my men expect it of me. I can't make exceptions—especially not for you. They're loyal *to a point.* If any one of them suspected there was more between us than—"

"You've been living with me for over three years and no one suspects anything." His "lil' señorita" was one of two maids they'd bought down in Mexico. Neither spoke a lick of English and Gideon kept them confused and wary with sporadic kisses and swats on the butt in front of the men.

"They will if you go callin' me Gideon and lookin' at me like you just did! Every day I put all I have on the line for you!"

"And I don't?"

"*Don't test me,* Nathan. You won't like the result."

"I wasn't trying to test you. You think I don't know what's at stake? I lost my temper! You don't usually let me down!"

"I haven't! I took care of Daines." He pressed his tongue to a new gap in his lower teeth. "Lost a tooth in the process. I truly hope he's dead." He stood and shrugged off his heavy duster.

Figuring both their tempers needed soothing Nathan

strode to the hutch on the far wall and retrieved two stout goblets. As much as he wanted to find faith in Gideon's confidence, he couldn't help but wonder if they'd stirred up a snake den of trouble. The Morgans had the kind of finances and connections any man would envy. Their spring colt sale had attracted buyers of political importance from all over the States. He'd hoped to have them as allies, not enemies.

Gideon crouched before the fireplace beside his desk and fed a log to the dying fire. Nathan picked up the bottle of bourbon and placed it on the small table between two high-back chairs. It had been Gideon's idea to move into these grasslands and expand their cattle trade to gain some notoriety. So far their plans had played out rather smoothly—until Margaret Grace had shown up.

Even as he reclined in a tall cushioned chair, bourbon warming his chest, tension continued to mount. "I'm not so sure your attack on Daines hasn't created a greater worry."

"You don't have to worry none about Daines. His outfit ain't that big."

"But his connections are. He's got strong ties with the Morgan brothers. This isn't a war I want to wage."

"Won't be no war." Leaving his boots by the fire, Gideon stretched out in the chair beside him, the cigar clamped in his teeth. "If Daines survived that beatin', he's in for a few surprises." He blew out a stream of smoke then smiled wide. "We got his brandin' iron."

"Which means?"

Gideon stared at him, his expression incredulous as he shook his head. "I know you got a lot of book schoolin', Nate, but you need t' step outta this office more often. You really do."

"We're both men of action in our own arenas. I have my job. I'm trusting you to do yours."

"Fair enough." He raised his goblet and downed the bourbon in one swallow. "It means cattle's been stolen. I'll bet my boots there'll be some Lazy J cattle in the stockyard next month with neighboring brands hidden beneath. Won't be nothin' the Morgans can do about it. Sometimes one of your own is just a bad seed. And in need of a hangin'," he added with a gleeful grin.

Nathan couldn't help but smile, and reached over to refill his glass.

"Ain't your judge supposed to be here this week?"

"Tomorrow." Judge Thornton would secure his hold on this county.

"He may be busy with cattle rustlers. That sheriff's been chompin' at the bit to arrest someone."

Finally the scales were tipping his way.

"Mad Mag is a whole 'nother animal. I gotta tell ya, despite yer distasteful view of women, this one's differ'nt."

"My view isn't distasteful, it's accurate."

"They're not all weak, Nate. Some are pure hell on fire an' bes' not to be nettled."

"When have you ever feared a woman?"

"Only had one fear as a kid," he said before tossing back the second glass of bourbon. "That was Mistress Florence and her whippin' stick. She run her orphan home like a battleship and could likely scare the starch outta any man."

Nathan laughed at the confession.

"Now, I know Mad Mag got your knickers in a pinch when she knocked you on yer ass. The old broad had some fun at your expense and you want 'er dead. Understandable. Trouble is, she's ferret-footed and slippery as a beaver. Huntin' her down could rouse attention you can't afford now that you're the mayor."

"We can't afford to let her live. Margaret Grace is not all that she appears."

"Margaret Grace?" Gideon smiled as he swirled the dark splash of bourbon left in his glass. "Don't keep me in suspense."

"Mad Mag, as she's called, is hardly an old woman. She's still in her twenties and she's a liability to everything we've built."

"How so?"

He'd never told anyone his family secrets. Those who knew the truth were dead and buried. That he trusted Gideon enough to confide in him came as a shock.

"If that mountain woman is an old lover of yours, I swear to God, Nathan, I'll be—"

"No," he said, amused by his sudden agitation. "She's my *sister*."

His brow creased with a scowl. "Thought all your kin was dead."

"So did I."

"You didn't know you had more than one sister?"

"There's just the one."

"Ain't she buried at the other house?"

"I buried her, all right. Apparently she didn't die as I had hoped."

"Oh, hell," Gideon said with a hoot of laughter. "You do keep life interestin'."

"Now do you see the severity of my dilemma?"

"I surely do." He flicked the last of his cigar into the fire. "Mayor Strafford can't have no dead sisters comin' back from the grave. But you don't need to worry none," he said, his eyes alive with mirth and a spark of desire as he leaned toward him. "I'll make sure she gets in that grave where she belongs."

Chapter Thirteen

All morning she managed to avoid the haunting allure of a room shrouded by heavy draperies. Streaks of light cut through the darkness, brightening silky pink wallpaper and piercing her memories, awakening images of another time—another life.

Instead of taking the stairs, Maggie stepped into the play of light and shadows of a parlor where dust lay thick on every surface. Fine-boned furnishings maintained a delicate beauty beneath the musty odor and a floating shimmer of intricate webs. A piano, alone in a corner, held her transfixed. Ghostly whispers of familiar melodies echoed in the back of her mind.

She hadn't seen a piano since she'd sat at her own. Her father's actually.

Play something sweet for me, Maggie.

His image drew her closer, his long frame relaxed in the pink tufted chair, his eyes closed, his silver hair a soft wave against his forehead. Her fingers reached toward ivory keys as she settled on the cool rosewood bench. Her father's favorite song trickled through her mind as her fingertips brushed the smooth surface, her light touch barely disturbing a silty film. Her hands moved silently over the keys, following the music playing in her mind.

Well done, button. Your mother could not have played any sweeter. It will be a lucky suitor who wins your delicate hand.

Her gaze fell to the scarred and callused fingers poised over the keys. Sadness rushed her heart at the thought of her father's disappointment. He'd loved her and had envisioned nothing but refined comfort for her future. He hadn't meant to leave her unprepared for the harsh realities of her life.

A prickling chill crept up the back of her neck. The internal warning she'd been too naive to recognize at the age of thirteen pulled her from her thoughts. She glanced over her shoulder and spied a tall figure looming. She gasped, lunging up. As she turned her hip banged against the piano. A clash of heavy vibrations exploded across the room.

"Maggie?" His rich voice eased her fright.

"Garret."

His face moved into a spray of light, casting off the dark pallor of old memories. The purple smudges beneath his green eyes and the puffy gash above his eyebrow reminded her that she'd been heading upstairs. "What are you doing out of bed?"

"Lookin' for my magpie."

Her heart fluttered at the endearment and she looked away. Her gaze collided with his bare chest and followed the dusting of crisp blond hair to denims riding low on his hips, the top button unfastened. His bare feet were the only part of his exposed body not baring bruises.

"Are you all right?" he asked, his concern palpable.

"You startled me. I wasn't expecting you to come downstairs."

Garret had been surprised to find her sitting at the piano as though giving a silent recital. Before sensing his presence she'd been a picture of perfect poise and grace, her shoulders squared beneath her buckskin tunic, her spine erect as her arms moved in graceful rhythm. And yet, the only sound she made was a light tap of her fingers barely touching the keys.

He reached her side and sat on the narrow bench.

"Your arm should be in the sling," she said, her expression firming as her gaze moved over his bare chest.

Afraid she'd fled before he'd fully roused, he hadn't taken the time to pull on more than a pair of Levi's. "My shoulder's doing good. Those hot packs and whatever you put in them sure helped with the pain and the swelling." Throughout the night she'd placed warm packs of pungent herbs on his shoulder and abdomen, easing his aches. But it was Maggie's heat, the feel of her settling back against his side that had truly soothed him.

Judging by the shadows in her eyes and the steel in her spine, it was his magpie that needed soothing. He slid his arm around her waist and pulled her onto the bench beside him.

"I didn't know you played," he said, tucking her snuggly against him.

"I don't."

He'd just seen proof that she did. He glanced at the sad curve of her mouth as she stared at the piano as though fearing it might somehow reveal her secrets.

"I did once," she amended, her voice just above a whisper. "But it's been so long...I don't remember how."

"That's a true shame," he said, certain he'd have heard a song played with perfect precision, had she applied any pressure to the keys. His finger clanked one of the ivory bars. The hollow sound echoed across the high ceiling. "I can't play a tune. Just like the wallpaper and fancy furnishings, the piano came with the house. The only time this thing makes music is when Chance's wife or my nieces drop in. Cora plays real well and has been teaching all the girls. When the twins sit down here together, it's like heaven opens up."

He trailed a finger through the dust on the keys. Maggie curled her fingers into her palms, as though resisting the urge to play. A tear, silent as her song, slid down her cheek.

"Was your childhood home so bad?" he asked, her quiet distress tearing at his heart.

She shook her head. "It was *wonderful*." She sniffed and wiped at her cheeks. She stood and stepped around the bench. "Can I assume it's been a while since your nieces have visited?"

He turned on the smooth seat and followed her gaze around the neglected room. "At least five months. This time of year is busy for everyone. Over summer and up until the snow hits the passes my sister and Cora take mercy on me and drop in near once a month. As you can see, I don't spend much time in this part of the house."

"It's a beautiful room."

"If you say so. Might actually get some use if I started storing tack in here. I spend more time in a saddle than anywhere else."

Her laughter was light, musical, and eased the tension in Garret's chest. He much preferred seeing her blue eyes bright with a smile than the shadow of painful memories.

"Come on," she said, holding her hand out to him. "You need some breakfast."

He closed his palm around hers. His teeth clenched as

he stood, the shift of bruised ribs and sore muscles reminding him he'd had the hell beat out of him the day before. Maggie's expression tensed.

"You shouldn't even be out of bed," she scolded.

"I can't heal if I don't move."

Her arm curved lightly around his waist as she stepped beside his side. He didn't mind her closeness, but he could walk without assistance.

"I'm not gonna fall."

"Not intentionally. If you did I don't think your pride, vast as it is, would cushion you."

"It would be a pure wonder if I had any pride left," he mused. "My woman coming to my rescue not once, but twice. A lesser man would take issue."

She smiled up at him. Liking that reaction, Garret gripped her waist a bit tighter as they walked through the dim corridor leading to the kitchen.

"Lucky for us you're not a lesser man," she said. "You're simply stubborn for no good reason."

"Isn't that the whole point of being stubborn? You don't have to have a good reason. What's your excuse?"

"I'm Mad Mag. I have to be stubborn."

"Part of your act?"

She laughed again, the light sound moving through him with such power, Garret knew for certain—he'd been thunderstruck by her.

"Is that what you think?"

"I think you're ten kinds of wonderful and the sweetest woman I've ever known."

She paused in the kitchen doorway, surprise lighting her expression as she stepped aside. "Then I'm clearly not being stubborn enough." She moved past him into the kitchen and Garret felt another nick in his pride. He breathed in appetizing aromas as his gaze moved over a spotless kitchen. Every hutch and cabinet had been dusted, their glass fronts sparkling beneath lit oil lamps. Pots and kettles steamed on the large stove. Maggie opened the oven and he noticed one of her flowery dish towels hanging from another handle.

She'd cleaned up after him.

He sat at the table she'd also given a scrubbing. Wasn't a damn thing he could do about the state of his house or his pride. She was here, which was exactly where he wanted her to be.

"You've been busy. My place is a site more run-down than yours."

"I don't run a ranch," she said, busily sorting through various canvas and leather pouches lined up across the drain board near the sparkling sink basin. "And I have a lot less to keep clean."

"Have you seen Boots this morning?"

"No, but Mitch came in earlier and said he's doing well."

She'd talked with his crew?

"I offered to take him," she said as she turned, a steaming coffee mug in her hands. "But Mitch said he'd rather keep him in the bunks until you were on your feet."

Garret was pretty sure the mug lacked the strong, dark brew his body was craving. The dull ache in his head needed *coffee*.

She stepped beside him, the barest hint of a smile on her lips, and he counted himself lucky to have her here, brewing the herbal tea she placed in front of him. She set the teapot at the center of the table.

"Thank you." He took a deep drink and was surprised

by the strong combination of woody herbs and sweetness, nothing like the tea she'd made him in her cabin.

"Do you like it?" she asked, still standing beside him.

"It's sweet. What is it?"

"Nothing poisonous," she assured him as she went back to the stove. "I barter a variety of wild herbs. Another reason Boots and I took our time in getting here."

"You sure know a lot about doctoring and herbs for a woman who keeps to herself."

"Trapping can be a hazardous trade. Weak and clumsy as I was in the beginning, Ira had to seek out an Indian camp when I had a cut that needed stitching." She turned with a plate in her hands, a smile on her lips. "I spent quite a bit of time with the Sioux, and I learned a lot."

Garret was taken aback by her easy delivery of information she'd held under lock and key up at her cabin.

"A little burnt," she said, leaning over the table to set a plate heaping with fried ham and potatoes in front of him. "I was keeping it warm and I'm not used to your stove."

"This isn't burnt," he said, taking a bit of crispy potatoes and tender ham. "It tastes good. Burnt is when you can't tell what the black coals used to be. We get that in the bunkhouse from time to time."

Maggie smiled as she sat across from him. She propped her elbows on the table, a mug of tea between her scarred hands—*skilled* hands that had nursed him back to health more than once. He doubted he'd be able to move his left shoulder today if not for her constant tending of herbs and hot packs.

"Thanks for staying last night, Maggie. You didn't have to."

"I had a feeling the Morgans would have knocked you

out and hauled you over the mountain if I didn't offer to stick around."

"They might have *tried*," he said darkly.

"They care about you. No harm in that."

"You haven't met my sister. Her caring can be down-right brutal."

The sudden chill in Maggie's eyes made Garret pause midbite.

"I didn't mean that literally, darlin'," he said, amused by her protective reaction. "She tends to hover, is all, like any good mother hen."

"She raised you?"

"Our ma died of pneumonia when I was five. Skylar had her hands full, driving stock for our pa and lookin' after me."

"I never met my mother." She lifted the teapot at the center of the table and refilled his mug. "She died shortly after I was born. I was named after her."

"A beautiful name for a beautiful woman."

"She was," she said, missing his intended compliment. "Our house was full of portraits of her. She was taller than me and had light brown hair and skin like fine porcelain. I take after my father."

"Did he live in Wyoming?"

"He did, but he was originally from Connecticut. He came West after Mother died." She stared down at the table as though staring into a window on her past. "We always had visitors from back East. Father would take them hunting and fishing. He loved Wyoming. He said it was the only place a man could step outside and see heaven."

"Can't argue with that. I've ridden through every state in the South and the Midwest and none are so beautiful as these hills and mountains. Have you been to Connecticut?"

"A few times when I was real young."

"Did you like it?"

"I don't know. I don't like to think about my life before Ira."

"Why not?"

She shifted her gaze to the wall behind him. "Your wife must have really liked pink. I have yet to find a room in this house that doesn't have pink wallpaper."

"My *ex*-wife didn't decorate the house," Garret said, not appreciating her new tactic of evasion. "She left with everything she brought with her. Every decoration in this house is the handiwork of Widow Jameson, the original owner."

"More?" she asked, glancing at his empty plate.

"No. Thank you."

She took his plate and scooted his mug closer. "Drink your tea," she said as she stood and went to the sink.

Her knack for giving orders hadn't changed. As sweet as she could be, he knew she also had a harshness to her—a reality he'd seen the night she took out Strafford.

Mad Mag has made herself a real nuisance, releasin' stock and vandalizin' ranches. We're goin' t' find 'er...

The man's Southern drawl had haunted him all night, along with images of Maggie surrounded by masked men. He wondered where else Maggie had been headed yesterday, why she'd come back and how in the hell he would convince her to stay. The thought of her traveling alone with such a band of men after her...

She stepped beside him and held up a fresh pot of tea. He pushed his chair back and set the mug on the table.

"Maggie, why did you come back yesterday?"

"I was headed north. I stopped by the river so Star could rest and have a drink. A group of riders rode past. I heard one of them say they'd shot a dog and might have killed the owner."

A chill raced across his skin at the thought of her being so close to the men who were hunting her.

"Your ranch was the closest." She set the teapot on the table and shifted her shoulders. "I wanted to make sure Boots was all right."

"Just Boots, huh?"

Her crooked grin put a kick in his pulse. "You don't spend two months with a pet and not get a little attached."

"Sassy." He grabbed her wrist before she could turn away and tugged her toward him.

Maggie gasped as she landed on Garret's lap.

Her hands touched down on his warm chest as she collided against his bruised side. His eyes flinched.

"Garret, you're going to—" The gentle glide of his fingers against her cheek stopped her protest.

"I've missed you, Maggie."

The admission softened her heart, weakening her hold on a storm of emotions she'd been fighting to contain all morning. "You've had a hard few months."

"I've had better. I've also had worse. Right now I feel damn lucky to be holding the prettiest woman in Wyoming."

"You keep talking like that," she said, unable to fight her smile, "and folks will start thinking *you're* the crazy one."

"You're not crazy, sweetheart. Just cautious. Can't say I blame you."

His understanding sent a wellspring of emotion spilling across her conscience. She leaned in and brushed her lips lightly over his, careful not to hurt his bruised mouth. Garret's hands slid up her back, holding her captive as he returned the gentle touch. The tip of his tongue skimmed the seam of her lips. Wanting his deep kiss, Maggie shivered, longing to kiss him in the way he'd taught her...in a dream. She sighed against his mouth at the memory and her arms drew a little tighter around his neck. Garret answered by kissing her with greater intensity. She returned every rhythmic touch, all thought of restraint forgotten. He groaned, his arms locking around her.

Realizing she was all but devouring him, she jerked back. Garret's tight embrace kept her on his lap.

"I wasn't expecting that," he said, staring at her mouth.

Her heart raced. Short of breath, she tried to draw air. "Neither was I." She broke away from his hold and stood. "Drink your tea."

"I've had a whole pot already," he said.

She dropped into the chair across from him, still trying to get her heart rate under control. "The herbs are good for you."

"I'm beginning to think passion is the best medicine," he said, smiling behind the mug.

He needed rest, not passion. The first pot of tea had definitely relaxed him and eased his pain, but the second was guaranteed to knock him out.

"Is there more between you and Strafford than that scuffle I saw in town?"

The unexpected question sent a shot of steel up her spine. "Why would you ask that? *Is he the one who did this to you?*"

"I was referring to the wanted posters he had issued for your capture. A five-hundred-dollar dead-or-alive bounty is usually reserved for murderers and train robbers. Mayor Strafford seems anxious for your capture."

"Mayor Strafford," she said, her voice drenched in

disgust. "Folks of Bitterroot Springs must be dumb, deaf and blind."

"Strafford can put on a pretty good show and he's been tossing money into their town. Being one of the newer ranchers in the area, he hasn't accumulated as many enemies as some of the other larger cattle barons."

"He's new to this area but he's not new to rustling. His cattle crew is too good at it to be new. Not that the rest of the ranchers are any better."

"We're not all ruthless thieves, you know?"

"You may be surprised by how many of you *are*."

"I am shocked that you know so much about the local cattle trade."

Maggie tensed, realizing she was revealing more than she should. "Just because I keep to myself doesn't mean I can't see what's going on out here. I follow the rivers through the spring and summer, which means I'm frequently near homesteads. I've seen the herding done late at night when no man should be driving stock. Mostly on the east side and north through the canyons. I didn't think you'd been having trouble."

"These days everyone has trouble. We haven't encountered more than small-time rustlers lookin' to fatten their herd. I reckon they're trying to make up for stock stolen to the east. I have a feelin' the problem is bigger than skimming herds. When I paid my dues last fall there were quite a few surprised and unhappy bigwigs. There are those who'd prefer to monopolize the market."

"Seems to me that those who have the most tend to want it all."

Garret couldn't argue. He was somewhat amazed and a whole lot impressed by her knowledge and observations.

He rested an elbow on the table and noted the ache in his ribs had dimmed considerably, while the weight of his eyelids seemed to increase by the second. "So, your deal with Strafford—"

"I don't have a deal with Strafford," she protested, her biting tone telling him she harbored some serious animosity toward the man.

"That day in town was your only run-in with him?"

Her slender eyebrows pinched inward. "Why do you ask?"

Hell. She didn't evade questions unless she had something to hide, and he didn't doubt that learning Strafford had sent his hired guns to his ranch to find her would set off the temper he saw brewing behind her angry blue eyes.

"Honey, those wanted posters are a real threat. The men who jumped me mentioned 'em."

Her blue eyes flared.

"They said they'd spotted you with Boots."

Worry replaced the anger in her expression. "Garret, did they—"

"They also told me to stay out of the stockyard next month. They'd have to beat me a damn sight harder to make that happen." He blinked against a sudden increase of weight in his eyelids. He felt awfully damn relaxed—too relaxed given their topic of conversation. His gaze fell to the empty mug in his hands.

She wouldn't.

He looked up. Maggie held his gaze from across the table.

"Maggie? What'd you put in that tea?"

Her sly grin confirmed his suspicion. "A few herbs to help you feel better and a bit of honey."

"You *drugged* me."

"I did." Smiling, she plucked the empty mug from his

hand. "You're hurting and you're stubborn. The madweed will help you rest easily. And unlike the whiskey, you won't wake with a headache."

He blinked several times, but the weight of his eyelids only increased. "You planning to sneak off while I'm passed out?"

"I'll stay until tomorrow."

Garret breathed a silent sigh of relief.

She walked around the table. "Let's get you up to your room before you fall on your busted face."

"Don't try to cushion my pride, now," he said, rising from the chair, sleep descending on him like a coastal fog.

Maggie pressed against his side. "I wouldn't dream of it."

"You can be a harsh woman, Magpie."

"They don't call me Mad Mag because of my needle-work."

Garret laughed, and hugged her close, not caring what name she went by, so long as she wasn't rushing off before he was able to look out for her. He'd find a way to keep her safe until he took care of Strafford.

A serenade of crickets echoed into the house as Garret poured himself a cup of strong coffee. He took a deep drink, the thick brew coating his tongue like tree bark and settling in his gut like warm mud.

"Perfect." He downed the cup, warding off any lasting effects of Maggie's *medicinal* tea. He was well rested after his herb-induced nap. He'd made sure Maggie napped right along beside him and he hadn't minded her serving his supper in bed, so long as she settled in with him.

He refilled the mug and started for the back door, knowing his nursemaid would be preoccupied for a good long while. He smiled at the thought of her slackened expression as he led her into the bathroom where a water-filled porcelain tub waited for her. He'd taken care to lay out one of the embroidered nightdresses he'd found in a bundle by the back door. His offer to stay and scrub her back answered with a glare, he'd left her alone. He'd bathed while she slept and felt like a new man after the long, hot soak.

He stepped into the cool evening air and shuffled down the back stoop. Following the racket of voices and guitar strumming, he headed for the bunkhouse. A full moon overhead dimmed the twinkling stars in the black sky. Movement near the corrals caught his attention.

Everett's brown hair stood out in the soft light, his bony shoulders silhouetted against a night sky. He sat on the fence, staring into the corral holding Maggie's horse.

"Everett?"

He turned. "You're up!" He jumped down and rushed over. "How are you feelin'?"

"Little worse for wear, but otherwise fine." Now that he could hold his eyes open for more than five minutes. "What are you doin' out here?"

"Nothin'," he said, his expression glum. "I counted the branding irons like you told me to and we're short one. Do you think the raiders took it?"

"Yeah," he said, taking a drink of coffee to wash down the sense of dread welling in his stomach. "I do."

"Clint wanted to talk to you about it this mornin' but Miss Maggie wouldn't let 'im."

"She wouldn't let him?"

"She said we'd have to wait 'cause she wouldn't wake you. She also said anyone who didn't knock on the back door before comin' in might not be walkin' back out."

Garret grinned, not doubting she'd told them just that. He hadn't thought about his crew clamoring in the back door as they usually did, and likely causing her a bit of fright. She'd never admit to it, but he knew it was fear that kept her wary. She'd likely instilled some in his crew of cowpunchers.

"She sure don't like me none," Everett said. "I only did what you told me to. If I knew they was—"

"You did the right thing, Everett. You brought help, just like I told you to."

"I'd have stayed and fought 'em with you," he insisted, his hands fisting at his sides.

"I know you would have, but it's just as well you didn't. Have the fellas been giving you a hard time?"

"No."

"You can bet they would if they thought you'd neglected your duty."

The kid shoved his hands into his pockets, seeming to ponder that thought.

"Come on," Garret said, nudging him toward the long-house. "Anyone ride out today?"

"Nope. Clint thought it best to stay close. We all found work on the ranch. Mitch and I finished the roof."

"Mitch is here?"

"Yeah. Two others from the Morgan ranch stayed on to help out."

Garret shuffled up the steps and was reminded of the sorry state of his ribs with each stride. He opened the door to a smoky room and a hum of guitar strumming and conversation. Jesse sat in his bunk on the far wall, strumming the chords to one of his cowboy ballads while Kuhana played poker at one of the long tables with Chavez and the two men from Morgan's ranch. Clint and a few others sat in the cushioned chairs spaced around the fireplace in the corner. He was talking to Mitch who lay on the floor before the fire. Boots was beside him on the rug, busily chewing on a bone.

"Evenin'," he said as he ventured farther into the lantern light.

Heads turned, eyes flinching as they looked in his direction.

"Damn," Kuhana said, tossing his hand of cards onto the table as he stood. The others followed suit with a combination of swearing and greetings.

Boots abandoned his bone and ambled toward him, favoring his front paw.

"'Bout time you showed your ugly mug," Clint said, his long frame unfolding from the chair.

"Looks worse than it is," he said, stopping to greet Boots. "My nephew Josh could have put up a better fight." He knelt down to inspect the patch of matted hair on his dog. "Boots and I were holding our own until one of those sorry cowards shot him."

"Get over here and take a load off," said Clint.

Pleased to find his dog on the mend, he continued toward the fire and eased into the chair Clint offered. "Thanks."

"Smoke?"

He glanced at the roll of white in Clint's fingers and recalled Maggie's reaction to the scent of tobacco when she'd entered the bunkhouse the day before.

"Nah."

"Figured your mountain woman still had you tied to the bed." Mitch grinned as low laughter rumbled from the men gathering around them.

Garret tensed, his hands curling into fists.

"For *doctoring*," he clarified. "I've got more sense than to make rude remarks about a woman with enough starch to stand the sight of you."

"She really Mad Mag?" Chavez asked, pulling up a chair.

His gaze moved from the cowhand's coffee-shade eyes to the dozen curious expressions fixed on him. Their curiosity reminded him of what it was costing Maggie to be here, the kind of exposure she'd avoided for years.

"Yeah. Her name's Maggie. Everett said she kept you out of the house this morning."

"Hell, we thought to come check on you," said Clint. "Yer little woman wouldn't have it and looked ready to skin anyone who thought to oppose her demands."

"You all appear to be unharmed," he mused.

"We not stupid," said Kuhana. "Do you know who jumped you?"

"We been trying to figure out why they would beat the hell out of you and not bother the herds," said Clint.

"I think they're more interested in controlling the stockyard than stealing my cattle."

"If they got your brand," said Mitch, "they're likely interested in hangin' you."

"Even if they managed to get me in a noose, my ranch goes to my sister, so what would they gain? This is about more than cattle. Mitch, can you ride back to the ranch in the morning and see if Tucker's been able to reach my attorney?"

Kuhana grunted. "You tell us which rancher, we go take care of it."

Flushing out the mayor of Bitterroot Springs wasn't going to be so simple.

"We're going to take care of him," Garret assured him. "But first I want to know exactly who I'm dealing with."

* * *

The familiar sweet scent of wildflowers was a welcomed and arousing distraction as Garret stepped in through the back door. Maggie stood before the warm stove towel-drying her hair. Instead of wearing the embroidered night-dress he'd set out, she wore a plain ivory shirt tucked into light buckskin britches with fringe running down the legs where it disappeared into the tall shaft of her moccasins.

Stubborn and beautiful as ever.

"How's Boots?" she asked.

"As spoiled as his master by the looks of it."

She smiled and he moved closer, drawn by the ease in her stance, the sparkling in her deep blue eyes.

"Did you enjoy your bath?"

"Yes. I must have been in that big tub for near an hour."

Breathing deeply, he closed the last bit of distance between them. "I love the scent of your soap." He lifted a sleek ebony lock from her shoulder and touched the damp hair to his lips. "It haunts me."

She eased back, her expression startled.

"I can't see a wildflower without thinking of you, and these hills are full of spring flowers."

Her answering smile broke the last of his restraint. He leaned in and she rose up as though meeting his kiss was a natural response. Desire flared as she clung to him, kissing him with equal passion. He slid his hands down her back, pressing her against the solid proof of the fire building inside him. He rocked his hips and her breath caught.

"Another effect you have on me."

"Nice to know all of you isn't broken." She kissed his neck.

He groaned against the pounding surge in his blood. He was sure he'd never been so familiar with any woman, and yet she surprised him at every turn. He'd sworn he wouldn't chase another woman—and he wouldn't. But he damn sure didn't plan to make it easy for her to walk away from him. He lifted her into his arms and started for the stairs.

"Garret! Your shoulder!"

"You bes' hold still until I get you up to bed."

Maggie tightened her hold as he started up the stairs, afraid she'd jostle his injury. "Who says I'm ready for bed?"

"I do. I have a mind to love you, Magpie."

Maggie's heart skittered as he carried her into the darkened bedroom. He sat her on the soft mattress. Moonlight poured in the through the second-story window, painting a milky glow across the bed, illuminating the lace canopy. Instead of reaching for the lamp, he reached for her shirt, undoing the button beneath her collar. His longs fingers pulled the bottom from her waistband while his eyes looked deep into hers. His eyes were a shine of colorless glimmer, his hair a glow of white while his body was cast in shadow outlined by silvery moonlight.

"Any objections?" he asked.

Objections? Anticipation sizzled beneath her skin, evaporating her breath. How she'd longed to be loved by him again. Realizing he waited for her response, she shook her head.

The warmth of his hands slid beneath her shirt and moved caressingly up her waist, stealing her thoughts as his gentle fingers found her breasts. He laid her back, every slow reveal of skin followed by the caress of his lips, his tongue, his teeth.

There was nothing hesitant in his lovemaking. He brought her shattering release again and again only to rebuild her passion until she was trembling, wild, frantic for their joining.

Chapter Fourteen

Maggie sat up in a tangle of bed linens. Disoriented and blinded by sunlight, she blinked up at an ivory canopy and instantly knew where she was.

Garret's bed.

"It's just the men." His sleepy voice came from the ripple of blankets beside her. It was voices in the yard that had woken her. Garret's arm snaked out from the covers and hauled her back down into the warm softness.

His lips found her neck and she snuggled against him, wishing she could stay here beneath this canopy forever.

"Good morning," he murmured against her skin.

"Mmm." She stretched, loving the feel of his body pressed to hers.

Garret eased back and smiled down at her. "I told you passion was the best medicine."

There'd been a few times last night when she knew his movement caused him a combination of pleasure and pain. She reached up, touching the cut near his eyebrow. The swelling was gone but his handsome face still bore a number of bruises.

"Am I healed?"

"A little more yellow today." She brushed her lips over a bruise on his chest. "How do you feel?"

"You tell me." He settled more firmly over her, hot and hard against her hip, the coarse hair of his chest tantalizing her sensitive breasts. "How do I feel?"

Maggie slid her arms around his strong back. *"Wonderful."*

"That's a good start." It felt more than wonderful to wake with her at his side, her skin pressed to his—it felt right. He kissed her neck and Maggie trembled beneath him. She tilted her head, giving him better access as he followed the curve to her shoulder. He eased farther down, one destination in mind.

A door slammed downstairs and Maggie shot up.

"Garret?" his sister's voice called out.

Maggie's wide gaze locked with his.

"My sister," he whispered.

A blanket slapped him in the face as Maggie pushed him away and flew out of bed.

"Garret?" Skylar called again, this time from the base of the stairs.

Maggie clutched a pile of clothes to her bare chest, her eyes frantic. *"Do something!"* she whispered.

"I'll be right down, sis," he called out as he strode to the door. "Can you start some coffee?"

"Okay. I'll meet you in the kitchen."

He shut the door and turned to find Maggie hastily buttoning herself into his shirt. Her expression thunderous, she struggled to stuff the long shirttails into her buckskin britches.

"Stop smiling," she snapped. "And put your clothes on."

"I would, sweetheart," he said, walking toward her, "but you're wearing my shirt."

She glanced down and her cheeks turned scarlet.

Garret grabbed her shirt up from the foot of the bed, tossed it over his shoulder and reached for the bottom of his. "Calm down," he said, kissing her forehead before lifting the ivory cotton away from her soft skin. Her arms covered her breasts as he pulled her shirt into place. She turned away from him to shove her arms into the sleeves and tuck in the bottom.

"I shouldn't be in your bed." She snatched up her boots. "I shouldn't be in this house."

Garret fastened his Levi's. "I wouldn't want any other woman in my bed or my house."

She looked up from lacing her boot, her eyes a shimmer of moisture before she turned back to her task.

When he was dressed but for the boots he'd left at the back door, Maggie stood near the window. Fully clothed, her arms crossed over her chest, her turbulent gaze was on the rise of mountains in the distance. If she truly had wings, he knew she'd be shoving up the windowpane and taking flight. He moved in behind her and encircled her in his arms.

"Ready to meet my sister?"

A blush stained her cheeks as she looked up at him. "I'll just wait here until she leaves."

"There's nothing inappropriate about you being here. I'm sure Tucker told her you stayed to look after me."

"I'm not so far removed from proper society to know that spending the night in your bed goes way beyond inappropriate."

"She doesn't know that you've been in my bed."

"But I do!" She pulled away from him. "I'll wait here."

He wouldn't have her hide up here, embarrassed and ashamed. "It would be rude to not come and say hello."

"I *am* rude."

"You can be, sweetheart, but we both know you're twice as kind. I wouldn't have you in my bed if you were some temporary fancy. I'd like to introduce you to Skylar."

He took her hands in his and drew them to his lips. Maggie nearly winced. When he looked at her that way, her resolve turned to mush and she doubted she could refuse him anything.

"Come meet my sister. You'll like her. I know you will."

"Won't matter if I like her or not," she said, grasping at the remaining shreds of her temper.

"It matters to me. I'll be the perfect gentleman, well…as close to a gentleman as this dusty cowpuncher can manage," he said, his smile not quite reaching his eyes. For the first time she sensed his easy grin was a mask.

Not since her father had she known such a gentle, considerate man, and her father had been the perfect gentleman.

Garret's fingers laced with hers and Maggie didn't resist as he led her from the room. Despite Garret's confidence in his sister, she doubted any woman would be pleased by her brother entertaining the likes of Mad Mag.

As they neared the kitchen, the sounds of activity at the stove made Maggie's stomach flop something awful. Her breath stalled as she spotted the tall woman setting coffee mugs on a tray. Even from the side-view, she could see that Garret's sister was strikingly pretty, and nearly as tall as Garret. Her long blond hair had a yellow tinge that Garret's lacked and was tied back at her nape with a white ribbon. A floppy hat hung from the chinstrap and rested on the back of her brown canvas coat. As they drew closer Maggie's eyes widened at the full sight of her. Beneath her coat she wore denim britches.

"Morning, Skylar."

Maggie hung back in the doorway as the woman turned. Skylar's blue eyes widened with shock and horror at the sight of her brother, reminding Maggie of the blackened eyes and bruising she'd gotten used to seeing.

"Oh, Garret."

"It's not as bad as it looks."

"I doubt that."

His arm slid around Maggie's shoulders and dragged her forward.

"Oh!" his sister said. "Hello."

"Maggie, this is my sister, Skylar Morgan."

Skylar's smile was as bright as her brother's.

"Good morning," Maggie managed to say, while resisting the urge to ram her elbow into Garret's bruised ribs for making her come downstairs.

"Skylar, this is *Margaret Grace*."

His formal introduction took Maggie by surprise. The pride in his voice made her chest ache and her eyes burn.

"I'm so glad to finally meet you." Skylar rushed forward and took her hand. "I can't thank you enough for all you've done."

"I haven't done much."

"Nothing but save my life," Garret said in a droll tone.

Skylar released her hand to inspect Garret's bruised face, lifting his hair for a close view at the gash near his eyes. "You look like you've seen the underside of a stampede."

"Honestly, sis, I'm on the mend."

"Bruises tend to darken as they heal," Maggie said, tucking her hands beneath her crossed arms while discreetly easing out of Garret's embrace. "He was hardly recognizable a couple of nights ago."

"And your shoulder?"

"Better every day." He shifted his shoulder, but his eyes revealed the stiffness in the joint.

"We've brought Mr. Patterson," Skylar said, a firmness seizing her expression.

"My attorney," Garret said to Maggie.

"He and Tucker are taking care of the horses. He was anxious to come. I'm hoping he has some news you can use."

"Will he know who attacked you?" Maggie asked.

"That's what we'll be discussing." Garret hoped Skylar would bite her tongue if Tucker had filled her in on Strafford's involvement. He preferred to take care of him without involving Maggie. "If you're here, Cora must have had her baby."

"A boy," Skylar said.

"About time I got another nephew. Poor Josh has been on his own with eight little girls. What'd they name him?"

"Tucker James. They're going to call him TJ so as not to confuse him with his proud uncle."

Maggie watched their shared smiles, sensed the affection and joy shared between them and felt a sudden sting of tears. She tried to steel herself against the unexpected burst of emotion.

What's wrong with me? she silently scolded. She knew his family was important to him. *As they should be,* she told herself. Most brothers didn't try to kill their sisters. And she doubted the men on this ranch would have stood idly by had he tried.

"How's the rest of the wild bunch?"

Skylar handed him a cup of coffee, her gaze sympathetic. "Far better than their uncle. And missing him, as well."

"Things have been...*hectic.*"

"Maggie?" Skylar said, holding out another cup of coffee.

Struggling with a tangle of nerves, her stomach roiled. "No, thank you. I should go check on Boots."

The concern in Garret's eyes told her she wasn't hiding her distress.

"It was really nice meeting you, Mrs. Morgan," she added, forcing a smile.

"Please, call me Skylar. I hope we'll have a chance to visit more." She picked up the tray of coffee and cups. "I'll be waiting in the study."

"I'll be right there," Garret told her, his gaze on Maggie. "Well?" he said when they were alone.

She didn't know what he was expecting. "She's nice."

"So are you." He pulled her close and the next thing Maggie knew she was clinging to him, kissing him with a passion he evoked in her so effortlessly. When he released her, it took a moment to catch her breath.

"*That* is exactly why I need to get going," she said accusingly.

"I think you've got that backward, honey," he said, looking rather smug and positively edible as he leaned against the table.

"*I can't stay, Garret.*"

"Have I asked you to stay?"

The realization that he *hadn't* felt like a blow.

"I know it hurts you to be here, and I wish to God it didn't. You're free to stay or leave, I'm not setting any trap-doors. I'd like you to at least stick around until I find out what my attorney's found out. Can you do that?"

"Yeah."

"Good." He kissed her lightly on the lips before turning away. "I'll be back."

Watching him walk from the kitchen, she felt drawn in a hundred different directions. She wanted Garret but she didn't belong here. With Nathan in the area, she'd never be safe. She couldn't lose another home, another person she loved.

Needing fresh air, she turned and hurried out the back door. Her gaze landed on the longhouse across the yard. She needed to look in on Boots. As she reached the steps of the bunkhouse Tucker's voice carried through the open door.

"…threatened to frame him for rustling if he didn't tell them where to find Maggie."

Hair prickled on the back of Maggie's neck. Garret hadn't told her any such thing.

"Strafford's man admitted to killing Duce, thinkin' he was holding out on how to find Maggie."

Nathan? Shock and rage slammed through her. He'd attacked Garret because of *her*—and Garret hadn't told her.

"Garret wants to keep it hush until he figures out an approach. He knows he can't just ride in and shoot the mayor of Bitterroot Springs without earning a noose. I'm sure he's tryin' to figure out how to go after Strafford while keeping within the law and his woman safe. By what his attorney's told me, Strafford has a knack for bending the law to his will."

"If Strafford's the one who got a hold on Garret's cattle brand," said Mitch, "Garret better act fast. If he's charged with cattle rustling—"

Maggie took a sliding step back, her heart raging as she rushed to the house. She knew just how crafty her brother could be.

Garret should have told me.

He couldn't ride in and shoot the mayor of Bitterroot Springs, *but she could.*

"She's a lot younger than I'd thought." Skylar smiled over a cup of coffee as she eased back in the striped armchair in his study.

"Yeah."

"And pretty," she added.

Garret grinned, knowing he didn't have to voice his agreement for his sister to see it.

"She's created quite a stir on our ranch. Ten of our workers lined up this morning, willing to ride over with us."

Garret tensed at the thought.

"I imagine most folks have never seen her up close. Chance's hostile reaction likely cooled their interest. I imagine she's not too comfortable being surrounded by curious onlookers."

"No, she's not." With just the two of them in the house it was easy to forget all that it cost her to stay with him, the fear she'd set aside to help him. She'd worked hard to keep herself hidden away from everyone.

Footsteps sounded in the hall before Tucker walked into the study. Jim Patterson trailed behind him. The man's slight build and tailored wool suit didn't hint at the aggressive man he knew the investigative attorney to be. Garret had sought him out after reading a newspaper article on the man's success and belief in thoroughly investigating plaintiffs and clients.

He stood and offered his hand to both men in greeting. "Tuck. Patterson."

"You look a world better than the last time I saw you," said Tucker.

"That's hard to believe," said Patterson, his slender hand giving a firm shake.

"I feel a world better."

"Shoulder functioning okay?" asked Tucker.

"It's getting there, thanks to Maggie. Have a seat." He motioned to the chairs Skylar had arranged around a low table holding the tray of coffee and mugs. "Patterson, Skylar tells me you've uncovered a good deal of information on Strafford."

"I have indeed." He sat across from him and removed his hat, revealing dark hair slicked back across his scalp. "I can't say I'm surprised Nathan Strafford is involved in all this. Of all the new ranchers in the area his property has expanded with the most notable speed. I haven't been able to connect him to Duce's death, but nearly all of those titles passed ownership following some sort of violence on the seller's end." He opened the valise on his lap and pulled out a fat folder. "His father was a former senator of Connecticut before coming to Wyoming. It would seem his son shares his political ambitions."

"The father still around?"

"No." He opened one of the folders and shuffled through a stack of papers. "Thomas Strafford died in an Indian raid back in seventy-five. Nathan Strafford returned home with a hunting party to find the rest of his family slaughtered. Here's a newspaper clipping I found."

Garret took the thin paper.

"With his family connections and knowing that Strafford recently brought in his own judge, I doubt it will do you any justice to file charges in Bitterroot Springs. I suggest we file with the territorial governor."

Garret's gaze was drawn to a small family photo. A

younger Strafford stood behind an older man sitting in a wing chair. A little girl in ribbons and a ruffled dress stood beside him, her hand on the arm of the chair tucked beneath her father's palm. Even in the black-and-white photo, he could tell her hair was pure black and her eyes...*were Maggie's.*

His gaze skimmed down to find her name. *Margaret Grace Strafford, age thirteen.*

"Damn."

"What?" said Skylar, leaning toward him.

"It's Maggie."

"Are you sure?" she asked.

Garret handed her the article.

"Who's Maggie?" asked Patterson.

Garret's mind drifted to the first day he'd met her in the alleyway, the shock on Strafford's face just before she rammed her rifle into his gut... He'd recognized her. And she'd laid him out.

Why did you stop me? Gentle society would be a better place without him.

She'd meant to kill him. And Strafford seemed to be doing his damnedest to return the sentiment.

"Shouldn't a man who's discovered his little sister survived an Indian attack be trying to help her, instead of putting a bounty on her head?"

"What exactly are you saying, Mr. Daines?"

"His sister's not dead. She's in my kitchen."

"There was a death certificate."

"It's not real." Strafford was her *brother.* He'd asked her point-blank and she hadn't told him!

Nothing worth mentioning. I know who he is, what he's capable of.

"You think the attack on his family was staged?" asked Tucker.

"I don't know. She's never mentioned how her family died. She only told me that Ira saved her."

"Perhaps you should bring her in here," Patterson suggested.

He glanced at the three of them. "She's not real fond of crowds. I'll talk to her alone."

"Does this change our plans?"

"No. I'm filing the charges for Duce's murder." He stood and started toward the door. "I don't mean to be rude, but I need to talk to Maggie alone. Can you give me a day?"

"Certainly." Patterson closed his case before he stood. "I need to prepare the paperwork. If there's a hotel you can recommend—"

"You can stay at our place," Skylar said.

"I'll come by tomorrow and then we can finalize everything."

"Perhaps you'd like Maggie to come and stay with us until all this is settled?" Skylar asked.

As much as he wanted to tuck Maggie away in a safe place, he knew full well her idea of safety didn't include a ranch teeming with people. "I don't know that I can even talk her into staying here."

"Should I draw up any paperwork on Miss Strafford's behalf."

Miss Strafford. "No. I can't speak for Maggie."

"If I could meet with her—"

"She wouldn't talk to you." He wasn't at all sure how she'd take being confronted about her connection to Strafford. A man concerned about his sister's safety wouldn't be sending out mercenaries like those he'd met.

"I'll talk to her. I don't want her brought into my battle. I don't want Strafford to know she's here." Not that she'd be here long after he started demanding answers.

He led them to the front door. "I really appreciate you coming," he said, stopping at the end of the porch.

"Tomorrow evening then," Patterson said, pulling on his hat as he strode to the barn.

Skylar looked back at him.

"My boots are on the back porch."

Skylar glanced at his stocking-covered feet and smiled. She gave him a quick hug. "Tell Maggie I hope to see her again soon."

"I will," he said, appreciating his sister's understanding. "Be sure to give Cora and Chance my congratulations. I'll be by tomorrow for supper."

Anxious to ask Maggie about her brother he made his way back through the house. She wasn't in the kitchen where he'd left her. His gaze was drawn to a splash of color by the stove. The dish towel baring his brand hung from the handle. An array of colorful flowers surrounded the insignia he'd stitched. His gaze shot to the corner by the door where her supplies had been for the past two days.

The corner was empty.

He hurried out the back door and shoved his feet into his boots. The paddock that had held her horse was empty, too.

Everett rode in from the side yard and Garret waved him over.

"Did you see Maggie leave?"

"Yeah. She rode out near twenty minutes ago."

"And you didn't think to tell me?"

"She's stayin' in the house with you. I figured you knew.

She came out with her gear and asked me to fetch her saddle. She packed up and rode out without sayin' another word."

She wasn't going to leave without a word to him. "Give me your horse."

"You sure you're in shape enough to ride?"

"Now!"

Everett's eyes widened and he stepped down from his saddle.

"She head south for the river?" he asked, gritting his teeth against the pain in his sides as he mounted.

"Nope. She rode east."

Garret's gaze moved across the miles of green hills to the east, dread turning his blood cold. Had she been listening outside the study?

Strafford's place was nearly a full day's ride—he'd catch up with her.

Chapter Fifteen

Like a swarm of bats dispersing into the darkness, Nathan's cowhands rode out for another night of rustling. As Maggie waited for the thundering hooves of twenty horses to fade into the distance, her brother's shadow moved past a lit window.

Anger surged hot through her blood. Crouched low near the house, she bid her time. The long ride to Circle S only served to fuel her rage as she remembered all he'd taken from her. Her family, her security. At the age of thirteen she'd been too naive to recognize the feeling of unease she felt in Nathan's presence had been warning signs of danger.

Nathan had moved into these hills like a plague. Garret had already suffered for helping her. She'd stop Nathan before he could cause further harm. This was a score she should have settled last fall.

Turning her face to meet a cool evening breeze, Maggie drew in a deep, calming breath. Her black hair a decent camouflage against the night, she'd left her hat with Star. Surrounded by the chirping of evening insects and intermittent murmurs from a bunkhouse off in the distance, Maggie straightened.

Clutching her rifle, a long blade tucked into each boot, she moved around to the front of the house. She kept her gaze on lights cast from bunkhouses farther out on the property as she ascended the front steps of his brightly lit porch. Her rifle resting against her shoulder, she stepped in through the front door.

No one stirred in the darkened foyer. The quiet house smelled of tobacco and wood smoke. Light seeped from a room at the end of the corridor, a door left slightly ajar. Her moccasins silent on the long carpet runner, she walked to the doorway. She stepped through the narrow gap, her gaze sweeping the dark paneled room. A fire crackled to her left. His boots had been left by the hearth. The only other light came from a small sconce on the far wall. A lit cigar sat in an ashtray on his desk at the back of the room.

He'll be back.

She glanced at a hutch to her right displaying an array of crystal cups and decanters as well as pretty plates of silver and gold. A white oval plate she remembered seeing in their parlor sat near the top, the center bearing three grapevines and the words *Sigillum Reipublicae Connecticutensis* inscribed around the outer edge.

Greed was what drove her brother. Her father had been a wealthy man. Nathan had wanted him to stay in Connecticut. She recalled their frequent fights when Nathan would visit, her father shouting that Nathan had attended the best college, that he'd supplied him all the finances he'd requested of him—but Nathan wanted it all for himself. Of course he wouldn't be satisfied with their father's estate, he wanted all of Wyoming.

She walked around the mahogany desk, the scrolling across the front and ornately carved legs jarring her memory. Her father's desk. She eased into the soft leather of Nathan's chair. A standard desk, she surmised, that had once seemed so massive to her young eyes. She leaned forward, placing her elbows on the polished wood, and leveled her aim on the door.

Fourteen years ago she'd been too young to stand up to Nathan. The world had been bending to his will for too long.

Footsteps approached, and Maggie's pulse began to pound.

The door swung wide and Nathan walked in wearing a pair of silky black pajama bottoms, his bare chest covered by a thick matt of black hair. His gaze fixed in the direction of the fire, he didn't see her as he walked to the chairs and lifted a glass decanter from a small table.

Maggie clicked back the hammer on her rifle. Nathan froze. His gaze shifted slowly toward her.

"Hello, Nathan."

The bottle slipped from his grasp and crashed against the floor at his feet as Maggie stood, her aim steady.

"Margaret Grace." His gaze moved to her rifle then back up, his throat working over what seemed to be a lump of fear in his throat. "This is…unexpected."

"I hear you've been looking for me."

"And here you are. You can't really mean to shoot me. As you can see, I'm unarmed." He held up his empty hands.

"I do mean to shoot you, Nathan," she said, a tremble in her voice, yet her hands were steady. "I wasn't armed the first time you tried to kill me. Perhaps you remember that day?"

Eyes as blue as her own narrowed with anger. "What do you know of that day, Margaret Grace. You were a child."

"And yet you tried to kill me!"

"Father forced my hand!"

"He was dead!" she shouted back.

"I sent him to the one place he truly wanted to be—the heaven he always talked about, with his angels."

"You *sent* him?"

Nathan found some amusement in her apparent shock. Sweet, naive Margaret Grace, even in her buckskin rags. God, how she made him sick. "Only you didn't have the good grace to join him."

"Show some respect, Nate."

He jumped at the sound of Gideon's voice directly behind him. Margaret Grace had a similar reaction, her blue eyes surging wide as he stepped beside him, her aim shifting. Hopefully Gideon had the forethought to grab his gun.

"That's no way to greet yer sister," he said, stepping forward, fully dressed, a blessed revolver in his beautiful hand. "Aren't you goin' to introduce me?"

Nathan drew an even breath, Gideon's relaxed presence helping to restore his composure. "Gideon Smith, Margaret Grace, my *dead* sister."

Gideon smiled and Maggie shifted her aim, clearly about to take her one shot at him. Nathan ducked behind the chair as Gideon lunged for her. Knocking the rifle from her grip he dragged her over the top of the desk and threw her to the floor.

"Sorry, little sister," he said, pinning her down, wrestling her arms over her head. "I've got far too much invested in your brother to let you do that."

Nathan placed a hand on the chair and tried to catch his breath. "Don't you have someone guarding the yard?" he demanded.

"Cabot should be at his post by now." Gideon looked up from his captive, his lips tilting with a grin as his gaze raked over him. "We'll finish this outside. You're coming along, so go get dressed."

"I wouldn't miss it."

Maggie stared up at Smith as Nathan left the room. He was a man of striking features and nowhere near Nathan's height, yet his presence was twice as menacing. His slow drawl was a contradiction to the clear sharpness of his eyes. Eyes that didn't blink as he stared down at her. All she needed was an ease in his grip to reach for her knife...

"E-e-easy, little sister," he said, tightening his hold as though reading her mind. His weight settled more firmly on top of her, revealing his fully aroused body.

Maggie stiffened.

Smith grinned and leaned close. "Don't get excited," he murmured near her ear, the stench of tobacco gagging her, the touch of his mustache forcing her to turn her head. "That's not for you."

"If you're going to kill me why not just get it over with?"

"Just between me and you, I'm a considerate man, an' Nate tends to fuss about bloodstains on his carpets. We're goin' t' sit up now, an' I'm expectin' you to be cordial."

His body shifted as he sat back on his knees and yanked her hands forward, hauling her up. Maggie used the motion to slam her clenched fists into his face. His head reared back but his hold on her wrists didn't loosen.

"Damn," he said, laughing as blood dripped from his lower lip. "I'll get ya back for that one. Ain't a wonder he underestimated you. Yer two of a kind."

"No, we're not!"

"Are, too. A fight to the finish, I like that in a person. But here's the lesson you won't get to learn twice, little sister—if Nate had caught you by surprise, he'd a saved the sentimental banter an' *pulled the trigger.*"

Her brother's laughter announced his return, adding to the sting of Maggie's error.

"Having fun?" he said to Smith.

"You know me, Nate. I always have a good time."

He whipped her up and spun her around so fast Maggie nearly lost her balance. "Just like dancin'," he said, twisting her arms behind her back until she thought her elbows would snap. A scream ripped from her lungs as he shoved her forward toward the fireplace. "She's already feelin' like the little sister I never wanted."

Keeping his firm hold, he stepped into the boots by the fire. They followed Nathan to the front and out onto the lit porch.

"Cabot!" Smith shouted.

"Smith?" A man rushed into the brightness in the yard. "I thought you rode out."

"Good thing I didn't," he said, ushering Maggie toward the steps.

"Where'd she come from?"

"The grave," said Smith. "Time to put her back."

A thick man with a wide face, Cabot stepped up to the base of the stairs. "She ain't all that bad lookin'. We got to kill her right away?"

"I don't know," said Smith. "What'd you say the goin' rate for Mad Mag was, Strafford, six beaver pelts?" He shoved at her back and sent her stumbling down the steps.

Maggie collided with the large man's chest.

"Tie her up. We're takin' her for a little ride."

Cabot grabbed one of her arms. Maggie reached for her blade with the other. Eyeing up Nathan on the porch, she turned and sent the knife spinning for his chest.

Smith shoved Nathan down and shouted as her knife pierced his upper arm.

Damn it! Cabot's thick arms locked around her, lifting her off the ground.

Smith ripped the blade from his arm. His hostile gaze locked on her and fear snaked through her.

A gunshot cracked through the air and Cabot dropped her. Maggie turned to see Cabot hit the ground, a hole blown through his skull.

She glanced into the darkness as she pushed to her feet. *Garret?*

"Oh, no, you don't!" Smith collided against her, a sting slashing across her arm as he locked her against him like a shield.

Gunshots exploded, splintering wood off the porch banisters, spraying them with shavings and keeping Nathan back. Maggie strained to pull out her second blade. Gripping the handle, she thrust it into Smith's thigh.

He stumbled back with a cry of pain. Maggie pulled away and dived for the ground. The next gunshot sent Smith to ground beside her, clutching his gut.

"Maggie, *run!*" Garret stepped from the shadows, feeding shells into his rifle as he cracked off consecutive shots. Men's shouts blended with the ringing in her ears and she knew ranch hands must be flooding from the bunkhouses.

Struggling to her feet, she ran for the cloud of gun smoke.

"Go to the horses," Garret told her as she reached him.

A roar of male voices rose behind her. She paused to look back.

"Move!" he shouted.

She did, running into the shelter of the night. Avoiding wide patches of moonlight, she ducked under branches and scrub as she made her way for the river. Garret was beside her a few moments later, his hand closing over hers like a steel vise, forcing her to keep up with his longer strides.

When they reached the horses she was out of breath and planted her hands on her knees.

"Gideon!" Her brother's shout rang clear as she struggled for a full breath.

"Are you hurt?" Garret whispered beside her.

"No," she said in a pant.

"We can't stop here." His hands closed over her waist and tossed her up onto her saddle.

His horse set off toward the west and her mare followed. As they splashed across the river one thought plagued her mind.

They'd shot the wrong man.

Maggie watched Garret's silhouette ride into another black outcrop of trees at the top of the hillside and knew he and the horses would outlast her. They'd ridden hard through streams, meadow and hillsides and her body ached with exhaustion.

Garret waited for her at the top of the rise just inside the first line of trees. He held the horse steady as he glanced over the moonlit ground they'd just covered. They'd stopped several times over the past hour to check for signs of anyone following their trail. She hadn't detected any but each time Garret would set off again without a word. She followed without question, his route no different than she would have chosen on her own.

He stepped down from his saddle and Maggie barely stifled a moan of relief as she reined in. He rubbed at his left shoulder as he walked toward her and she knew his bruised body had to be hurting after a full day of hard riding. Before she could dismount, he dragged her from the saddle and set her firmly on the ground before him. His hands slammed down onto his hips. As her eyes adjusted to the shadows she realized his expression didn't show a trace of pain—he was *furious*.

"Garret—"

"Just what the hell did you think you were doing?"

"Trying to kill that rotten bastard," she ground out.

"They nearly killed *you*," he shouted at her.

"I was handling myself," she raged right back. "You keep forgetting who I am!"

"Oh, I know who you are, Margaret Grace Strafford. The most stubborn, infuriating woman I've ever come to know!"

"No one asked you to come after me!"

"All the fires of hell wouldn't have stopped me! They could have killed you, Maggie."

"People die, Garret! Grow up!"

"That supposed to be advice, coming from a woman who's so afraid of life she hides herself away from the whole damn world?"

"I'm not hiding!"

"You use those mountains like a fortress. You live in a cave and have folks believing you're some crazy old woman so they'll leave you alone. And what's keeping you from admitting you fancy me, but fear?"

"I doubt my fancying you is a big secret! Fear doesn't control me. Lately it seems to be lust and I have no more morals than a—"

"You finish that sentence," Garret said through gritted teeth, "and I'll have you standing before a preacher by sunup. If all I wanted was sex, I'd visit a brothel. And if I wanted just any woman for a wife I'd snag me one on my ride out of town. I want *you,* Maggie! You have to know I care about you."

"I don't understand any of this—least of all you!"

"Which part don't you understand, sweetheart? That I'm crazy about you? Or the thought of you risking your life rather than trusting me makes me mad as hell? Do you think so little of me?"

"You aren't the problem, Garret!"

"I am sure glad to hear that. Then you should have no problem with being courted."

"I may be inexperienced with relationships, but I'm quite sure we've passed the courtship stage."

"I'm ready to risk marriage if you are."

Maggie stared up at Garret's fierce gaze, hardly able to believe his words. "They must have cracked your skull."

"Was that a refusal?"

"Of what? You didn't propose."

He dropped to one knee and pulled her hand into his. "Then I'm asking."

Her heart clenched at the picture he made, kneeling before her…he couldn't be serious. She shook her head. "Garret, *don't.*"

"Marry me, Maggie."

"No!"

"Why not?"

"Because you don't mean it!"

"The hell I don't," he insisted, straightening to tower over her. "I just blazed across fifty miles to keep you from killing yourself!"

"I wasn't trying to kill myself—I was trying to kill my brother!"

Silence stretched as he stared at her and she knew she'd just hit on the root of his anger.

"Which brings us back to that trust issue," he said, his voice a rumble of barely controlled fury. "How could you not tell me, Maggie? Did you think I wouldn't fight for you?"

"This is *my* fight."

"Anything that affects you, affects me. *I love you, Maggie,* and if you can't understand that, then there's no point in even talkin' to you right now!"

Garret turned away and shoved his hands through his hair. He wanted to hold her, to hug her, but he was afraid if he touched her he'd find a way to stuff her into his back pocket. He struggled to gain a grip on his temper as a combination of rage, fear and adrenaline stormed through his system.

Had he just demanded she marry him?

Holy hell. As if they didn't have enough against them, he knew better than to grab a rattler by the tail!

Leaves rustled behind him and he turned to find her sitting in a patch of moonlight, her arms strapped around her knees, her hair covering her face as she looked down at her feet. Dark streaks on her buckskin shirt filled him with new alarm

"Is that blood on your sleeve?"

She glanced at her arm as though just remembering she'd been cut. "Yeah. It's not deep."

He crouched beside her and reached for the matches he kept in a pouch on his belt. She'd nearly been killed by her brother and he'd just raged at her instead of checking her for injuries.

"What are you doing?" she asked, hearing his movement.

He struck the match and she flinched away from the light. "Let me see your arm." She held out a mostly severed sleeve which had him swearing before he caught sight of the five-inch slash in her soft skin. The cut wasn't too deep but blood still seeped in spots.

"That needs to be bandaged." He shook out the match and went to retrieve her pack from her horse. Star stood just a few feet away, grazing on patches of tall grass. He removed her pack and found all he needed. She looked up as he knelt before her and he saw exhaustion clear in every line of her face.

"Let me patch you up," he said, reaching for the belt at her waist.

She didn't resist as he removed her belt and then her buckskin shirt. He cut away the sleeve of the cotton shirt beneath. Once he rinsed the long cut and wound a strip of clean cloth around it, he pulled another soft buckskin tunic over her head.

"We've about gone through your winter supply of hand towels, haven't we?"

Her lips shifted slightly as she shoved her arms into the sleeves. She sniffed then wiped at her cheeks.

"I'm sorry, Magpie," Garret said, sitting behind her. "I should have been checking you for injuries before now."

"I'm not crying because of that little cut."

He pulled her into his arms and felt a rush of relief as she relaxed against him. "I'd say you're entitled to some tears. Your own brother just tried to kill you."

She drew a shuddered breath. "Some things just never change." She moved closer, leaning up to kiss his jaw. "Thank you," she said, so softly he barely heard the words spoken against his skin.

"For what?"

"Coming for me."

He stroked her back softly, wishing he knew the right words to ease the grief he heard in her voice. "Nothing could have kept me away. You never should have gone there alone."

She looked up, her eyes searching his. "I've always been alone."

"You're not alone anymore, Maggie."

He touched her chin. She leaned up to meet his light kiss. Maggie hugged him tight and Garret counted his blessings.

She was safe. *For now.*

"We have two choices, sweetheart. We can make camp or ride through the dark for a few more hours. Either way it will be late afternoon before we reach the ranch. Your call, honey."

She melded against him. "Five more minutes and I'll be asleep in your arms."

"Then we'll make camp."

He stood, taking away her warmth. "Wait here."

"Garret?" Maggie looked up to find him gone, his retreating shadow leading their horses farther away.

As much as she wanted to curl up on the ground and fall asleep, images of Nathan's angry glare kept her eyes open.

You're not alone anymore, Maggie.

He'd come for her.

Garret returned a short time later and fanned a blanket over the ground beside her. "I left the horses saddled," he said as he sat down, using her canvas pack propped behind him for support. "Com'ere," he said, opening his arms.

That was all it took for her to go to him, to let him guide her down between his raised knees and lean her back against the warm support of his chest. He fanned a second blanket over her as she snuggled against him.

"Here," he said, holding up a long strip of dried venison.

Realizing she was hungry, she took the dried meat.

"We can't risk a fire tonight." He set a canteen on the ground beside them.

Completely drained of energy, she leaned into him as she chewed on the tough meat. They ate in silence, nothing stirring but a cool breeze. His lips intermittently brushed her hair as his hand gently caressed her back, melting away her anxiety.

"How's your shoulder?" she asked as her eyes began to droop.

"Just fine. How's yours?"

She smiled. "Fine."

"What were you thinking, Magpie?" The gruffness of his voice told her he'd soothed her anxiety while holding on to his own.

"That Nathan needed to pay for what he did."

"You should have told me."

She turned to look at him. "This is my fight."

"*Our* fight. We'll find a way to beat him together. One that keeps us both from hanging."

"It would have been worth it. He'll be after your ranch now."

"Magpie." He brushed his lips over hers. "I would *never* choose my ranch over your life. I'll walk away from my business before I see you come to harm. You have to know I care about you."

"*And I care about you,*" she said, leaning back against him. "Fighting for something you care about is never in vain. You taught me that."

Garret shook his head, flattered and infuriated by her reasoning. He closed his arms around her middle and brushed his lips over the shell of her ear.

"I'm the reason he attacked you, the reason your partner was killed."

"You didn't kill Duce. You weren't the one who sent henchmen to my ranch. I'm not going to let anything happen to you."

She shifted, her cheek resting on his chest as her arms slid around him, and Garret thanked God he held her, safe and unharmed.

"Rest. I'll keep watch."

Just when he thought she'd fallen asleep her whispered voice broke the silence.

"We didn't get him, Garret."

"We will," he said, his arms tightening around her.

Chapter Sixteen

A gray sky loomed overhead as thirty-seven men gathered around the double grave site. Most of them ranch hands and cowpokes Nathan had never met, he couldn't have named five of them if his life depended on it. He stared at their downcast faces in a kind of wonder as words of a eulogy droned in his ears.

He knew their ranch had expanded considerably, but he had no idea just how many men he employed. Gideon had handled all the ranching particulars. Outside his personal security consisting of Gideon's gang, he'd never given the rest of them much thought. They'd be looking to him to give orders now.

A strain of panic flared inside him. He *needed* Gideon. It had been a mistake to allow someone to become so integrated in his life.

The men beside him stepped forward and Nathan watched as the five remaining men of Gideon's gang lowered his casket into the ground—the only men he had entrusted with Nathan's safety. The moment they stepped back, others from the cattle crews began filling in the wide grave. As he watched dirt spatter onto the wood casket grief and rage clawed at the numbing cloak that had settled over him as he had watched Gideon breathe his last. Even as death had encroached on him, his blood spilling through Nathan's fingers, Gideon's first thought was to protect him as he pressed his revolver into his palm. *"Damn it, Nate, take cover."*

Nathan tucked his hands into his coat pockets, his right hand sliding over the gun. His eyes felt hot as a fist seemed to squeeze his lungs. Not about to disgrace his memory by showing a shred of weakness, he turned away and strode to the house.

"Mayor Strafford?"

He glanced back. One of the cowhands hurried toward him. Gideon's posse closed in fast behind him. They hadn't shrugged their duty simply because their leader was laid into the ground.

The cowhand stopped before him and tugged on the brown hat he'd been holding.

"What can I do for you, Mr....?"

"Rawlings. Jim Rawlings."

Jim Rawlings glanced side to side as Gideon's men encircled them.

"Gentlemen," he said, his unease revealed in his tense expression. "Real shame what happened to Smith and Cabot."

"It was," Nathan agreed.

"I figure you'll be needin' a new foreman to manage the crews straight away and I've been workin' with cattle my whole life."

"Is that a fact?" Jim Rawling's *whole life* couldn't equate to a full twenty-five years. "You think you have what it takes to run this place?"

"I do. Ain't nothin' I don't know about managing stock and I got experience with rough ridin'. Spent some time working jobs with a gang down south, if you know what I mean."

"Yes, I believe I do." The man was a braggart, which meant he likely lacked skill. "I see you wear a Colt .44." Nathan held his hand out. "May I?"

"Well, sure." Like the young fool Rawlings was, he passed over his firearm. "It's a fine revolver. Seen me through a lot of trouble."

Nathan closed his hand over the grip and tested the weight of the gun. He glanced at the men beside him and noted their slightly amused expressions.

"Smith preferred a .45 Schofield Smith & Wesson. I bet he has two dozen in the house." He knocked open the carriage, glimpsing a full round. "Impress me, Mr. Rawlings. Who, exactly, were the notable rough riders *under your command?*"

"Well, sir, I rode with—"

"You *rode with?* Did you lead or did you follow, Mr. Rawlings?"

"I held my own," he said, squaring his shoulders, his young features firming.

"Either you lead or you follow, Mr. Rawlings, or you have no loyalty. These men rode for Smith. Smith did a hell of a lot more than simply *hold his own*. He demanded respect and loyalty. Now I'm curious, how does an unarmed man who claims to merely hold his own expect to run my ranch and evoke such loyalty in his men?"

"Well, I—"

"What do you say, boys?" Nathan glanced at the men standing at his side. "You think Mr. Rawlings here can take the place of Smith?" Rage put a tremble on Gideon's last name.

"No, sir," his men answered, their narrowed gazes fixed on Rawlings.

Nathan looked back at the man who dared to compare himself to Gideon as dirt was being shoveled over his grave. "Guess that's a no," he said, watching his eyes round as he raised his gun and emptied the chamber into Rawlings's chest. The blasts echoed across the silent plains as Rawlings fell, dead before he hit the ground.

Nathan tossed the gun onto his bloody shirt and glanced at the wide-eyed crowd watching from a short distance. "Anyone else interested in being my foreman?"

"No, sir," came a chorus of low mumbles.

He glanced at the men beside him. "Bury him down by the river and get the sheriff out here. We've got murderers and rustlers to round up."

He turned back to the house and didn't slow his stride until he was inside.

"Señor Strafford?" His maid approached with a silver tray holding his breakfast.

"Not now." The moment he shut the study doors, the heavy scent of cigar smoke swirled around him, and a pain like he'd never known gripped his chest. His legs buckled. His knees hit the floor as his vision blurred. He tried to drag in a breath as grief ripped at his lungs. He crumpled forward, pressing his hands to the flood of tears scalding his face.

She'll pay for this. He'd see the both of them *dead!*

Chapter Seventeen

He wasn't about to wake her. The sheer wonder that Maggie had slept soundly so far past sunrise was testimony of her exhaustion.

After easing away from her and tucking her into the warmth of the blankets, Garret had prepared and eaten a small breakfast. He sat by the low fire, still trying to fight the images of Maggie held at knifepoint from his mind.

She sat bolt upright in a tangle of blankets and appeared disoriented.

"Magpie?"

She didn't look at him. Her complexion pale, her expression tense, she glanced to one side and then the other.

Something was wrong.

"Honey, what's—"

She threw off the blankets and darted into the woods.

What the hell? Garret lunged up and chased after her.

When he caught up to her she stood leaning forward, her hand on her knees.

"Maggie—"

"I'm okay," she said in a pant. "Just…go."

Go? His heart was about to thump clean out of his chest. "What can I—"

She leaned over and retched into the shrubs. He stepped close and she waved him off. "Go on. I'll be fine in a minute."

Garret went back to camp and wet a bandana. When he returned she was reclined against a tree, her hand on her stomach. Her slow, deep breaths suggested she was still fighting the nausea.

"Here," he said, holding out the bandana.

"Thanks." She held the wet cloth to her face. "I don't usually get sick this early."

This early? "It's midmorning."

She looked up, seeming shocked by the sun's high position in the overcast sky.

Garret's mind flashed with the two times in the past few days he'd seen her sick to her stomach.

She sighed and leaned back against the tree as she shut her eyes.

"You gonna be sick again?"

She shook her head. "It'll pass. Just a nervous stomach."

A nervous stomach? Last night she'd had reason to be nervous aplenty but she hadn't gotten sick. He only knew one ailment that caused a woman to be sick in the morning.

"Holy hell," he muttered beneath his breath. Was she hiding a pregnancy from him, as well?

She wiped her face with the cloth again and straightened as she drew a deep breath. Her cheeks began to take on some color. "Thanks."

Garret moved beside her and pressed his lips to her hair. After fighting last night, he wasn't ready to start another just yet.

"There's hot water on the fire," he said as they walked

into the small clearing. "I wasn't about to toss in herbs and have us both knocked out."

She grinned up at him as she set to the task. "You've been up for a while," she said, glancing at the skillet. "Why didn't you wake me?"

"You needed sleep." Garret settled beside her as she steeped her tea. "I fried up some of your venison and potatoes. Don't suppose you feel up to eating?"

"I'm starving."

Garret served her what was left in the skillet. She dug right in, not the least bit hampered by the queasy stomach that had her doubled over not ten minutes ago.

She polished off her breakfast in minutes, but her gaze remained fixed on the low fire, her thoughts having taken her miles away.

Garret took her plate. "What are you thinking about, Magpie?" he asked as he stood and began packing up the rest of their supplies.

Her frown deepened before she looked up at him. "Nathan told me he killed my father."

"You didn't know that?" Garret asked, surprised.

"No. When I woke they told me he'd had heart failure. When Nathan found his will and saw provisions had been made for my dowry and to send me away to an expensive school, and he went crazy. He chased me down and started beating me. Our staff was there, but no one would help me. They just stood there...*watching*."

"Different folks have different reactions to fear. I've seen a lot of men freeze up and even die when they couldn't react to what was happening around them. Or maybe your brother wasn't working alone. How did you get away from him?"

"He got winded and I ran for the woods. He came after me."

"That's when Ira found you?"

"Nathan had knocked me to the ground and Ira…he just appeared. I was so scared. For days I thought someone would come after me. But they didn't. Nobody looked for me."

"Your father wasn't the only one to die that day."

"What do you mean?"

"My attorney showed me a newspaper clipping about your father's death. Seven people died that day. *Six* actually. According to Nathan's accounts there was an Indian raid and he returned home to find everyone slaughtered."

Maggie shook her head. "No."

"I reckon he made sure there was no one left to oppose his claims of how he came into his full inheritance. I would imagine he had people in that house who sided with him."

Everything packed, he went to Maggie and held his hand out to help her up.

"He killed them because of me?" she said as she stood.

"No." He pulled her close. "He killed them because he has no value for anyone's life above his own. This sure explains why he's put so much effort into finding you. Murdering his family would be a hell of a thing to come to light if he's counting on a seat in the senate once Wyoming's granted statehood."

"He's going to be after both of us now."

The fear and regret in her eyes tore at his heart. The reminder that she'd gone to face him alone had him tightening his hold on her. "Fine by me. Because I'm going to be after him."

He released her and picked up the supplies. As they

reached the horses he shifted the pack into place behind her saddle and Maggie began tying them down.

"You still feeling okay?" he asked.

"Yeah. Especially since I ate."

"How long have you been having an upset stomach like that?"

"Just since leaving my cabin again."

"A week?"

She gave him a questioning glance. "I guess."

"And only in the morning?"

She secured a knot in the rope and seemed to ponder the question. "Yeah."

"Have you thought something other than nerves might be upsetting your stomach?"

"Like what?" Finished with her task, she stepped back, her blue eyes wide with curiosity as she gazed up at him. She wasn't hiding anything from him—she didn't have a clue.

"Like, maybe you're *with child?*"

She reared back, her expression creased as though he'd cursed at her. "I'm pretty sure my belly would swell up instead of turning inside out."

"Takes about four months before you'd see any signs in your belly."

"Oh. Then why would you think—?"

"You've been sick every morning for a week. Have you had your monthly since we were up at your place?"

Her mouth dropped open. Color flamed into her cheeks as she stared at him and Garret realized that was likely a personal sort of question—no more personal than the woman he loved carrying his child.

"Maggie?"

She shook her head. "I haven't. I thought…that maybe…"

"You're pregnant."

Maggie felt as though the breath had been knocked from her. She never once guessed… "I can't be." She'd accepted long ago that hers was no kind of life to offer a child.

Oh God. "I can't have a baby."

"Here," he said, pressing the reins of her horse into her hand. "You're coming back to the ranch with me."

"Garret, *I can't.*" She'd had enough years behind her to realize her longing for a baby had been selfish and immature. She'd long since given up all hope.

"You're obviously not thinking clearly. I'm not about to let you ride off alone, sweetheart."

"I've caused you so much trouble already."

"Hey," he said, the slide of fingers over her cheek capturing her attention. "You aren't to blame for the actions of your brother. I'm glad to know you, Maggie. I want to marry you."

"I wouldn't be a good wife, Garret. Or mother."

"Guess I don't want a good wife. I want *you,* Magpie, the woman of my dreams. And I know firsthand that it doesn't take a dress or any fancy manners to make a fine mother. You're the finest woman I know. So get used to the idea."

Her heart clenched at his description. She touched a hand to her belly, shock staggering her mind as the realization took hold. *A child.* Garret's child. Her heart didn't hold a deeper desire than to be loved by him, to love him in return.

That she now had so much to lose horrified her. She'd once lost all she loved—she wouldn't survive losing Garret, the promise of the life he'd just described for her.

"He wants you dead, Maggie. That part's clear enough. I'm not leaving you alone. You're coming home with me."

"Okay."

Her easy acceptance surprised Garret. The bleakness in her eyes as she looked into the distance sent a cold wave of dread crashing through him. He knew, too well, the expression of a woman trapped in a fate she didn't want.

The sun neared the western rim of mountains by the time they reached a high point on the riverbank near his ranch. Even at a good distance, Maggie could see there were an unusual number of horses in the yard.

She reached into her saddlebag and pulled out her brass scope. "Here," she said, holding it out to Garret. "Be careful of the sun's position. It can reflect off the lens."

"I am aware," he said, his lips slightly tilted as he looked through the telescope toward his ranch. "The sheriff."

"And Nathan," she said, knowing by the chill in her skin he was among those gathered in the cluster.

"And Nathan," he agreed. "I want you to stay here. I'll circle around before I ride in to see what's what. If—"

"*No.* You said we'd stay *together.*"

"I'll come for you. If I'm arrested, you go to my sister's—"

"They could hang you, Garret!"

"Not with a dozen witnesses on my ranch. Worst Bartley will do is arrest me."

"And then they'll hang you!" she whispered harshly. "That's what they do to rustlers—no questions asked, drop-you-from-a-tree *hangings!*"

"I've known Sheriff Bartley for ten years—"

"I've known Nathan my whole life—what the hell difference does that make!"

"Nathan brought the sheriff out here because he's trying to win and save face as mayor. Could be Bartley just wants my statement on what happened. *You* have a dead-or-alive bounty on your head. Promise me you'll stay here or head on to my sister's. Either way, I'll come for you."

"If anything happened to you, I'd never forgive myself."

"*Trust me,* Maggie."

"It's *them* I don't trust. I'm staying right here and keeping my sights on any man who's near you. So long as no guns are drawn and no ropes aimed for your neck, I won't pull the trigger. That's my promise. I'll wait here until they leave."

"And if I'm arrested, you'll go to my sister's."

If he was arrested that would mean Nathan had him. "I don't want you to go," she admitted, fear shaking her voice.

"Strafford is not going to just go away and I won't have you anywhere near him. I need to know you'll be safe. Think of our baby—"

"Don't say that!" she whispered harshly. She rushed forward and closed her arms around his waist. He didn't hesitate to pull her close. "I'm too afraid to hope," she whispered, her cheek against the warmth of his neck.

"I'm not leaving you, Maggie," he assured her, hugging her tight. "If he intended a quick kill, he wouldn't have brought the sheriff." He eased back until she looked up at him. "Let me protect you."

"I'll keep watch."

"And?"

"If I have to…I'll go to the Morgans."

He kissed her lips. "Wait for me to come for you."

Maggie rode toward a massive two-story farmhouse more than twice the size of Garret's Victorian home. The sun nearly set, light glowed from the many windows. Her gaze moved over a vast expanse of horse corrals. A few men in the yard watched her approach.

I'm trusting him, she reminded herself. It had taken all her restraint to keep from opening fire as the sheriff of Bitterroot had arrested Garret, cuffing his wrists while her brother had stood an arm's length away. Garret's men outnumbered Nathan's two to one. All of them had set off for Bitterroot.

She reined in before a wide porch and dismounted. Sucking in a deep breath, she ascended the steps. A hum of conversation from inside carried through the rough-wood walls.

I'm keeping my promise. She'd only promised to come here—she hadn't promised to stay. If she had any other options to help Garret she'd have used them. She wanted him back. The Morgans would know what to do.

She rapped on the door.

The noise inside seemed to increase before the door opened, a boy appearing in the narrow gap. His white wavy hair caught Maggie off guard. Skylar and Tucker's son. Around ten years old and about her height, he was the spitting image of Garret but for his deep green eyes.

"Evening, ma'am," he said.

"Is Chance here?"

"Yes, ma'am." He turned and shouted, "Uncle Chance!"

"Right here, Josh," his approaching uncle said from behind the door. "No need to shout the house down."

Chance stepped into view, his eyes widening at the sight of her.

"Maggie."

She stared at the pink-cheeked infant tucked into the crook of his arm. Cora's baby, she recalled. And Chance's, and yet the tiny bundle held so gently against his chest didn't fit her image of Chance. No more than she could envision herself with such a delicate bundle.

Oh God. It had been too many years since she'd entertained any such notions—to do so now terrified her.

"Well, come on in," he said, opening the door wide as he stepped back. "Isn't Garret with you?" he asked, looking past her.

"No," she said, her gaze falling on the source of all the clatter and chatter. A roomful of children sat at a long dining room table just beyond the foyer. An array of blond braids and orange curls, little girls of varying ages surrounded the table. She'd never seen the like. The room quieted as so many little faces and wide, curious eyes looked in her direction.

Have I told you that I have eight nieces? They've taken great pride in teaching their uncle the finer points of tea parties and needlepoint.

Tears threatened at the memory.

"Maggie?"

Her gaze snapped up to Chance still waiting at the open door. Reluctantly she stepped inside to a welcoming warmth and the scent of baked chicken.

"What's happened?" Chance asked.

"It's Garret," she said, glancing briefly at Garret's nephew standing beside him. Surely she couldn't say what needed to be said before a roomful of young children.

Skylar stepped through a doorway on the far side of the dining room. *"Maggie?"* She seemed to see her distress. Lifting the hem of her full skirt she hurried toward them. "Girls, finish up," she said as she passed the table.

"Who's Maggie, Mama?" one of them asked.

"A friend of Uncle Garret's." She offered a slight smile. "Is everything all right?" she asked softly, looking from Chance to her.

Maggie could only shake her head.

"Joshua, run down to Zeke's house and tell Mr. Patterson our guest has arrived and he's to come at once."

"Yes, Mama." The boy darted past her and out the door.

Chance put a hand on her shoulder. "Let's go have a seat in the front room."

He stayed beside her as they moved into the room on the left. Fire crackled in a stone fireplace covering the high wall at the end of the great room. Chance motioned to one of the leather-padded chairs and sat in the one beside her.

"What's going on?" Tucker asked, his boots coming into view first as he descended from the top of the stairs.

"Maggie's just arrived," said Skylar.

As Tucker stepped beside his wife, Cora came in from the dining room, wiping her hands on her apron. Unlike the first time she'd met Chance's wife when she'd been in tatters and on the run, her auburn hair was swept up in a tidy bun, her burgundy dress spotless.

"Maggie," she said. "Is everything all right?"

"Garret's been arrested." She glanced at all four of their shocked expressions, noting that whereas Chance and Tucker were truly identical, their wives didn't share a single similar feature. Cora was short and rounded, her skin pale against her dark auburn hair. Skylar, tall and thin, had a tanned complexion and light hair. "He told me to come here, to tell you."

"Arrested for what?" demanded Tucker. "By who?"

"For cattle rustling and murder most likely. *It's my fault,*" she said. All the trouble that had befallen him was because of her. "He followed me to Nathan's ranch last night."

"Nathan Strafford?" asked Chance.

"He's my brother. I meant to kill him."

"Did you?"

She shook her head. She'd let him distract her with memories of the past. "Garret showed up and he shot the two men trying to hold me. When we got back to his ranch this evening Nathan was waiting with the sheriff. Garret wouldn't let me go with him. He said to come here and tell you."

"Who all rode out with Garret?" asked Chance.

"Everyone on the ranch, as well as Nathan and six of his men."

Skylar turned her wide eyes on Tucker.

"I'll go pack my saddlebag and head out now," he said. "Chance, you'll stay and see what Patterson has to say about all this?"

"We'll meet you in Bitterroot," he agreed.

Skylar followed her husband up the stairs.

"Don't worry," Chance said to Maggie. "His crew will stay with him."

"I'll put the girls to bed," said Cora. "Maggie, can I get you some tea or coffee?"

"Tea. Thank you."

Cora hurried back to the noisy dining room. "Everyone into the kitchen," she said. "One cookie before bed."

The chatter of happy children rose up and then faded as they moved into the other room. Maggie looked at Chance who watched her silently from the chair beside her. Her gaze strayed to his infant son cradled in his arms and the ache in her chest became unbearable.

"I'm sorry to have interrupted your supper," she said, struggling to maintain some composure.

"You haven't. We were expecting Garret and fed the

children early so that he could have a quiet meeting with Patterson."

She couldn't look away from the sleeping baby, his rosy cheeks and soft tufts of blond hair...so tiny and perfect. She didn't know the first thing about tending babies.

"Callie Mae," Cora's voice called from upstairs, "you get back into this room."

The patter of footsteps and giggles filtered down from the stairwell.

"You certainly have a brood."

Chance laughed. "Yeah. You won't find a quiet moment in this house until bedtime—and even then we have our share of noisy moments. How are you doing, Maggie?"

"I'm worried."

The front door opened. Joshua stepped inside followed by a man in a dark suit. His face lit with a smile at the sight of her.

"Miss Strafford!" He rushed toward her, extending his hand.

Maggie surged up.

Chance stepped forward, intercepting his exuberant greeting. "Patterson. Why don't you have a seat? *Over there.*" He motioned to a sofa on the other side of a low table.

"Oh. Yes, of course," he said.

Maggie sat down as Patterson sat across from them.

"I had hoped to have a chance to speak with you, Miss Strafford."

"Call me Maggie."

"Maggie," he corrected. "Is Mr. Daines here?"

"He's been arrested," said Chance, and proceeded to fill him in on all that Maggie had told them. By the time he'd finished and Patterson had shuffled through some folders,

Cora and Skylar had joined them. Cora took her infant to a chair near the fire while Skylar sat on the sofa beside Garret's attorney.

"Do you know who exactly arrested him?" Patterson asked.

"Garret called him Sheriff Bartley," Maggie said, sipping a strong, bland tea.

"Sheriff of Bitterroot Springs," Chance confirmed.

"That is unfortunate. Any proceedings held in Bitterroot will most certainly be slighted to Nathan Strafford's favor."

"You can't help him?" Maggie asked.

"I'll do all I can. Knowing that Nathan Strafford is working outside the law makes that job more difficult. Especially when I can't find any evidence to use against him."

"I know where he's grazing his stolen stock. Is that evidence?"

Patterson smiled. "It is. Though I'm not sure the good it can do. If his judge is working for Nathan it may not be enough. He can order those claims be verified and stock can be moved. What could help us the most would be to tear down the credibility of Mayor Strafford's character. Presently he's being hailed a Good Samaritan of the people, a man victimized who overcame tragedy after his family was brutally murdered by savages."

"*Lies,*" she said. "Nathan is the savage! He killed our father and then found out his will was not written as he'd assumed. My father had made provisions for me and rather than carry out those provisions Nathan tried to kill me. He would have if I hadn't been rescued by Ira Danvers."

"That's how you came to be with Ira?" Chance asked. "I didn't know."

"Of course you didn't know. It's not your business. I

didn't come here to talk about my past. I came here to *help Garret.*"

"I believe it is your past that can be of most use to him," said Patterson. "Would you be willing to repeat what you just told us in a courtroom?"

"Hold on." Chance leaned forward, splaying his hands wide. "She's not going into Bitterroot."

"She is the best option we have for destroying Strafford's credibility."

"We take her into town and Garret will have our heads. They have a five-hundred-dollar bounty on her, *dead or alive.*"

"I'll go," she said. "Whatever it takes to clear Garret's name."

"I won't mislead you. With Nathan Strafford controlling the justice system in that town, we aren't up against the best odds."

"Do we even know that the charges will go to trial?" asked Skylar.

"I was in Bitterroot Springs earlier this week," said Patterson. "Those folks are anxious to set their new judge to work. If word spreads that Garret Daines has been apprehended as the cattle rustler who's been plaguing their ranchers, they'll want to see some quick justice."

"Then they should hang Nathan," Maggie snapped.

"If we can't count on a fair judge, we might be able to convince the people. If we get a big enough crowd, they can oftentimes sway the verdict."

A big enough crowd? A chill snaked through her at the thought of going before any size crowd. Townsfolk tended to greet her with apprehension and scorn. She hadn't forgotten the angry rumble of the mob filling the alleyway on her last visit to Bitterroot—or Garret standing between them, shielding her, a woman he didn't know beyond the rumors of Mad Mag. Her heart broke when she thought of all the hardship he'd endured all because he had dared to defend her.

"It's settled," she said. "I'll go."

"Garret wouldn't want us to put her at such risk," Chance insisted. "She can tell me the location of the cattle and I'll testify."

Patterson shook his head. "Maggie is the evidence we need to prove Strafford is a murderer as well as a thief. Our best defense is going to be destroying his character."

"And what if they don't believe her? It will be her word against his. He's the town hero and Maggie's…not known for her sweet and gentle nature."

She nearly grinned, his description far too kind for what folks really thought of her. "I'll take that chance," she said.

"Garret sent her here to keep her out of this, not thrust her on center stage!"

"He said we'd find a solution together. I'm not afraid to face Nathan. I'm afraid of what could happen if I don't."

"They'll arrest you the moment you step foot in that town," Chance argued. "They've got wanted posters for Mad Mag on every street corner."

"I'll turn myself in before I'll see Garret hang!"

"That won't be necessary."

Cora's voice drew everyone's gaze to the rocking chair closest to the fireplace. She stared at Maggie as she patted the bundle on her shoulder. "You said *Mad Mag* is wanted, right?"

"Yeah," said Chance.

"Well, we're not talking about Mad Mag. We're talking about Margaret Strafford."

"What do you mean?" asked Maggie.

"I don't like it." Chance shook his head.

"I think it's brilliant." Skylar's eyes sparkled as she smiled. "Folks in Bitterroot Springs have never met Margaret Grace Strafford."

"I believe it's time they did," Cora said as she stood.

Both women stalked toward her, and Maggie suddenly felt like an animal caught in a snare.

Chapter Eighteen

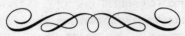

"Let's go, Daines." Sheriff Bartley stood on the other side of the cell door, handcuffs in hand. He didn't look eager to open the cell. "Clint, you better stand down."

Sitting on a cot against the wall, Garret's foreman gave the sheriff a puzzled glance. "The glare off that badge must be blinding you. I haven't moved." The night before he'd blackened the sheriff's eye for accusing his crew of being rustlers, earning himself the neighboring cot. "Stupid and blind as you've become, it's a good thing you don't work on the Lazy J no more. I'd have fired your sorry hide."

"Put your gun on him," Bartley said to his deputy.

Garret laughed and got to his feet as Clint shook his head in disgust.

"Stick your hands through the bars," he instructed as Garret stepped up to the door.

"Damn, Bartley," he said, holding out his wrists so he could slap the metal bands on them. "Why in hell are you acting like I'm some crazed criminal?"

"'Cause he's stupid and blind," Clint said from behind him.

"You murdered two men," said Bartley.

"While defending my woman!"

"You and Mad Mag? Hell, Garret. Even I don't believe that. Even if she *was* Strafford's sister. You bes' come up with a better story 'fore you go in front of that judge."

Bartley ushered him toward the door leading to the main room of the sheriff's office.

"Where are we going?"

"Judge is ready to see you."

Garret stopped just before the door. "They can't make me go to trial before my attorney arrives."

"They sure can. Lucky for you, your fancy attorney rode in a short while ago. Don't know the good it will do ya. Heard the judge sayin' that a man who needs a lawyer has somethin' to hide."

"Whose side are you on?" The moment he stepped into the office he got his answer. Strafford and two of his men stood among eight of Garret's ranch hands.

"Mayor Strafford," Bartley said in a cheerful tone.

Kuhana and Mitch stood at the center of the room as though they'd been blocking Strafford's advance.

"Sheriff Bartley, once you clear out this garbage, I want a posse assembled to hunt down Mad Mag. She's a danger to my good citizens."

"Yes, sir, Mayor Strafford," Bartley said.

"Unless Mr. Daines would be so kind as to reveal her location right now. If he's innocent of rustling, he should be willing to turn in Mad Mag."

"I don't know a woman by any such name," he said. "Maybe I should ask your *sister.*"

"We all know who Mad Mag is," Bartley snapped impatiently.

"You feel it, don't you, Strafford?" Garret said as he stepped beside him. "The sins of your past catching up with you?"

"You're going to hang," Strafford said with dark certainty. "With any luck you'll live just long enough for me to find her."

"Mayor Strafford, if you'll kindly step aside, we're on our way out."

"Certainly. I'll see you in the courthouse." Strafford and his cronies walked outside and Garret glared at Bartley.

"So that's how it is? I can't believe I didn't see it sooner."

"See what?"

"The imprint of Strafford's back pocket across your face."

"I'm just doin' my job."

"The hell you are. It ain't a wonder you haven't caught any rustlers. Take me to my attorney so we can get this over with."

"You hear that?" Everett said when they stepped outside. Sounded like a swarm of bees. The steady buzz grew louder as they walked along the boardwalk. Reaching the end of the block, Bartley swore beneath his breath.

It looked as though every citizen of Bitterroot Springs swarmed around the small courthouse, making the white building look more like a circus big top. As they caught sight of them the hum of conversation became angry shouts.

"There he is!"

"The cattle rustler!"

"Traitor!"

The deputies and ranch hands closed in around Garret and pushed into the scrum of people.

"Let us through," Bartley shouted. "Courthouse won't open until one o'clock."

Shouts and jeers followed them up the steps.

"This is not good," Kuhana said from behind him.

Bartley banged on one of the double doors. "It's the sheriff. Let us in."

A gray-haired man looked out, then opened the door for them. The men at the back of their group were quick to shut out the noise and mayhem.

"It's crazy out there," said one of the deputies.

"First trial in the new courthouse," the older man said.

Everett stepped beside Garret. "Looks like a church, don't it?"

Rows of chairs on each side of the room led up to what did look to be an oversize pulpit. The room reeked of fresh paint.

"Sure does," he agreed.

Bartley and his deputies led them to the room to the left of the judge's podium. He opened the door so Garret could pass through and said, "The rest of you can wait out here."

"You can wait out there, as well," Patterson said, greeting them in the doorway. "I need time to confer with my client."

"I'll be right outside the door."

Garret moved into the small office and spotted his sister in her Sunday best beside Tucker. Chance held the arm of a woman bound in a shiny royal-blue gown and topped with a fancy black-feathered hat. Half Cora's size, she wasn't his wife.

"Lucky for us they kept him handcuffed," said Chance.

Garret tensed. The woman in blue pushed back the black mesh on her hat, and Garret stopped breathing.

Maggie.

"Get her out of here!"

"Calm down," said Skylar.

"I told you," Chance muttered.

"I trusted you!" he shouted at Chance.

"This was your attorney's idea!"

Garret turned his glare on Patterson. *"You're fired."*

"Garret, we've—"

"Strafford just told Bartley to assemble a posse to hunt her down and you *bring her here!*"

"I'm here of my own volition," Maggie said as she stormed toward him.

"He's in the next building."

"We just walked right past him and he didn't recognize her," said Skylar.

Holy hell.

"Everyone thinks she's my wife," Chance informed him. "Cora Mae's never been to Bitterroot Springs."

"I'm here to help you," Maggie said.

"I won't risk your life."

"I won't have one without you!"

"She's not going into that courtroom," he shouted to his attorney.

Maggie's hands on his chest stopped his protest. The sheen in her eyes took the fight out of him. Her gloved fingers fisted his shirt, tugging him toward her.

"I'm glad to see you," she whispered.

He lifted his cuffed hands and she stepped close, banding her arms around his waist as his arms encircled her. Holding her didn't ease the panic raging inside him.

"I don't want you to become part of this trial."

"Lots of things happen in life we don't want," she said, looking up at him. "You told me we'd face Nathan *together.* That's what we're going to do."

He looked to the men standing behind her, frantic for backup.

"Don't look at me," said Chance. "I was up against three strong-minded women and your slick-talking attorney."

"She has every right to be here," said Patterson. "And we need you on board with our defense."

"I'm paying *you* to defend me."

"I *am* defending you. But I'm not a magician! You've admitted to going onto Mayor Strafford's ranch and shooting his men. You say Maggie was in danger, they say she's your accomplice. He says you were trying to steal his cattle and this town is eager to hang a cattle thief. Were we merely talking about missing cattle, Maggie's testimony wouldn't do more than earn a double hanging. This is why our defense is not to defend your actions, but to expose the truth behind Nathan Strafford's and that lies in your lady's testimony."

His lady wasn't fond of crowds and she hadn't eased her hold on his waist. Her tight embrace told him she was terrified, a fear that didn't show through the determination burning in her eyes.

"I'm doing this, Garret. I want them to see him for what he really is."

"If he recognizes you—"

"Haven't you noticed? *I'm wearing a dress.*"

Despite the tension eating a hole through his spine, he grinned. "I noticed. You look beautiful." He touched his lips to hers. "You look beautiful no matter what you wear."

She leaned up, whispering into his ear. "I didn't tell them I'm wearing buckskins and a blade underneath."

He laughed and pulled her closer. "That's my girl."

The door thumped behind Tucker, jostling his shoulders as he reclined against it.

"Hey!" Sheriff Bartley shouted from the other side.

"Best release her," Chance said in a low voice. "We got 'em convinced she's Cora Mae."

"Are you sure about this?"

She tugged him back to her lips. "You're worth the risk," she whispered, giving him a quick, hard kiss.

Any other time he'd have been elated by such a confession.

She stepped back and he reluctantly lifted his arms.

"If anything goes wrong," Chance said as Bartley pounded on the door, "we'll get her out."

"Not unless I'm dragging you with me," Maggie said to Garret.

"Maggie, promise me—"

"Don't even ask," she said, the steel in her voice telling him she wouldn't be swayed on leaving him.

Tucker stepped aside as the sheriff gave a hard shove and stumbled inside. The murmur of folks packed into a crowded courtroom followed him. His narrowed gaze whipped around the room. "Time's up. Judge wants everyone in the courtroom."

Chance slid his arm around Maggie's shoulders. "Time to take our seat, *darlin',*" he said, and tugged down the veil of her hat to hide her face.

"Don't get pushy," she warned, her gloved hands lifting the hem of her blue skirt.

"Wouldn't dream of it, dearest," he said, ushering her out the door behind Skylar and Tucker. He glanced back at Garret, his hard gaze telling him he'd fight her tooth and nail to get her to a safe place should all hell break loose.

Sheriff Bartley stepped up to him. "You find a better alibi?" he asked.

Even worse. His alibi, dressed in royal-blue, had found him.

* * *

The heat and stagnant air were nearly unbearable. Maggie tried not to fidget beneath the constricting mass of blue taffeta and bulky petticoats. Wedged between the broad shoulders of the Morgans, she felt all but invisible in the massive crowd of nearly a hundred onlookers who'd met Nathan's attorney's depiction of Garret as the mysterious cattle bandit of Bitterroot Springs with an outpour of applause. They had since been fairly silent.

At the front of the room Judge Thornton reclined in his chair, his thick gray eyebrows pinched in a scowl. His threats to issue fines and clear the courtroom upon further interruptions had been taken seriously.

"How can you claim his innocence when he admits to shooting both men dead?" asked the judge.

"Self-defense," said Patterson.

Maggie watched as he looked at Garret.

"They were about to kill an unarmed woman," Garret told him.

"So you claim," the judge replied, his expression unmoved. "The infamous Mad Mag?"

Garret glanced at Patterson who gave a nod. "No, sir," Garret answered. "Her name is Margaret Grace Strafford, the mayor's own sister."

Gasps ricocheted through the room followed by an eruption of conversation.

"I won't have him insulting my family!" Nathan shouted. "You know my sister died years ago," he said to the judge.

The Morgans leaned in, as though to hold her in her seat. She wasn't anxious to stand, and hadn't forgotten Patterson's instructions to wait until he'd called her.

"Quiet down!" Judge Thornton rapped his gavel and waited for the room to settle to a hush of soft whispers. "Mr. Patterson, you'd best confer with your client because I will not tolerate such lies in this courtroom."

"He's not lying," Patterson answered directly.

"I don't know what you're trying to pull," he said, looking at Garret, "but I can attest to the passing of Margaret Strafford. I was a frequent guest in the Strafford household and I attended her funeral."

"You were misled," said Patterson. "We'd like to call our first witness. Margaret Strafford."

Patterson's request was met by a charged silence. Maggie knew Nathan must be searching the room, but she kept her gaze on Judge Thornton. Shocked that he'd attended her funeral, she wondered if she should recognize him? Her father had many guests to the house, both local and from back East. She glanced at the nameplate on his desk, William P. Thornton.

"You ready?" Chance whispered beside her.

She stood, as did both of the Morgans.

"This is an outrage!" Nathan shouted. "Putting that woman in a dress does not make her my sister. Arrest her!"

Chance and Tucker stayed at her sides as she moved into the center aisle. Maggie glanced at Garret as she reached the attorneys' tables. His gaze didn't waver from her brother sitting on the other side.

"Young lady." Judge Thornton's voice boomed over Nathan's protests. "Do you understand that lying in this courtroom is a punishable crime?"

"Yes."

His eyes narrowed as he stared at her.

"Come here."

She stepped forward, the Morgans moving with her.

"Just the lady," the judge instructed.

"Your Honor," said Patterson, "we have obvious concerns for her safety."

"Sheriff, escort the lady to the bench."

Bartley rushed forward, his eyes wide with disbelief as he held his arm out to her.

"I won't stand for this," Nathan raged.

"Mayor Strafford," the judge shouted, "you will sit down."

"That woman is not my sister. Arrest her or I will!"

Ignoring his threat, Judge Thornton leaned forward as she approached him. "What is your name? I'll warn you to think hard on that. I had supper at the Strafford table many times."

William. That was what her father called him. The passing years had aged the dark-haired man she now remembered as a friend of her father's. "I do recall," she said softly. "I believe I ruined one of your white shirts with a slice of cherry pie."

He stared at her a long moment. "My God," he whispered. He slighted a quick glance in her brother's direction, the indifference in his expression hitting Maggie with a fresh wave of fear. Just because he believed her identity didn't mean he wouldn't side with her brother.

"Garret hasn't stolen any cattle," she said in the same hushed tone. "The rustler is Nathan. Just as he killed our father to claim his inheritance, he's been forcing folks off their land and stealing cattle. I know where he hides the stolen stock. I could even draw you a map."

Judge Thornton's gray eyebrows shot up, the first shift in his staunch expression. "And you, where have you been all these years?"

"The mountains."

"Are you the one they call Mad Mag?"

She hesitated, his reaction not giving her any indication how he intended to use all she'd revealed so far. "I am."

"What is she saying?" Nathan shouted. "I won't have lies said about me in my courthouse."

Judge Thornton stood. "This is my courthouse, Mayor Strafford."

Maggie didn't trust herself to look at him.

"You will sit down."

"The hell I will!"

A rash of screams split the air. Garret shouted her name and Maggie looked back. He leapt over the table like a madman. Gunshots exploded as he dived for her.

He slammed her to the floor as several blasts echoed through the room. His palms cradled the back of her head as his body crushed her.

Maggie struggled to catch the breath he'd pounded out of her.

"Are you hurt?" Garret eased back. "Maggie?"

"No," she said in a shallow breath.

He stood, lifting her in the same motion. She glanced in the direction of her brother but couldn't see anything beyond the barrier of Garret's crew and the Morgans.

"Out!" the judge shouted above them. "Everyone out!"

Garret pulled her close and Maggie startled at the sight of blood on his upper arm. "Garret!" She reached for the tear in his jacket. "You were shot?"

"Barely a nick," he said, glancing briefly at the injury.

Nathan had tried to shoot her, and would have if Garret hadn't tackled her.

A sigh broke from his chest as he pulled her close. "You're hard on a man's health, Magpie."

The ranks of men around them having loosened, she

caught a glimpse of the prosecutor's table, and Nathan. He lay facedown over the table, his blood pooling onto the floor.

She shivered and Garret shifted, blocking her view. "I've got you," he whispered, holding her tight. Maggie shut her eyes and tried to absorb the comfort of his embrace.

"I had to shoot him," Sheriff Bartley said to the judge. "He wouldn't drop the gun."

"Take Daines back to the jailhouse," Judge Thornton instructed. "We'll take statements later."

Maggie tightened her arms around his waist as Sheriff Bartley moved toward them.

"I'm not leaving Maggie out in the open," Garret protested. "He's had a group of hired guns after her!"

"I will not allow Miss Strafford to come to further harm. She can wait under guard in my chambers."

"Not unless my sister and brother-in-law accompany her."

The judge stepped down from his high seat, his gaze hard on Garret's as he approached them.

"Very well. If you will unhand her, the Morgans and the deputies will escort her safely to my chambers."

She stepped back, feeling his reluctance to let her go.

"Why not just set Garret free?" asked Skylar.

"Proclaim him innocent and we'll leave," Chance said from beside her.

"This is my court, Mr. Morgan. I don't give rulings while blood is dripping on my floor! Garret Daines will remain in custody until I say otherwise! Sheriff, get him locked up *now.*"

Garret released her, his eyes dark with worry.

"I'll be all right," she said.

It had been hours since the judge had asked her to draw the map of the canyons and had left with the sheriff and his band of deputized citizens to investigate her claims. Maggie slumped in the overstuffed chair behind his desk while Skylar sat with Tucker and Chance near a small fireplace on the other side of the room. She didn't feel up to being social or eating the meal a deputy had brought over for them. Just like the night spent in the Morgan house, she felt caged in. She wanted *out*.

A high window revealed a patch of blue sky. She wasn't going to spend another night in forced confinement.

"Mag?" Chance moved to sit on the edge of the desk. He glanced at the untouched food on her plate. "You feeling okay?"

Movement at the door saved her from another awkward conversation. She straightened as Judge Thornton walked in.

Garret didn't follow, delivering a sharp sting of disappointment.

"Sorry for the long wait," he said. "We rode out to Strafford's place and sent men to the locations you'd specified."

"Did you find the cattle?" she asked.

"We did."

"So the charges against Garret have been dropped?"

"They have."

She surged up and moved past Chance. "We can go?"

"Not just yet."

Maggie bristled.

"Your brother's death has left a few unresolved issues."

She noticed a parcel of bound papers tucked beneath his arm. Her apprehension mounted.

"I can still remember you quite well as a young girl," he said. "Your father was a good friend and mentor of mine."

She didn't want to talk to him about her father. She wanted to see Garret.

"We were told you'd been killed by Indians," he said.

Maggie shook her head. "It was Nathan."

"Had I even suspected…"

"It's all right," she said, ready to leave.

"No, it's not. You won't have to scavenge in the mountains any longer."

Scavenge? She didn't scavenge!

He held out the thick parcel of bound papers. "All of the Strafford estate belongs to you now."

"What?"

"He wasn't married. Had no children. You are the sole surviving relative and beneficiary to his estate."

"I don't want it." She took a backward step and bumped into Chance. His hands closed over her waist to steady her, which she instantly brushed away. "Half of that land was stolen."

"Then it would seem you have a chance to set things right."

"No. Not me."

"You can choose to appoint someone to oversee the estate. I'm sure your intended will know how to go about doing so."

Her intended? Maggie stared at the parcel, her mind reeling at the thought of owning…*anything.*

When she didn't move to accept the documents, Chance took them.

"Should you need advice or anything, my door is always open."

Maggie didn't want anything from him. She just wanted to leave.

"This has all been quite traumatic for her," said Chance.

"You can use my chamber as long as you need," he said, taking a step back. "Mr. Daines is taking care of some paperwork but should be here shortly. Mr. Morgan. Mr. and Mrs. Morgan."

Garret was safe. That had been her only reason for coming here. She couldn't stand another moment of it, this room, the people, these clothes….

"Maggie?" said Skylar.

"I'd like to be alone," she said, not caring if her request was rude. She couldn't breathe.

"All right. We'll be right outside."

The moment the door shut she began tugging at shiny buttons and satin ties.

She couldn't do it. She didn't belong here.

His magpie had taken flight.

It was a sharp slap of rejection, staring at the pile of blue fabric heaped on the judge's desk. A breeze swirled in from the open window above a bookcase.

She's going to make me chase her.

"We shut this door not fifteen minutes ago," said Tucker.

Garret picked up a stack of bound papers from the folds of silky fabric. "What's this?"

"Titles to Strafford's estate most likely. Judge came by and told her she'd inherited all he had. She seemed pretty shaken by the announcement. In fact, she tried to give it back to him."

"No wonder she ran." He hoped it was the titles and this town she'd run from—*not him*.

"She ran because she's wild," said Chance, "and being stuck in this room was driving her crazy."

"She's not wild!"

"The hell she's not. She was ready to claw these walls down to get out."

"I felt the same way in that damn jail cell."

"I'm not trying to put her down, Garret. I know you care about her. I'm calling it like I see it. Just because she's softer beneath the surface than she appears doesn't change who she is."

He grabbed the clothes and documents and shoved them at Chance. "I love who she is. If I have to live in the wild to be with her, so be it." He paused beside his sister, giving her a quick squeeze. "I'll send word when I get home."

"What do you want me to do with this?" Chance called after him.

"Put it in a safe place."

He knew where to find Maggie.

The mountain.

Garret rode into the yard and could hardly believe his eyes. Several miles back he'd stared at the shift in direction visible in the pitted ground, not sure he wasn't merely seeing what he wanted to see—Maggie's tracks leading him home. In the fading light of dusk he saw Star in the paddock beyond the bunkhouse.

Leaving his horse in the yard to find water, he hurried toward the light shining through the window on the back door. Through the curtains he saw her sitting on a kitchen chair, petting the dog relaxed at her feet. She sat back, pushing her tangled hair away from her red-rimmed eyes as he stepped inside.

"*Garret.*" She went to him and he opened his arms, holding her tight as she fell against his chest. "What took you so long?"

He smiled against her hair. "I came as quickly as I could. I thought you'd gone home to the mountain."

"I wanted *you*."

His hold tightened as her words eased his fear. *She was his.* "Magpie."

He'd never loved anything the way he loved her. She'd been through so much today. When he thought of how close he'd come to losing her, her mountain hideaway didn't sound like such a bad idea.

"I tried to wait for you," she said, "but I couldn't breathe in that town."

"I know. It was a brave thing you did, going in front of all those people. I can't say I'm sorry Nathan's dead, but he was still your brother. I'm sorry, sweetheart."

"I can't grieve for him. I don't want his things. I don't know what to do."

"You don't have to figure it out today. All you have to deal with right now is *me*."

She relaxed against him. His hands moved over her back, melting the tension beneath his palms.

"Will you marry me, Maggie?"

She eased back, her lips quirking with a smile. "I will." Her smile didn't last a full second. "I don't know anything about babies, Garret."

"A few days in my sister's house will fix that."

"One night was enough to terrify me."

"Ten kids is a lot to take on at once," he said with a laugh. "I've had enough diapering experience for the both of us."

His assurance didn't ease her worried frown.

He touched his forehead to hers. "We can do this, Magpie. We can do this."

"I believe you."

Her open trust dissolved the last remnant of his worry. "We likely have bigger worries here than diapering, anyhow."

"Such as?"

"With your ebony hair and my cotton top, our kid's liable to come out zebra-headed."

She laughed.

"It's a worry," he said, kissing her smiling lips.

"I love you."

"I love you, too. I'd do anything for you, even live up in that wild country if I had to."

Her eyes hazed with moisture as her smile brightened. "I find I'm rather partial to sleeping beneath your lace canopy."

Seemed what he thought to be a useless weave was good for netting magpies. "My saving grace," he said, and lifted her into his arms.

She tightened her arms around his neck as he carried her from the kitchen. "What now?"

"I'm getting you into a warm tub while I've got you wooed."

"Do you have a mind to love me?" she asked, her smiling lips seeking his.

"I surely do. For the rest of my life."

Epilogue

Six years later—Strafford Estate

It had been twenty years since she had stood on the front steps of her childhood home. Maggie had been surprised to discover the large house she remembered was in fact a mansion. The massive Victorian now stood at the center of a large township, and moments ago had been revealed as the new Strafford Music Center—the many rooms and parlors converted to classrooms and performance theaters.

She smiled up at the ornate gold placard on the door proclaiming the name of the music center in memory of Thomas Strafford. She held a plaque presented to her during a lovely dedication ceremony. The moment the planning council had approached her with interest to purchase the estate, she knew this was something her father would have wanted. She was glad Garret had talked her into attending the opening. Their boys had enjoyed the train ride across Wyoming and had been on their best behavior all afternoon, an amazing feat for her three-year-old and five-year-old sons. After two days of travel and an afternoon of tours, ceremonies, pleasantries and finger sandwiches, her boys were likely as exhausted as their mother. She was ready to shed the cumbersome lavender gown Cora had sewn, adding extra pleats at the midsection to accommodate six months of pregnancy.

"Mrs. Daines." Mr. Hudson, head of the music council, took her gloved hand in his. "Thank you again for your generosity. Your donation means so much to this community."

She pulled her hand away. "I'm glad my father's house will be of good use," she said for the hundredth time today. While she meant it, she was anxious to be on her way.

"If you'll excuse me, I need to find my family." Holding the dedication plaque to the tight bulge of her belly, she started down the steps, searching for her husband in the hundreds of guests spanned across the grounds. Her crew of cotton tops was easily identifiable on the lawn. Garret waved, bringing an instant smile to her face. She started through the crowd, never losing sight of Garret.

He looked dashing in the dark tailored suit, his pale hair a ripple of incandescent waves over the back of his collar. Oblivious to the number of admiring gazes fixed in his direction, he held Jonathan's hand and appeared to be in deep conversation with Zachary. Her oldest stood a few feet off from his father, his hands tucked into his trouser pockets, the hard curve of his mouth suggesting he'd rather be in a saddle than all slicked up and standing in the yard of his grandfather's estate.

He caught sight of her approach and his blue eyes brightened.

"There's our girl," said Garret. "Let's see it."

She held out the plaque for the boys to see. Garret crouched between them.

"Shiny," said Jonathan.

"Will look real nice on the mantel," said Garret.

"We get to take it home, Mama?" asked Zachary.

"We do."

"On the train?" Jonathan asked.

"On the train." Both her boys beamed excited smiles.

"Aunt Maggie!"

She turned to see eight-year-old Callie Mae approaching with her parents and the entire bouquet of Morgan girls. Cora and Chance had brought Skylar's daughters. Maggie had been so touched that they'd all made the long journey to share this day with her. The ceremony couldn't have come at a worse time, the Morgans' preparing for a colt sale and Garret in the midst of spring roundup. Yet they'd made an event of it, sewing a flurry of new spring dresses just for the occasion.

"You really grew up in that house?" Callie Mae asked, flouncing to a stop in front of her.

"I did, but they've made a lot of changes."

"It's so pretty, and *huge.*"

"It really was a lovely ceremony," said Cora. "Seems a fine school."

"Can we go look at the birds on the pond now?" asked TJ, tugging on his father's jacket sleeve.

"Sure," said Chance.

"Can Zach and Jonathan come, too?"

"Can't," Zachary said, his expression mournful as he shook his head.

"Why not?" Maggie asked, shocked that her son would decline a chance to explore the willows and grasses around the wide stretch of water curving around to the backside of the mansion. She'd spent a good deal of time chasing ducks and picking flowers along those shorelines.

"Promised Daddy to not get dirty on account it's your special day."

"I see mostly grass around that pond. You should be able to stay fairly clean."

Hopeful blue eyes shifted to Garret. At his daddy's nod Zach and TJ set off across the lawn.

"Don't get wet," Maggie called after him.

He came to a hard stop and looked back at them. "What if I get *pushed* in?"

Garret chuckled.

"TJ," Chance said dryly, his arm sliding around his wife's shoulders as they strolled after the boys, "don't be pushing your cousin into the pond."

Blond curls swayed above wide brown eyes as TJ shook his head. "I won't."

"Come on, Jonathan," Grace said, holding her hand out to him.

Her youngest took his cousin's hand and followed the rest of their clan.

"You do realize Zach will find a way to get wet?" Garret said as he pulled her into his warm embrace, discreetly caressing the rise in her belly.

Maggie smiled and leaned against his side. "Most likely. He's a lot like his father."

"How 'bout you, Magpie, you want to go see the birds?"

"I'm ready to head for the hotel," she whispered. "But it's been a nice day."

"It has."

"Thank you for making me come here."

"You wanted to come. You just needed a little nudge."

Garret was sure the fancy crowd milling around them would likely be surprised to know his wife preferred cotton over silks and rarely socialized with anyone outside of the family and her business contacts for their ranch. Yet she'd gone before several hundred strangers with the poise and grace of a duchess to help commemorate her father.

"Your father would be proud of you, Magpie. I am, too."

Her smile never failed to set his heart racing.

"Would it be highly improper for me to kiss you right now?"

Her eyes widened. "Yes, it certainly would." She lifted onto her tiptoes, whispering, "Kiss me anyway."

"Still my wild woman," he murmured, before giving his wife a purely improper kiss.

* * * * *

MILLS & BOON

Historical

Don't miss Carole Mortimer's third instalment of
her glorious series

THE NOTORIOUS ST CLAIRES

From Mills & Boon® Historical

You've read all about Hawk and Lucian – now it's the turn of
Sebastian, the *Ton*'s most desirable rake...

The Rogue's Disgraced Lady

Gossip has kept Lady Juliet Boyd out of society since
the suspicious death of her husband. Starved of
affection, the scandalous Sebastian St Claire is irresistible
to Juliet. But does Sebastian really want her – or
just the truth behind her disgrace?

Find out in February 2010!

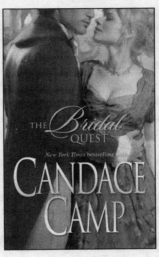

millsandboon.co.uk Community

Join Us!

The Community is the perfect place to meet and chat to kindred spirits who love books and reading as much as you do, but it's also the place to:

- ■ **Get the inside scoop from authors about their latest books**
- ■ **Learn how to write a romance book with advice from our editors**
- ■ **Help us to continue publishing the best in women's fiction**
- ■ **Share your thoughts on the books we publish**
- ■ **Befriend other users**

Forums: Interact with each other as well as authors, editors and a whole host of other users worldwide.

Blogs: Every registered community member has their own blog to tell the world what they're up to and what's on their mind.

Book Challenge: We're aiming to read 5,000 books and have joined forces with The Reading Agency in our inaugural Book Challenge.

Profile Page: Showcase yourself and keep a record of your recent community activity.

Social Networking: We've added buttons at the end of every post to share via digg, Facebook, Google, Yahoo, technorati and de.licio.us.

www.millsandboon.co.uk

✓ 2 FREE BOOKS
AND A SURPRISE GIFT

We would like to take this opportunity to thank you for reading this Mills & Boon® book by offering you the chance to take TWO more specially selected books from the Historical series absolutely FREE! We're also making this offer to introduce you to the benefits of the Mills & Boon® Book Club™—

- **FREE home delivery**
- **FREE gifts and competitions**
- **FREE monthly Newsletter**
- **Exclusive Mills & Boon Book Club offers**
- **Books available before they're in the shops**

Accepting these FREE books and gift places you under no obligation to buy, you may cancel at any time, even after receiving your free books. Simply complete your details below and return the entire page to the address below. You don't even need a stamp!

YES Please send me 2 free Historical books and a surprise gift. I understand that unless you hear from me, I will receive 4 superb new books every month for just £3.79 each, postage and packing free. I am under no obligation to purchase any books and may cancel my subscription at any time. The free books and gift will be mine to keep in any case.

Ms/Mrs/Miss/Mr_____ Initials _____

Surname _____

Address _____

_____ Postcode _____

Send this whole page to: Mills & Boon Book Club, Free Book Offer, FREEPOST NAT 10298, Richmond, TW9 1BR